10/20/18

PIG FARM

PIG FARM

Todd Parnell

Acclaim Press
MORLEY, MISSOURI

P.O. Box 238
Morley, MO 63767
(573) 472-9800
www.acclaimpress.com

Book & Cover Design: M. Frene Melton
Cover image by Amber Hansen

ISBN: 978-1-948901-08-6 | 1-948901-08-0
Library of Congress Control Number: 2018909236

First Printing: 2018
Printed in the United States of America
10 9 8 7 6 5 4 3 2 1

"This shining water that moves in the streams and rivers is not just water, but the blood of our ancestors."

Chief Seattle
The Earth is Precious

"Any reasonable man cannot look upon these marvels in their pristine state without feeling an innermost sense of awe and humility."

Dr. Neil Compton
The Battle for the Buffalo River

"Have I done all to keep the air fresh?
Have I cared enough about the water?"

Chief Dan George
Tsleil-Waututh

"A paradise found, in just a few generations, can all too easily become a paradise lost."

John Dillon
Ozark Mountain Daredevils

Contents

Foreword

Following a successful career in banking and a stint as president of his Alma Mater, Todd Parnell found his true muse telling stories. Stories about his family, stories about the Ozarks where he grew up, stories about his great passion for the beautiful rivers and streams of the region. Perhaps more than any other characteristic, these water resources have defined the Ozarks and Todd has been their advocate and champion.

For many years, before being sold to a national corporation, the Springfield newspaper carried the catch phrase on its masthead, "Tis a privilege to live in the Ozarks." Todd's stories have borne testimony to that sentiment, reflecting an organic sense of the people, land, water, culture and history of this distinctive region.

Pig Farm is Todd's latest novel and incorporates all of these organic characteristics. The story line engages you quickly and draws you into a tale of two families over succeeding generations. It's a story of adventure, lust, love, humor, violence,tragedy and resourcefulness with the inevitable tensions between the two families a compelling dynamic.

The story is set in the Ozark mountains of Arkansas near a "beautiful river" which anchors the fiction of the families in the reality of a defining natural resource. The line between fiction and reality narrows when the pristine river is threatened by development of a commercial hog farm in the watershed. The resolution of this new tension is left undone with the implicit suggestion that the reader become involved.

Todd Parnell has combined two of his great passions in this book. One is his appreciation for a family's deep roots in the Ozarks. The second is his love for the rivers and streams he often floats and cares for so deeply. These passions and his commitment to seeing them continued through successive generations have inspired this novel. It's a good read and might even involve the reader in these commitments as well.

Dr. John E. Moore, Jr.
Retired President, Drury University
Retired President, Upper White River Basin Foundation
Retired Chairman, Wonders of Wildlife Board
Bee Keeper

Author's Note

The Ozarks. This vague notion of land, water, and culture in southern Missouri, northern Arkansas, and even eastern Oklahoma, some say. Ask a native where the Ozarks begins and ends and you will get as many answers as questions asked.

The Ozarks. Home to colorful characters, legends, and lore.

The Ozarks. Where seven generations of my family, going back to the 1830s along the Buffalo River and in north central Springfield, MO, the 1840s next to Swan Creek in southern Missouri and Flippin Barrow in northwest Arkansas, the 1870s along Bear Creek in northwest Arkansas, the 1880s in Kirbyville, MO, and, since its founding in the early 1900s, in Branson, MO, have toiled, loved, and thrived. Two new generations carry the line forward, nine in all.

The Ozarks. A land that has been good to my clan over the nearly two centuries we've dwelled here. The Parnells, the Caseys, the McHaffies, the Hoggs, the Wardens, the Hiblers.

The Ozarks. Where I am blessed to have been born, to grow through childhood, and to return to for my most productive years. I hope to die and be buried here, my ashes mingling with theirs.

The Ozarks. Once the fresh water capital of the world. With thousands of springs bubbling up through porous karst topography and thousands of miles of uniquely beautiful streams pulsing and carving through layers of limestone, and polishing bedrock bottoms with exotic color. All derived from ancient ocean and violent upheaval.

The Ozarks. A rugged beautiful land, discovered and settled relatively late in the American saga, paradise to Native Americans, explored by many whites who were escaping something. Exploited, abused, but never totally subjugated. Raped of its native hardwood forests and shortleaf pine, decimated of wild turkey and deer, and farmed out by the end of the Great Depression; dammed into large lakes in the interest of flood control, energy generation, and tourist dollars; and yet forever resilient, regenerative, a region of great beauty and promise, facing a new set of challenges to its unique natural infrastructure.

The Ozarks. I love the Ozarks, however one measures or describes it. It's a love of place that embraces beauty, history, tradition, humor, lore, and reality.

The Ozarks. I worry about the Ozarks as well because I want my grandchildren and theirs to know it as I have, if such is possible. Unfettered development, overpopulation, sedimentation and pollution of water resources, and encroaching corporate farming are but a few dark clouds on the horizon. In the end, they all merge together. It's all about the water, as it has been in the Ozarks forever.

The Ozarks. One hundred years from now, seven generations from now, ten centuries from now, the Ozarks will likely out last us all. Perhaps there is hope in that.

Todd Parnell
September 16, 2017
Jude Ranch, on a beautiful, rainy morning, surrounded by water, beneath a canopy of turning trees.

Lineages

THE SNARKLE LINE
(8 Generations)

Polly
(1788-1877)
↓
Jebediah and Sunshine
(1818-1900) (1817-1838)
↓
Bear and Fannibelle
(1838-1927) (1833-1910)
↓
Bear Jr. and Sadie
(1858-1927) (1862-1930)
↓
Sam and Mai
(1900-1997) (1910-1999)
↓
Nathaniel and Layne
(1929-1995) (1934-1996)
↓
Skeet and Betty Sue
(1958-) (1960-)
↓
Jebediah Snarkle Jr.
(1983-)

THE HENSBELL LINE
(5 Generations)

Jamon and Dulcetta
(1856-1877) (1859-1905)
↓
Tyson and Glory
(1877-1893) (1877-1893)
↓
Tyson Jr. and Honey
(1893-1987) (1900-1980)
↓
Tyson III and Tillie (Snarkle)
(1931-1971) (1931-2001)
↓ ↓
Lester Tyson Hensbell, IV (1971-)
Molly (Snarkle) (1970-)

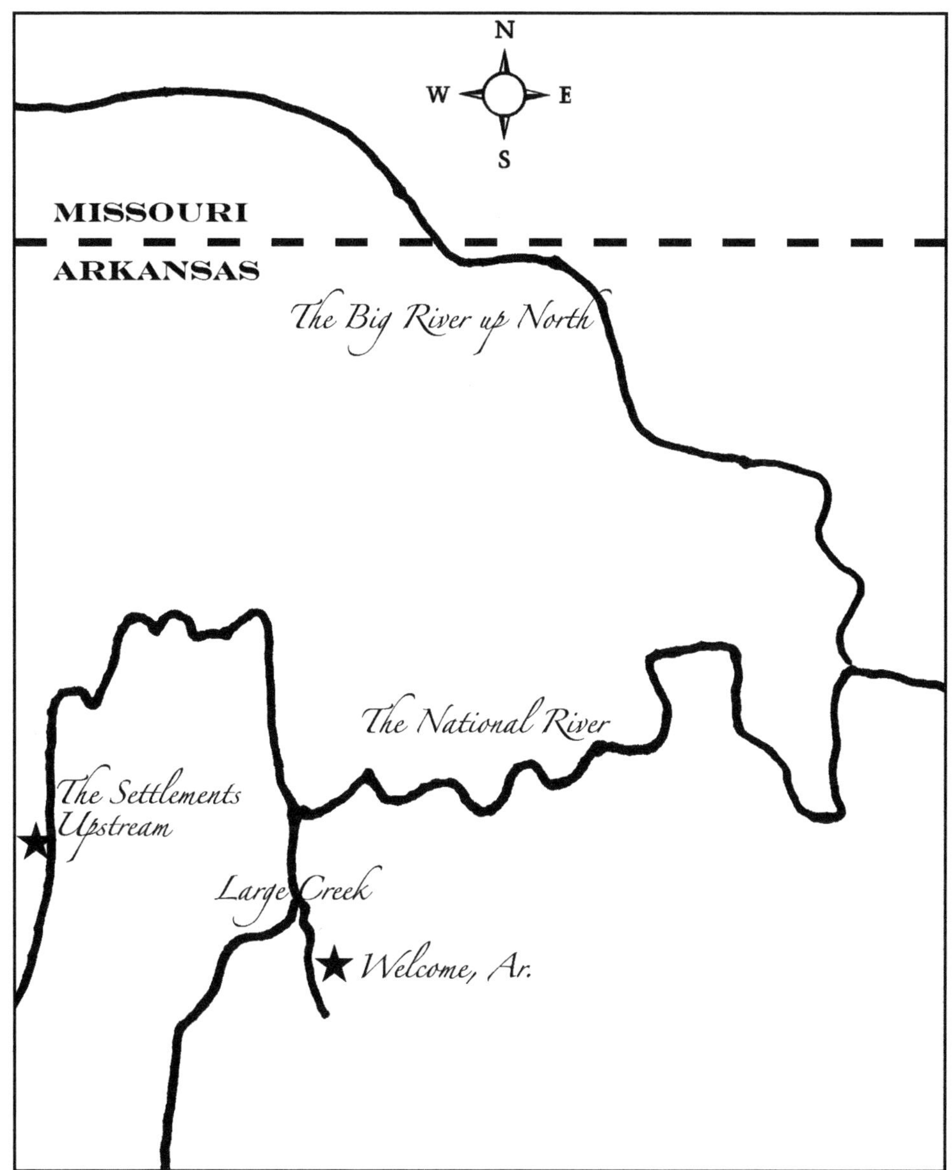
N
W
E
S
MISSOURI
ARKANSAS
The Big River up North
The National River
The Settlements Upstream
Large Creek
Welcome, Ar.

Dedication

This book is dedicated to three brave grandmothers—Carol Bitting, Lin Welford and Dr. Nancy Haller—who have gone to court to try and stop the Buffalo River CAFO, and to the passionate opposition, including the Buffalo River Watershed Alliance and others, who have led the way.

> "Someone had to take a stand for the river and it seemed to each of us that it was our turn."—*Carol Bitting*
>
> "How long can we feed the world if we wreck our land and water resources in the process?"—*Lin Welford*
>
> "If we can't protect a river that has been set aside as a national park, is any waterway in this country safe?"—*Dr. Nancy Haller*

As with those who saved the Buffalo from being dammed in the 1960s, we on the sidelines owe them all a great debt of gratitude. May they, too, prevail, for all of our sakes.

Todd Parnell

Left to right: Lin Welford, Carol Bitting and Dr. Nancy Haller

Preface

In August 2012, the state of Arkansas, through its Department of Environmental Quality, granted a permit for a 6,500-pig industrial farm (CAFO) near Mt. Judea, just six miles from the Buffalo National River itself, along a major tributary, Big Creek. C&H Hog Farms was the permittee, with international agricultural conglomerate Cargill Foods as co-conspirator. Funny thing. Many locals didn't know about it, especially those impacted most directly.

I first learned of this travesty on July 7, 2013, just one day before my 66th birthday, from an editorial in *The Springfield News-Leader*, and couldn't believe it was true. My confusion turned to anger as I read more in the local press, and even *The New York Times* later in the year.

CAFO? Don't you just love the sound of it? CAFO. Confined Animal Feeding Operation. These are open-air houses with pigs (or chickens or turkeys) crammed snout to butt (or beak to tail feathers) and all their waste pooled beneath or washed into outdoor storage lagoons, prior to being sprayed on adjoining fields.

True confession. I love ribs and pork chops, chicken thighs, and turkey breasts like most. It would be hypocritical for me to rant and rave about CAFOs. What sets me off is when these CAFOs are stuck next to fragile, irreplaceable waterways and water tables, or small communities who don't want the stench of corporate farms as neighbors. Like next to America's first national river.

In this case, approval was granted under the cover of darkness, without proper notification of those most directly impacted or adequate environmental impact studies. The National Park Service, which administers the Buffalo National River, was even left in the dark. Sure, "they" followed all the rules. There just aren't very many. It was a political deal all the way, greased with contributions and silver tongues.

At full capacity this CAFO will produce as much putrid annual waste as a city of 30,000. But, a city treats its waste. Where does the CAFO's waste all go? Most is sprayed on surrounding fields, including, in this case, those adjacent to Big Creek, where between rain and our unique karst topography, it will find its way into America's first national river.

Makes a lot of sense, doesn't it? Of all the potential sites in Arkansas, the first CAFO permit in the state is issued in the heart of the Buffalo National River watershed.

And that doesn't even take into account the possibility of a breach in the adjoining waste lagoon, which was built to comply with only a 25-year flood event. That is a blink of an eye in the life of a river.

Corporate farming has snuck in the back door of a paradise it has no business even being near.

This is a story through time of how it might have come to be.

IN THE BEGINNING...

In the beginning was water. Lots and lots of water. A shallow ocean covered the Ozark Dome, 300 million years ago. Then thermal heat drove tectonic plate movement to uplift soluble limestone and non-soluble chert skyward. Physical and chemical weathering, and raging river flow, fueled the give and take of time to carve striking bluffs and rugged rock faces. Carbonic acid caused dissolution and karstification of soluble limestone to form a topography characterized with subsurface drainage systems, and featuring springs, sinkholes, and caves, which speed a hydrologic cycle through subterranean arteries to cleanse and nourish the veined infrastructure over time.

In the beginning, as now, there was lots and lots of water.

And there were natives, real native Americans, Stone Age Indians without horses or wheels, then bluff dweller Indians, then groups of hunter gatherers and hunter farmers. Later white priests and explorers invaded hunting grounds, spreading disease and laying claim to the land for their foreign government. And eventually native tribes were removed to the west to allow for more permanent white settlers to move in.

PIG FARM

Chapter 1

Paradise (1838)

Jebediah Snarkle had never seen a more beautiful place in his world. He looked down from the top of a ridge onto a crystal clear stream cutting through a narrow valley, leaving rock edges and ledges carved with random precision over a long time. Millennia came to Jebediah's mind. A big word his mother had taught him in the context of God and Religion, with a capital R. He recalled it meaning something like forever, even beyond that constraint.

Jebediah's mother had also given him his name. She called him Jeb for short, and Jeb learned early on to never doubt his mother's decisions.

She explained that his name had Hebrew roots and loosely translated into "beloved friend," which in fact is what Jeb's mother became to him. Unfortunately, his father did not.

Jeb Snarkle was born on a dirty blanket in backwoods Tennessee. The year of his birth was 1818, or 19, or 20. He was never quite sure. His mother had recorded it in a beaten up family Bible that his father later burned in a drunken rage, accusing his mother of preferring sex with a make-believe deity over her own husband. That was actually one of the few things he was ever correct about.

His father's name was Elmer, and he hated it as much as he did most things. Hers was Polly, and theirs was not a marriage made in that real or imagined deity's home turf.

How they got together was beyond Jeb's imagination, as soon as he was old enough to have one. Elmer was gone most of the time, to the family's great relief. It was when he returned that life took on a sour color.

Jeb's family consisted of his beloved mother and six older sisters who treated him as if they were also his mother. It had taken Elmer seven impregnations, with three miscarriages sprinkled in among the labors, to get the boy he demanded of Polly.

That was family as far as Jeb was concerned. He did not consider his father part of it in any way.

It was, in fact, Jeb who finally provided closure. He stabbed his father in the back as he was forcing himself on his mother for the last of countless times. He just couldn't take it anymore, seeing her bear silently and stoically the pain and humiliation of Elmer's intrusion.

Jeb would never forget the look of pain and anger Elmer gave him through glazed eyes as he rolled off his mother and tried to grasp his son's throat. The blood issuing from his throat confirmed that Jeb had struck pay dirt and rendered Elmer powerless. As Polly pulled a cover over her tired, withered body, she flashed a brief look of gratitude at her son, her youngest and last baby. Jeb was a baby no more.

And so it was that Jeb Snarkle led his family of five siblings and one mother out of Roane County under the cover of darkness, leaving his fat, stinking carcass of a father to rot in summer's heat.

Jeb Snarkle led his band of female refugees through western Tennessee, across the vast Mississippi, and into the new state of Arkansas. He ultimately encountered a mighty river called the White and followed it upstream, losing three of his sisters to frontier men along the way. They each seemed happy in their own way, though Jeb harbored doubts about at least two of the three trophy males they claimed to have landed. They were rough-cut brothers who said that they had carved a comfortable and survivable way of life out of the wilderness and simply needed female companionship to round it out and produce offspring. He wasn't sure what that meant, but had enough to worry about without them. His mother shared his pessimistic outlook, sensing a sameness in their choice that had led her to Elmer, but offered her blessing. Neither mother nor brother would ever hear from any of those sisters again.

They earlier had lost another sister to dysentery just after crossing the Mississippi on a ferry.

Along the way Jeb heard of land to the west of great beauty and unprecedented natural resources, from pristine water to abundant game. He was told that it was rugged but rewarding terrain on which to settle. And it was land that was available to first comers, land that had been freed by forced indian migration to reservations further west, land that manifest destiny made available to his kind.

As he drove deeper north and west into the wooded hills, he paid a river man to ferry what remained of his family unit across the White.

He encountered a small group of Cherokee fringe dwellers, left behind and overlooked during the white man migration, who had established a tiny agricultural outpost on the western outskirts of the river, near where he set foot on solid ground.

Jeb approached the community to buy food for his tired, undernourished family and was surprised by the welcoming he received. He had heard bits and pieces about savages who waged fierce and cruel war against settlers moving west. The atrocities reported, from rape, to scalping, to mutilation and torture, had sketched an expectation in his mind. The greeting he received could not have been further from that expectation.

The warm and welcoming embrace he and his three remaining women folk received included an invitation to winter at the camp, which he quickly and gratefully accepted.

Chapter 2

Love

Jebediah Snarkle fell hard in love that short, cold winter.

She was both shy and sensuous at the same time. Dark skinned like the dusk, radiant as in rising sun, full lipped and supple bodied, she was the picture of desire, and propriety, if such is possible.

Jeb first saw her sitting outside her lodge, stitching skins together for winter clothing. She glanced at him briefly as he passed by, eyes darting to connect with his, then back to the task at hand in a blink.

Jeb was stunned at the magic in that moment of engagement. He began to find reason to walk by her lodge more often.

Polly quickly took notice. She cautioned Jeb about the differences between his strain of humanity and hers that extended well beyond appearance and culture. Centuries beyond.

"She's an indian, Jeb. The daughter of a red man. Her kind will find our world hard to fit in over time. She has been run out of her homeland by such as ours, and likely harbors both anger and resentment for her family and tribe's loss. There is little room for kindness and love in that vacuum."

And still, Jeb found reason after reason to walk by. He also found that she stationed herself outside, even as fall turned to winter, with increasing regularity, finding some task to occupy her hands with.

She also chose to be more open to his glances, even smiling slightly on occasion. There was the time that Jeb stared intently a bit too long and tripped over a large rock that rimmed the path, falling face first at her feet. This caused her to laugh out loud for a second or two before regaining her stoic dignity. He stretched out to touch her only to find her slide quickly beyond his reach.

The small village was home not only to those Cherokee who farmed its perimeter and grazed livestock about, but an odd assortment of visitors headed west, from small families with young children, to older couples set on adventure beyond children, to wayfarers in twos and threes who rarely lingered. Jeb, his mother, and his two remaining sisters were among only a few who settled in for winter.

Villagers intermingled easily with passer-throughs, bartering food and deer-skin clothing for wool blankets and colorful trinkets. Campfires lit and heated common areas. Tents and teepees dotted the landscape with even a covered wagon or two tucked in on occasion. There was a balance in their interactions with only one operational rule. No alcohol. By order of the village head man. No exceptions. Those who violated were asked to leave immediately. If they refused, they were moved out.

Winter mornings began to take on a welcome chill beyond flat out frigid. Days lengthened and spring, with all of its beautiful foliage, began to peek through the drab.

Jeb and Polly talked through the days about departing. They knew that land to the west was rugged, but longed to sample its beauty and potential. Neither sister seemed to be in any hurry. One had taken up with a singleton passing through mid-winter and shared his tent on occasion. He was intent on heading south rather that west, and she wanted only to be with him. The other fancied one of the indians she had met. It was unclear what had passed between them, but as spring grew so did their displays of affection. It was clear she had no plans to go anywhere.

"I don't want to go anywhere without her," Jeb suddenly burst out one morning to his mother.

"Who is 'her' my son? Is she the one I warned you about?"

He ignored his mother's broadside. "I call her 'Sunshine', for that is how she warms my heart. I have even whispered it to her in passing by on occasion. Sometimes she nods in agreement, which is enough name recognition for me," Jeb countered.

One evening after a warming day, Jeb noticed her leaving the village as he was making his rounds. He pretended to ignore, but trailed her at a distance. It soon became clear that she was headed toward one of the small tributaries to the great river. He heard splashing and crawled on his hands and knees through the rough underbrush to a tree-covered knoll. He looked down in awe.

Her clothes lay in a neatly folded pile next to a small fire laid next to the creek. She spun and turned in the water in a spring body cleaning ritual, clearly enjoying the feel of cold water mingled with warming air.

Jeb had never seen anything so beautiful in his life.

She slowly emerged and crouched next to the warming flames. What she did next changed Jeb's life forever.

The young lady rose slowly and turned to face Jeb full frontal. His gasp brought a smile to her face. She spread her arms in welcome toward the spot where she knew Jeb lay spread eagle, then beckoned him with one arm.

Among the many things bursting out in Jeb's mind was the cautionary reminder that he had never done anything like she was asking him to do in his life. Sex to Jeb was his drunk father ripping off his mother's clothes, pinning her to the bed or ground, and pounding into her from above as she lay silent and helpless. Beyond that he hadn't a clue.

She beckoned again, inviting beyond doubt for Jeb to join her. She even laid her coat on the ground and motioned to it.

Jeb rose hesitantly from his hiding place and stepped toward her, one foot in front of the other, he kept reminding himself, keeping his eyes fixed on the ethereal vision ahead. When he finally reached her, she reached out and began to unbutton his shirt. She then motioned for him to sit on the blanket and knelt to remove his boots, followed by his leggings and remaining undergarments.

She then moved over him and squatted, guiding him into her. Jeb had never felt or seen anything so divine in his life. He finished too quickly and knew he had, but reached up to squeeze her with all his worth.

Unsure of what to do next, he rose when she extended her hand, then followed her back into the chilling water, where they frolicked and splashed about like children, drawing each other together for warmth before playfully pinching a body part or bare backside, then drawing close again.

Jeb did better on his second try, whispering "Sunshine" into her ear at the consummate moment of pleasure.

Chapter 3

Sunshine

"She shines like the sun, inside and out," Jeb told his mother. He hesitantly shared with her the gist of their shared intimacy.

Polly had known something was up with Jeb the past several weeks. He was gone a lot. "Wandering through the woods," he generally claimed. And, the woods were enchanting with their spring finery. White blooms, pink ones, lush green canopy, springs of blue crystalline water. It reminded Polly of Tennessee, just more primitive and untouched.

Several times Polly caught Jeb and the young indian maiden locking eyes for more than a passing moment. She even began to notice them vanishing from view and reappearing on roughly the same schedule.

Jeb and his young lady gathered at the river more than once, finding excitement and electricity in each encounter. She spoke rudimentary white man talk but their communications ran far deeper than language. It soon became obvious to both that theirs was a relationship to be nurtured and joined, not ignored or separated.

Jeb finally asked his Sunshine if she would go west with him, leave her family behind, and become the central figure in his own. When she nodded her concurrence, both shed tears. Tears of fear. Tears of joy. Tears of certainty and eternity.

It was time for Jeb and his mother to move on, to follow the dream they set out to pursue.

Jeb pronounced his intention to take Sunshine west with them. Polly reluctantly concurred. She worried that Jeb would get hurt, not by the young lady, but because of her. In the end, Polly was attracted to her quiet dignity and the calmness that emanated like a mist from her presence. It would be nice to have another set of hands with them in the wilderness, especially since neither of her remaining daughters would be accompanying them. It also warmed her heart to see Jeb so enveloped in her presence, physical and emotional. She had never experienced such inspiration as a young lady, or even to today.

Jeb would approach her father with a formal proposal. If he refused he would take her anyway. He loved her as he had loved no one in his life, and was confident she shared his feelings.

"What will you give for her, son?" Polly asked.

"All my love," he responded.

"Not enough," she replied.

"What do you mean?"

"You need to provide something tangible, something physical to her father in exchange for his daughter. That's their tradition."

"Like what?"

"Ask her. And speak to him her using her own name, not the one you have assigned her."

"I don't know what that is, mother."

"Find out."

"So what is your indian name, Sunshine?"

"Yanasa," she giggled. "Yah-nah-sah, is how you say it white boy."

"What does it mean, Sunshine?"

"Buffalo."

"Odd name for a pretty young lady."

"Why?"

"Buffalo sounds big and powerful."

"Buffalo sounds sleek and beautiful, too."

"So, you're one of those?"

"My father thinks all of the above. I am special to him."

They had just lain together again, this time deep in the woods in a bed of mayapples. Both were giddy.

"I am ready to ask your father for permission to take you west with my mother Polly and me."

"Are you sure?" Sunshine whispered back.

"I am, beautiful Sunshine. Are you?"

"I am."

"What shall I offer your father to gain his permission? I understand that is a tradition which must be upheld."

"Yes. What do you have?"

"Nothing we don't need. Just myself."

"You will need more. Bring him the skin of a black bear and see if he smiles. If he does, I will be yours. If not, it will register as an insult, and I will never be yours."

"I get only one chance?"

"Yes."

"If he says no, will you come with me anyway? I will sneak you away under cover of darkness and take you somewhere he will never find you."

"Yes. Gv-ge-yu-hi, white boy. I love you and I will go with you if it comes to that. But you will need to be ready to kill one or more of my brothers. My father will surely send them to bring me home."

"I will be ready to defend you."

"So how about this bear, Miss Sunshine? Where do I find one of them?"

Jeb knew about bears from his youth in Tennessee. He had never seen a live one up close, but knew from those who hunted that they could be ornery and cantankerous. Even dangerous.

She pointed west, to a heavily wooded mountainside in the far distance. Jeb left her side and reclothed. He kissed her hand and left her snuggled under the blanket.

"I will fetch my rifle and knife, and be back soon. With the skin of a bear."

In his urgency to kill a black bear, Jeb forgot to ask Sunshine about the bump in her belly that he noticed in passing as they had made fierce love.

Chapter 4

Yonu

"Yonu," Yanasa's father grinned broadly. "Skin of very big Yonu. Very good, very good."

Jeb stood in front of Sunshine's, make that Yanasa's, father holding a large, freshly skinned black bear coat. Sunshine lurked in the shadows hoping for a positive reaction. She had helped Jeb clean the pelt for presentation, as well as treat the deep wounds on his arm. She was relieved that he was okay, and pleased with her father's reaction. But still…she was his youngest daughter…and remained unsure of a final verdict.

Jeb tried not to smile too broadly, but sensed a connection with Sunshine's father. How he had gotten from then to there had not been easy.

When Jeb had left Sunshine's warm flank he felt more desire than fear. That changed as he plowed more deeply into the tangled underbrush guarding the densely wooded mountainside in the distance. He knew what he was seeking, but was relying on Sunshine's vague directions to find it. He slept one night tied in a tree along the way and thought he had heard grunting sounds during the night. But he couldn't be sure. The extraordinarily large pile of fresh scat he stepped around not far down the animal trail he followed confirmed his instincts. He would slow down and move quietly going forward.

Further up the mountainside he saw an indentation in the rock. On closer inspection he determined that it was a small cave and that there were two sets of tracks, one large, one small at its entrance. Perhaps a mother and her cub he reasoned.

Jeb was savvy enough to know that he would never want to be trapped in close quarters with a sow and her baby, so he settled in behind a large boulder to await their exit. He occasionally nibbled at the jerky in his pocket and sipped from a skin canteen, but otherwise he sat dead still.

Hours later as sun began to recede and a chill frosted the air he heard noises from inside the cave. A large female black bear issued cautiously from within, sniffing and snorting, before turning back to urge a young cub out. He really didn't want to kill a mother and leave her baby unattended, but he wanted Sunshine more. It was a choice he was spared of.

A fierce roar from behind and above, accompanied by the crashing through trees, alerted him to his dangerous dilemma. He had no more time than it took to spin on his back and aim his rifle up to defend himself from the assault of a huge and very angry charging bear. As it rose above him, filling the air with noise and foul odor, he fired.

As true as his shot was, the beast landed on him, and sunk its teeth into his arm, shaking and twisting it like a small animal. He feared it would come off as he grabbed his long knife with the other hand and began plunging it into the eyes and neck of his assailant. Blood flowed everywhere, to the point of Jeb losing consciousness for a brief moment or two.

And then it was over. The huge carcass that lay on him ceased to move beyond a death tremble. Its head was a mass of knife wounds and its teeth remained lodged in Jeb's arm. The mother and cub had retreated into the cover of the cave.

He feared their return, so after separating the bear's jaws so as to dislodge their grip on his mangled flesh, he quickly reloaded using his good arm, rolled from beneath the 300 pounds pressing on his body, and took aim on the entrance. He lay that way for at least a half of an hour, knowing that he was losing blood at an alarming rate, but afraid to be unprepared for a second attack.

None came and Jeb tied a rag above his wound to staunch the blood's flow, before passing out for real. When he awoke, his arm throbbed and still oozed blood, and the air was filled with the smell of death.

Jeb rose slowly to assess his situation. He was far from the village, at least a day and a half of heavy trekking. He had lost the use of a limb and what seemed like buckets of blood from the surrounding puddles. He was likely in close quarters with another protagonist. He could not begin to think in terms of hauling the huge carcass at his side anywhere. Simply getting it off his body had taken more strength than he possessed at the moment. Jeb really didn't have a clue as to what to do next.

Suddenly trees rustled to his left. He raised the rifle with his good arm, uncertain as to whether he could draw down on anything, let alone pull the trigger, with any hope of accuracy. He waited, trembling in fear.

An old indian with long gray braids and regal bearing walked slowly toward him, mumbling something that he didn't understand. Jeb felt comfort, not threat, before sinking slowly to his knees and passing out again.

When he awoke he found the deep wound on his arm dressed, bandaged, and reeking of some strange poultice not known to him.

His arm was in a deerskin sling and his rifle lay across his chest. Perhaps most remarkable, the skin of a large black bear covered him for warmth. A stash of dried meat and fruits lay within reach, as did his full canteen.

Jeb lay, then sat for several hours, nibbling as he could on the provisions left at his side, wondering who or how to thank, ever wary of an angry black bear sow charging from the dark corners of the cave. He lost all track of time but felt his strength slowly returning, and the pain of his wound diminishing. At one point in the process Jeb even wondered if he had died and been reborn, or at least entered an alternative life cycle. He simply couldn't explain much of anything to his own satisfaction.

"I want to marry your daughter, o' wise one. I want to take her with me to settle in the wild lands toward the setting sun. I want her to bear many children who will carry your brave blood. I present this black bear coat as a token of my appreciation for your consideration."

Jeb turned from the father and beckoned Sunshine from the shadows.

"Gv-ge-yu-hi, Yanasa," he said staring deeply into her eyes. "I love you, Yanasa," he repeated.

"Is this all true my daughter? Does white boy love you to your satisfaction and are you willing to leave and live with him?"

Sunshine stood tall and proud, and answered with a single nod of her head.

"It will be so white boy," her father said with emotion. "She is my final daughter, one I never expected to adore so much. It is important that she be happy and that no harm come to her. Forever."

"And so I promise, wise one."

"We will celebrate before you leave. And you may sleep with her in my lodge tonight, and until you depart, white boy."

As they lay locked together in the aftermath of reunion pleasure in the far corner of her father's compound, Sunshine asked Jeb again about the strange visitor that came upon him in his hours of distress, weakened, wound bleeding, in and out of consciousness, another bear lurking near.

"What did he look like, white boy?"

"Since I've been accepted into the family can you at least call me Jeb?"

"You don't call me Yanasa. Okay, Jeb, tell me again."

"He looked like an old indian warrior of regal bearing. Timeless. Ageless. Ancient."

"Nunnehi, Jeb. Nunnehi. One of the 'travelers' who live forever and look after Cherokee over the eons, who protect them, who intervene on their behalf. I have heard tales of the spirit race all my life. Every now and then another will surface from one of my neighbors."

"But I'm not a Cherokee, Sunshine."

"No, you are not, Jeb. But you love one. And this intervention must mean your love is selfless and true, or the Nunnehi would have let you go. He is protecting you for me, for our future together, and for this one," she said patting her belly.

"You are pregnant, Sunshine?" Jeb asked in horror. "Oh my, will your dad want out of our deal now?"

"No, he will turn his head the other way and be grateful for it. If it's a he, we will name him Yonu."

"Yonu?"

"Yonu is 'bear' in my language."

"Are you kidding? A bear almost killed me!"

"But it didn't, Jeb. And bears are viewed by my people as strong, brave, mighty, and wise. They attack only when they are provoked, and in your case you were threatening his sow and cub. He was only defending them, which he did to the death. My people coexist with Yonu, and respect him. Your Yonu met an heroic end, and his coat earned you me. It is only wise to honor this legend with a name. If he is a boy."

"Bear Snarkle does have kind of a powerful tone to it," Jeb laughed.

"It will be a boy, and we will name him Yonu."

Chapter 5

Into the Wild

One thing Jeb Snarkle was certain of was that he didn't want to go west in the direction of that mountain which had almost cost him his life. No, they would follow the great river north, this time on the south side, until they could find a river valley to explore. He was told that there were several of great beauty and length, with few people and limitless possibilities. It was what he and Polly had dreamed of since the dark days in Tennessee, and what he and Sunshine wanted for their future, and that of their baby to be.

They would travel with the livestock Sunshine's father had granted them at the going-away celebration. Two pigs, four chickens, a goat for milk, all carried in pens in the back of a wagon drawn by Jeb's horse. He walked, leading the procession, while Polly and Sunshine shared a second horse. And thus it was mile after mile, game trail after game trail, up and down rugged mountainsides for day after day. Very rough going, very beautiful country. They all agreed on this.

Polly and Sunshine bonded quickly. Sharing a bareback horse either joins or separates in a hurry. In their case it brought them together.

Polly had lost all of her six daughters. One to illness, three to ne'er-do-wells along the way, one to an indian suitor, another to a man headed south rather than west. She missed them, some more than others, but their company had helped carry her through the dismal years of abuse from her worthless dead husband.

Polly felt she had a new daughter, one more beautiful and spiritual than any of her own had been. A daughter to lean on, and to depend on her as she carried Polly's first grandbaby, at least that she knew of.

After a month or two – time was so hard to keep track of in endless transit – they came upon a large and beautiful tributary to the big river.

Jeb wondered if this was the one so many had talked about as he shared his dream of finding a remote and beautiful water source to trace to its headwaters and settle. They would explore it a bit before moving further north.

It certainly fit the descriptives as they moved slowly upstream. Westward-sourced pristine water, rugged limestone bluffs, bottomland to farm and graze livestock, and heavy timber to build structures. Game, fish and water-fowl all about, and no one else around.A stunning and isolated land of plenty.

No one had been able to provide Jeb with a consistent name for the beautiful tributary to the great river, the largest they had yet encountered. Indians called it many things. White men didn't know or care; there was nothing wrong with a river without titling. It gave everyone graced by its beauty a chance to call it what they wished.

Jeb would do just that. He would name it Buffalo, in honor of his love for a new bride, and because just like her, it was big and powerful, sleek and beautiful. The Buffalo River it would always be to him if indeed they found the place of their dreams alongside or overlooking it. And, with that flourish, Jeb decided that they would follow it toward its source.

Sunshine blushed when he told her. Polly smiled. Her son was crazy in love, full of life and adventure, and about to become a father himself. Polly's world was right.

The next two months and many miles were brutal. The land was rugged and filled with summer discomforts. Ticks and chiggers set the travelers to itching endlessly, briars and thorns tore their skin beneath clothing, poisonous snakes appeared out of nowhere. Polly knew them all from her days in Tennessee.

One snake struck her horse, throwing both Polly and Sunshine to the ground and hobbling the horse on a swollen leg. Fortunately neither rider was hurt, especially Sunshine and the baby. And, the horse survived.

The summer heat was unbearable, so Jeb took to setting up camp early morning after riding from dusk to dawn.

The only comfort they found the entire summer was traipsing down to the river from whatever vantage point they stopped, and soaking in its healing waters when time allowed, which became more frequent with each stifling day. Nudity replaced modesty, and each became adept at the "throw off your clothes" shedding ritual that preceded each river bath. This was at first difficult for Polly in that she had been treated all her life as if her body was inherently ugly. But watching the baby bump fill and grow in Sunshine's beautiful and statuesque frame eased her embarrassment and brought much needed comfort and relief in the end.

The livestock was particularly at risk from the heat and shared the water with them when possible.

The few humans they encountered along the way were white, crude, and dirty, frontiersman to the core. Most were standoffish and remote.

One morning as all three lay sleeping under a canopy of trees, Sunshine snuggled up next to Jeb, he awakened to a pistol resting on his forehead and a toothless leer. He at first wondered if he was dreaming, but the foul smells accompanying the intrusion quickly dispersed that notion.

The invader announced that he needed sex and wondered if the pretty little indian lady would be available for a price. Sunshine spat in his twisted face, which caused him to renounce his offer and simply reach down and pull Sunshine to her feet, gun now pointed directly at Jeb's head. He ordered her to get naked or he would shoot her man dead.

Sunshine cast an apologetic look at Jeb and began to remove her clothing. She pulled off her top first and turned to shield her breasts and baby.

"Ha," he laughed. "I get a pregnant one. Haven't had one of those in a long while."

He then turned to Polly never moving his pistol's line of fire from Jeb's head, waving about his state of arousal. "Maybe the old lady would like a piece of this when I finish with the pretty one. I'm sure I can be up to it."

As Sunshine bent to slowly lower her bottoms, the ape smacked her bare bottom, and Jeb prepared to charge, bullet in the head or not. He would not stand by and see his true love ravaged without dying first.

He paused only when he thought he saw a glint of something in Sunshine's hand. With her pants at her ankles and her body open to assault, Sunshine turned in a flash, stuck the blade of an "Arkansas toothpick" into the fat belly of the poor excuse for a man, and ripped it upwards through his gullet, wiping away his heinous smile and deflating his erection in one last moment of life.

She then turned slowly to face her dead assailant, stepped over his bulbous body, squatted, and peed on his upturned face.

Jeb was senseless. He couldn't speak, he couldn't move, he could only look on in wonder at his love's calm demeanor and ultimate act of revenge.

Polly began laughing out loud. "If only I had the presence of mind to do that to my shithead ex-husband," she cackled.

"I didn't know you carried a knife, Sunshine," Jeb gasped.

"Only when we're not making love," she responded. "An indian never knows when they will run into a white man who hates them."

"And your final act of defiance?"

"All you white boys think we indians are savages. Just getting my money's worth."

"Please don't call me white boy."

Chapter 6

Along the Trail

Not long after the "unfortunate hillbilly" encounter as Polly liked to call it, always with a grin on her face, she had one of her own.

As hot summer nights picked up a whiff of fall, Jeb went back to daytime traveling and nights of sleep. It took a few nights for everyone to adapt, but soon they were all sleeping like rocks and taking both morning…and evening river baths. Sunshine had taken on a rosy glow as her baby grew and began to squirm in the womb. Polly explained that it was all a natural extension of the birth process and a healthy indicator of what was to come. Given her extensive experience, Sunshine didn't question her analysis.

One evening as they were headed back up the trail to their sheltered campsite in a small cave, reclothing along the way while leading their animals by ropes, they ran full frontal into a visitor, who immediately and politely covered his eyes. Polly was horrified in that she was leading the parade, had not yet covered her topside, and harbored a memory of prior guests that sent shivers up her naked spine.

Jeb cursed himself for not having his rifle, given their most recent encounter with an intruder, but took some comfort in the man's attempts at modesty.

With everyone finally and fully covered up, he announced to the stranger that it was okay to look, walked up to him and carefully extended his hand in welcome. The man grasped and shook it, introducing himself as Sam.

Sam was a gray haired, grimy old man, who clearly needed a bath himself. He blushed deeply when introduced to Polly, still feeling guilty after his brief but intrusive glance at her nakedness. In that Sam was coming from the direction they were headed, Jeb invited him to share supper and sleep if he wished, in the hope of finding out more of what lay ahead.

Sam accepted with gratitude and apologized for his rough appearance. Jeb tossed him a piece of lye soap and pointed toward the river. Sam returned a half an hour later, smelling less, and even wearing a relatively fresh set of clothes that he must have been carrying in his backpack. He began a fresh round of apologies, which Polly hushed by handing him a cup of coffee she had just brewed. Jeb motioned for him to sit next to the fire while Sunshine pushed a plate of mush and squirrel his way. All ate in silence.

Sam finally broke the evening lull with a hearty "thank you." He explained that he was returning downstream from the most beautiful and bountiful country he had ever seen. In response to Jeb's "why," he responded with "too lonely."

He had headed west after losing his wife to illness, hoping to escape the emptiness her passing left behind. He just couldn't get beyond the shadow of her loss, regardless of the great and glorious waters and land he found, so he was headed back home to Tennessee, to die within range of kinfolk. It was apparent that Sam was a decent, heartbroken adventurer who had lost his sense of adventure.

Jeb inquired about the others he may have encountered along the way.

"Not many," Sam responded. "There are a few small settlements up river, generally peaceful folks seeking to escape from something, and supportive of one another when a bad guy shows up. I liked everything about these people and places, except the hole in my heart they couldn't fill."

Jeb noticed both Polly and Sunshine leaking tears in the fire's glow.

"It's also pretty clear that the earliest settlers have the largest upstream village organized and functioning in the interest of their families. The Caseys and the Whiteleys have pretty much locked up the good property parcels and business opportunities at the headwaters. Things like a gristmill, cotton gin, and sawmill, as well as a church and a school. They seem like nice folk and hearty settlers, but pretty intertwined, including intermarried."

"But there was some land in between there and here that was near paradise and seemed left alone. I ran into it on my way out. If I were you, I would give it a long look."

"Maybe it's unclaimed because most settlers came in from the north across the mountains, and settled in a fertile valley a ways upstream."

"That is in fact how I came in. You've taken the hard way here according to most, which is why I wanted to go out this way. There is nothing easy about my life these days."

Sam rose slowly, carried his backpack to a nearby tree, leaned back against it, and pulled a tarp over himself.

"Sam, you're welcome to crawl in a corner of the cave, it won't bother us none," offered Jeb.

"No thanks, you all have been kind enough already. I'll just settle in here and head out at morning's light."

Jeb retreated to the cave with Polly and Sunshine. At about the same moment each whispered something to the other about wishing they had Sam to help them find the property he mentioned.

"It would be so much easier if we had him to guide us."

"He seems like a decent guy."

"He is so sad and alone, it might be good for him to have us around."

Jeb volunteered to make the offer.

True to his word, Sam arose early and quietly to depart. Jeb had been lying awake most of the night, wondering if this was the right thing to do. He did not want to submit his flock to more risk from an unknown wanderer, and yet they were all united in their observations. He particularly noticed a seriousness in Polly's reactions. He would ask Sam to join them.

"Sam, wait please," Jeb hollered as Sam slipped silently from view.

Sam turned and sat down in a hollow of underbrush as Jeb caught up.

Jeb squatted down next to him.

"Sam, we don't know you. And yet we trust you in a way that's hard to explain. We also sense a need from you."

"I have a wife, Sam, who is expecting not long from now. I have a mother who is looking for a new life after a long, unhappy, and unhealthy one. I killed my father for abusing my mother. We are a mixed up, fired up, crazy, small group in need of wisdom, experience, and guidance. With the concurrence of Polly and Sunshine, I want to invite you to join us, if only for the journey to your 'near paradise.' Would you consider at least leading us there?"

Sam sobbed out loud. He hadn't been wanted since his wife had closed her eyes for the last time. And now these folks say they not only want, but need, him. He was quiet for a bit.

"Why? I'm an old heartbroken man with nothing left to give? Why me?"

Unbeknownst to Jeb, Polly had slipped up behind him and Sam. She walked up to Sam, looked up at him straight in the eyes, and reached out to grab his hand.

"OK," said Polly. "I'm an old heartbroken woman with nothing left to give either. I promise nothing to you. I ask nothing of you. But…I see nothing but you in our future. I add my invitation, no strings, to Jeb's. Please stay with us, Sam, and help us find the paradise of which you speak. If you later choose to stay and share it with us, so be it. If not, please at least help us get started. We're trying to go where you are coming from. It only makes sense that you help us get there."

Sam stayed silent, but did not release Polly's hand. He had not held a woman's hand since he had felt the life leak out of his dear wife. It felt right and good.

"I will," he finally muttered. "I will take you there and assist you in setting up a homestead. If you will have me, I will likely stay. I can't tell you how vital you have made me feel with your challenge. I will help you in any way I can."

"By the way, Sam, do you have a last name?" Jeb asked.

"No, I left it with my deceased wife. I'm just Sam now."

He finally released Polly's hand, but not before instinctively bending down to kiss it. This brought a smile to Jeb's face.

Polly did not bed down alone again.

Chapter 7

Settling In (1838)

Which brings us back to the most beautiful place in the world. Sam had not exaggerated. It was exactly how he had described it: a heavily wooded ridge looking down on a strip of fertile bottom land bordered by a crystal clear stream cutting through a narrow valley rimmed by limestone bluffs with rock edges and ledges, and even a stunning waterfall in the distance. A spring bubbled up from beneath a rock indentation adjoining the field to add glory. Wood, fresh water, more water and pasture, all naturally sheltered. All that was needed to build a future lay beneath their gaze.

And, all to themselves, Jeb hugging Sunshine, Polly and Sam with arms entwined.

It had taken them several more weeks of increasingly up and down trudging to reach the mouth of the tributary that Sam had explored on his way to them, and then another two days of walking the creek to reach the stunning promontory.

It was hard on Sunshine as her baby filled rather than bulged. Thankfully the cooler weather lessoned the strain of summer and leaves took on bright and diverse colors.

Sam never left Polly's side. When she hinted that she wanted to share herself with him, Sam hesitated, explaining that he was an old man who had not been with a woman since well before his wife died. Polly countered that it had been years for her as well, but that she still remembered how if Sam did. This made him laugh.

"So where do we sneak off to?" Sam asked.

"We'll let them fall asleep, take our blankets, and slip around that big boulder up there."

"Are you sure you want to go through with this?" Sam queried. "What if I'm too old to fulfill my duties? What if I can't, you know…?"

"That's my job," Polly countered.

"What if you fall asleep while I'm fumbling around trying to find myself?" This made her laugh.

And in the end, their laughter simmered down to pleasure and sweet connectivity. Both were renewed in their sense of worth and purpose.

As they lay in each other's arms, Polly confessed that she had never really loved like this before. Sex had always been forced on her, first by a boyfriend who didn't know any better, then by her violent husband who always resented her sleeping with another before him, and took it out on her any time he wanted. Only two men in her entire life, and neither worthy of her affection. She had never been touched like Sam had touched her, never not rushed through the act itself, never savored the moments of shared pleasure.

"Thank you, Sam, for catching me up on fifty years of not knowing what I was missing," she whispered in Sam's ear. This got Sam stirring again and they passed the night without much sleep.

Jeb had heard them sneak off, as well as an occasional grunt or yelp.

He feigned sleep when they slipped silently back into the fire circle. He was happy for their shared passion, and grateful that he had both to lean on as Sunshine neared her moment of truth. She had heard them too and whispered to Jeb that she couldn't wait to resume their pursuit of pleasure.

Jeb pointed to a corner of the field below, far away from the issuing spring, and suggested that they build pens and shelter for the livestock as a first act of civilizing the site. Sam nodded his agreement.

Jeb then scanned the ridge for a building site for themselves. Sam said he preferred a more sheltered location midway down the hill. He spoke not only in terms of weather but also privacy. Jeb welcomed his suggestion and again was glad to have his wisdom and experience to lean on.

Sam also indicated that they would be needing two cabins, not one, which meant more work, but brought a smile to Polly's face and heart. Sam would indeed be staying.

All agreed that they needed to get to work at once in order to be sheltered by winter.

Not long after they commenced to saw down trees and lay out their respective cabins, a stranger sauntered into their camp. He introduced himself as Feral Feester, and proclaimed to be lost. He had wandered down from up north, settled for a bit with the families upstream, but lost their favor when he took a shine to one of their daughters, and had been asked to leave. He was looking for a group to join forces with over winter and was happy to have stumbled onto them. Feral claimed that he was handy with building things, and a quiet but reliable man who was comfortable staying within himself.

Jeb quickly noted that there were no available women around, pointing to his pregnant wife and Polly and Sam holding hands, but reckoned that if he wanted to pitch in and help them get their cabins up before winter, that they could assist him in finishing some kind of shelter for himself, if he located it around the corner of the valley, out of sight and sound.

Feral said he understood, and was ready to go to work immediately. Jeb suggested he scout out a place to settle in first, then come back to help. They would include him in supper plans for this evening.

After Feral left, Polly expressed some concern about inviting strangers into their midst, but agreed that Feester seemed harmless enough.

"An honest pair of hands is always welcome," Sam reasoned.

"If he's honest," Polly added.

The next several weeks were busy ones. Logs were assembled, stacked, and joined with a rudimentary mud-sourced mortar. Stones were formed into a fireplace at one end of the structures for cooking and warmth. Bed frames were constructed and cloths stuffed for mattresses. Goats provided milk like they were supposed to, and chickens began to lay. All settled in to a comfortable routine of building, hunting, tending, and loving. Feral's contributions were invaluable, and they saw little of him when he wasn't working with them, which suited everyone just fine.

When the two log cabins were ready, Jeb and Feral moved on to the site Feral had selected and helped him erect a smaller version, more lean-to than cabin, but suitable for surviving winter's cold and wet.

Sunshine's time came near.

Sam volunteered to hike back to the upstream settlement to acquire basic supplies for the winter and supplement daily game. Polly didn't like the thought of him going it alone, but no one was comfortable leaving the two women alone. They were off the beaten path but stragglers still wandered in, as Feral had done, including an indian or two on occasion. It was simply not worth the risk and Jeb did not want to leave Sunshine's side so close to birth. So, Sam would go alone and take one of the horses to load up. He guessed it would take him no more than two weeks to complete the round-trip journey.

Shortly after Sam's departure, a strange storm like none of them had seen before covered everything with a layer of ice. It was impossible to function outside the cabin beyond crawling on hands and knees. Temperatures plummeted and the ice remained thick and solid. And then more came down. Even Jeb could not figure a way to hunt for food or get down to the spring for fresh water.

He finally crawled down to Polly's cabin to drag her back to his and share the misery together. Polly worried greatly about Sam. Jeb reassured her that he was holed up somewhere sitting it out like they were.

"But he's so…so…so old," Polly blurted out after one of her weeping spells.

"Not too old to put a smile on your face on occasion, Mom," Jeb countered. Polly blushed, then nodded in agreement.

In actual fact Sam was burrowed beneath his cold dead horse on a treacherously steep hillside, trying to stay above freezing himself, and hoping against hope that he and his shelter would not slide down the icy slope into the river.

Sam had tried to push through the early stages of the storm in hopes of getting to the settlement before travel was completely shut down. He had heard of ice storms like this and knew how demobilizing they could become. His horse was jumpy on the slick ground and even reared a couple of times. It was the last one that had brought it down hard, leg crumpling beneath full body weight and snapping in several places. The horse screamed in agony and fought to stand, only to fall and thrash about again. Sam was clipped hard in the shoulder by a flailing hoof as he scrambled to stay clear. It knocked him to the ground as well.

Sam knew the horse would be of no use to him even in good weather and put it out of its misery. He then began walking down the slackened game trail, falling several times immediately, once on his damaged shoulder, sending shots of pain down the whole side of his body. He got up cringing and slipped again.

Sam knew he was in trouble. He couldn't walk on the slick, crusted trail, and crawling would get him nowhere. He looked around for shelter but saw only ice-covered trees with limbs breaking off, gunshot sounds in real time, and the river running cold and deep below. So he went back and crawled under his dead horse, still warm with coagulating blood, but cooling fast. The way Sam figured it, he would either freeze to death, slide down to a water-chilled grave never to be found again, or somehow hang on to life beneath the horse carcass until the storm slowed or someone stumbled onto him. Neither outcome was pleasant to contemplate, so he thought about Polly instead, wishing that it was her warm welcoming body he was hollowing under instead of a dead horse.

In the midst of all this misery, Sunshine cried out in pain. First Polly, then Jeb, stumbled to her side. Her face was a deathly gray and her eyes were clinched shut. "Jeb," she screamed. "Jeb, it hurts so much."

Polly pulled back her cover and saw blood issuing out between her legs in great quantities. She also saw a baby's crown amidst the carnage. She grabbed the head and pulled, taking some comfort in the muffled cries. She wiped the baby as best she could, severed the chord to his mother with Sunshine's nearby knife, and ordered Jeb to heat water in the fire place.

Yes, it was a him.

Jeb stood in shock, unable to move until his mother screamed the order at him again and handed the crying baby to him.

Polly sensed they were losing Sunshine but knew she had to staunch the bleeding from within if they were to have the slightest chance of saving her. She grabbed another rag, dipped it into the cold water, and jammed it as far up Sunshine's vagina as it would reach.

Sunshine opened her eyes long enough to search the room for Jeb who was holding her baby out to her.

"Gv-ge-yu-hi," she whispered before closing her eyes again.

"She's bleeding to death, Mom, do something," Jeb screamed clutching the baby to his chest.

Polly jammed harder with the rag, but the blood still flowed around her fingers. She placed her ear to Sunshine's chest, held for a minute or two, then raised her head with tears pouring down.

"We've lost her, Jeb. Your wife is gone."

Jeb let out a moan that bespoke grief and fear. Polly tried to take the baby from his clutch, but he wouldn't allow it. It was all he had left in the world.

"I need to clean and warm your baby boy, Jeb, or we will lose him too."

Jeb handed his son to his mother and buried his face in his wife's chest, sobbing uncontrollably.

"I want to die with her!" Jeb screamed.

As sun revealed the frozen fields below, and began to drip the melting ice downhill toward the swollen river, Polly sat cuddled with the newborn infant next to the dwindling fire, Jeb squeezed his dead wife, Sunshine, on a bed of dried blood, and Sam crawled out from beneath his stiff horse to resume his journey for supplies, all weak and suffering, each in their own way.

Chapter 8

Beyond Death

"Jeb, you've got to get up and help me or we will lose your son."

"I can't, Mom."

"You must Jeb, or Sunshine will have given her life for nothing. What I hold is all that remains of that life, the ultimate gift she could have left behind. You must help me honor it, and her. We must save your little boy, Sunshine's little boy. I can't do it without you."

Jeb's first trek was to the firewood stack outside the cabin. The icy glaze was giving way to slush, and provided traction enough for him to slosh through. Which is exactly what he was doing in his own mind, sloshing through the loss and gain of life simultaneously.

Next was a trip to the spring for fresh water, to heat over the fire, bathe the baby, clean the blood from his beloved in preparation for burial, and from himself and Polly, if he could even bear parting with this last remaining touch of her. The baby was also desperate for liquid of some kind to ingest.

Then it was to the animals to make sure they had survived, and if so, feed them. He would try and coax some milk from the goat to substitute for Sunshine's breasts.

It would take a week for the baby to show signs of surviving beyond the next breath or nap, and for the ground to thaw enough to consider laying Sunshine to rest.

Feral had trudged up to see how they had weathered the storm, and broke into tears himself when he saw Sunshine's blanket-covered corpse in the corner. He excused himself and returned shortly thereafter with dressed squirrel ready to cook over the fire and dried fatback for nourishment.

He mentioned in passing that he had taken in a stranger who had wandered in during the storm.

And still no sign of Sam.

Sam struggled into the settlement, shoulder ablaze with pain, dragging one leg behind him, and barely ambulatory. He was shaking with chill and weak with worry.

One of the Casey families took him in, bathed him in warm water, and provided nourishment for several days. It was a neighborly thing to do and probably saved Sam's life.

Sam slept soundly and stopped shaking for the first time in days. As he regained his strength, he sat about to accomplish his original mission – acquire supplies to get his small family unit through the winter and seed to plant the coming spring.

He found most of what he needed at the trading post that had been established as the town took root. He paid in cash and found that with what he had left he could afford to replace the horse he had lost as well as add some livestock to the mix. He couldn't be sure if theirs had survived the storm and knew that more would be better in the event they had. One could never have enough to eat and drink in the wilderness they inhabited.

He also sought direction on how to lay claim on the land they had settled. He learned that it was likely in a newly-incorporated county and that the county seat was not that far from their property. He should file and record a claim as soon as possible as word of their paradise was leaking into the land up north, and more adventurers would surely be making their way into the region. Virtually all the indians had moved west and the land was for the taking, first come, first served.

Sam lost track of time amidst his near death and the multitude of tasks that present in terms of establishing their own little settlement. When it finally struck him that Polly might be worried, he quickly wrapped up his business dealings and prepared to return.

One of the acquaintances he made during his stay was a traveling preacher name of Rev. Chester Divine. When Sam asked if that was his real name the preacher responded, "That's what the good Lord calls me even if my mama named me something else. You can call me Rev for short and everyone will be happy."

There was something about the Rev. Chester Divine that drew Sam in. He wasn't sure if it was his naiveté or stupidity, but Chester seemed to operate in another space and time.

The first time Sam met him he was near death following his harrowing experience. The Casey family had called Rev. Divine in when Sam was too cold to communicate. They assumed he was in the throes of death and the least they could do was send him off with a proper blessing. The good reverend had immediately administered the "Last Bill of Rights" as he called it. Sam had heard of the Last Rites of the Catholic tradition from his first wife, whose mother had been raised in that religion. He vaguely recalled that it involved confessing sins and taking communion among other prayers and recitations. Rev's goodbye ceremony bore no resemblance to that ritual, and in fact had caused Sam to laugh out loud at one point despite his distressed condition.

Such things as "the right to bear arms if you are dispatched to hell," "the right to live if you can con God into it," "the right to one last act of sex if God turns you down." And on and on. Sam had never heard anything like it and in fact had passed out several times during the lengthy recitation, causing Rev to skip to the end each time with a dramatic "Godspeed, Godsend, Goddamn, and God bless you my child." Every time Sam regained consciousness, Rev appeared to pick up wherever he had left off, as best as Sam could remember.

When it became apparent that Sam's condition was not as dire as originally feared, and that he appeared to be resting more comfortably, all present applauded and cheered, patting Rev. Divine on the back as he exited with a victorious smile.

When Sam was feeling stronger he asked the Casey woman what the good reverend's ceremony had been all about. She had shrugged in confusion, and responded that "sometime it works, and sometime it don't."

That was as close as Sam could get to grasping Rev's philosophy until he ran into him one night in the small local saloon. Sam was not a heavy drinker but it didn't take him long to ascertain that Rev. Divine was drunk, drunk as a skunk, drunk as blind lemming. Sam thought it might be fun to follow him on this one occasion. The more they drank, the more Rev spouted. Inane stuff. Religious stuff. Sacrilegious stuff. And in the end, the truth, as interpreted by Rev himself, varied from case to case, subject to subject.

At one point in the proceedings, Sam raised the delicate question, "Do you even believe in God, Rev. Devine?"

"I don't know," responded the good Rev, "but I'm guessing it would be pretty bad for business if I didn't, now wouldn't it?"

Sam always respected an honest answer.

Sam had not had a more entertaining evening in a long while. They closed the place down and staggered to their respective beds to recover.

Sam knew it was time to go home. He knew Polly would be worried. He knew Jeb and Sunshine's baby had probably arrived. And, he knew spring was just around the corner. These were all good things. He thought.

He also had another thought, this one particularly random. He and his adoptive flock were going to build a village. Someday. They were already on the path. Jeb, Sunshine, and little Snarkle. Polly and himself. Feral Feester. The makings were all there for growth and self-sufficiency. What any settlement needed though was what this one had. A holy man of the cloth. Or some semblance thereof.

Sam wondered if he could steal Rev. Divine on the pretense of starting a new flock. Whether he could convince him of that as his next calling, and encourage Rev to return with him. He decided to make the ask.

To Sam's surprise, Reverend Devine didn't hesitate to say yes.

When Sam apologized to his kind hosts who had speeded his recovery through days and now weeks, their response surprised him as well. They wished Sam and Rev well, and safe passage without a hint of regret, almost a good riddance kind of gesture.

Sam explained to them that his community had recently expanded with the addition of Feral Feester, who he understood had left their village under a cloud of disapproval because of advances on a young lady.

Mr. Casey laughed out loud at that one. The cloud and advances were correct. But it was a young guy, not gal. Feral Feester was a queer, and had almost gotten strung up on the spot when the young lad's dad had stumbled onto the two buck naked, and engaging in unnatural acts. Feester had exited the community with only the shirt on his back and pulling up his trousers as he ran away in abject fear.

Oh my, thought Sam to himself. A religious leader who didn't believe in God, and a homosexual. He wondered if his sense of community was misplaced.

Time and Jeb Snarkle would tell.

Chapter 9

A Sense of Community

Sam knew something was wrong the moment he turned the bend and headed through the field and up the mountain toward home. There was a pile of fresh dirt looking out on the beautiful valley with a wooden cross sticking in it.

Sam's first thought was Polly, which he screamed with all his might. He dismounted quickly and raced up to their cabin. "Polly! Polly! POLLY!"

The cabin door flew open and Polly raced down the hill toward Sam.

Both cried tears of joy as they embraced and fell to the ground. Unfortunately, Sam landed on his damaged shoulder and screamed in pain, sending Polly into a tizzy.

Jeb emerged from his cabin wearing one of Sunshine's large paternity dresses and carrying a swaddled baby.

Feral came running up from around his bend to see what the commotion was all about. He was followed not far behind by a very young man.

This was the scene that greeted Rev. Divine. He briefly turned his horse around to head back upstream, then reversed course and bellowed in a loud voice, "God, descend on this mess and help me right it," before dismounting and walking up the hill to introduce himself.

"First things first," Rev. Divine proclaimed. "I am the right Reverend Chester Divine, and I have been sent by God Almighty to minister to you. You may call me Rev for short, but never shortchange God."

"Who died and have they had a proper burial ceremony?" Reverend Devine continued.

"Sunshine," Polly responded, "and no."

"Who are you?" Rev queried.

"Sam's friend, Polly"

"Are you married?"

"Not officially, but certainly in word and in deed."

"Who is the guy in the dress?"

"Jeb Snarkle, husband of the deceased."

"Who is the baby he is clutching to his chest?"

"No name Snarkle, son of the deceased and his father, Jeb."

"Hello, Feral, do you remember me?"

"Yes, Rev. Divine, I do."

"And, who is the young lad holding your hand?"

"That would be Randy, my friend."

"OK, Jeb Snarkle, Sam, Polly, Feral, Randy, and baby, we have work to do, rituals to follow, and God's blessing to bestow on this gathering."

"Jeb, hand the baby to Polly, take off the dress, and put on your real clothes. Polly, hand the baby to Sam, draw him a warm bath to soak his shoulder in, and get in with him to clean you both up. Bathe the baby while you are at it. Then each of you put on the best and cleanest clothes you possess. Same for you, Randy and Feral. Polly, when finished, return the baby to Jeb, fresh and swaddled. All meet back here when the sun is straight up for a burial, a christening, and two weddings."

"Dear God, take your beloved servant Sunshine into your kingdom and grant her peace from this strange place on earth. Strengthen her love for those she has left behind at your command, and help her smile at all who remain. Amen."

"Jeb Snarkle, place Sunshine's large dress on top of her grave, and never touch it again."

"Next, Jeb Snarkle, lift your baby to the sky and repeat after me: Jesus, Alien, imbue your offspring with the strength and courage needed to survive the loss of his mother, a cross-dressing father, and a community in need of your saving grace."

"I'm not a cross-dresser, Reverend Divine. Just trying to stay close to my beloved Sunshine," muttered an embarrassed Jeb.

"Who is this Jesus, Alien?" Polly whispered to Sam.

Sam shook his head in confusion. That one hadn't even surfaced at the saloon that long night.

Rev. Divine inquired of Jeb what he intended to name the baby.

"Yonu, Rev, Yonu."

"Strange name, Snarkle, what does it imply or mean?"

"It means 'Bear' in Sunshine's native tongue. I promised my beloved that we would name our first son Bear in honor of the Nunnehi who saved my life from a vicious bear."

This was more information that Rev. Divine could process at once, so he simply nodded his approval.

"Jesus, Alien, please accept our praise and humble gratitude for this new life sprung from the love of this unusual father and dead mother, and light its way to its new name, Yonu. Actually, Bear sounds better."

"Bear Snarkle, please accept Jesus, Alien as your personal guide through the life that lies ahead of you. I formally and reluctantly christen you Bear, for this life."

"Polly and Sam, Feral and Randy, please step forward."

"Dearly beloved, we are gathered here…"

"Wait a minute, Rev," Sam interrupted. "What is this Jesus, Alien stuff you are blessing us with? I've never read anything about it in the Bible and my first wife read to me from it daily."

"It is a new and novel interpretation of the scriptures. I received it in a dream on the way to here. Trust me on this one and I will delve more deeply into it in my first sermon. Speaking of which, I will need a place to stay until we can build my church from which to minister to you."

"You can stay with me and the baby, Rev. Divine, until then," offered Jeb, "and Sam, Feral, Randy, and I will commence work on your church and adjoining living quarters as soon as you marry these couples in need of God's blessing. Thank you for being here, Rev. Divine."

Chapter 10

Welcome (1858)

Over time, people came and went to and from the small settlement that finally grew large enough to consider a name.

As usual, Rev. Divine played a crucial role in gaining consensus for that name.

Discussions began not long after the population of the adjacent hills and valleys swelled to twenty or so, depending on the time of year. An elderly couple, the Daniels; a stray indian family who refused to give their name for fear of being discovered by authorities; a farming family of Italian roots with working children, the Pompassies; several unnamed young men looking for adventure who passed through on a seasonal basis; and a couple of tradesmen—Rubert Gas and Erasmus Henry. Rubert launched Gas's Trading Post and provided a limited supply of needed goods. Erasmus was a man of color who was a smithy. Rubert and Erasmus didn't have family, but seemed to attract an ample supply of rotating girlfriends, rumored to be shared on occasion, among themselves, and with young passer-throughs, for a price.

Jeb Snarkle began to take pride in his pig farm. Between the four founding piglets and their normal reproduction over the years, the few added from adjoining farmers, less natural family and community consumption, he counted more than fifty of the porkers in his pens. He had become the major pork provider in the immediate area, though others kept small counts. He allowed all to free range, and was constantly moving their confinement areas so as to allow fertilization of other fields for community row crops and grasslands for other livestock to feed on. He maintained a wide strip of trees along the riverbank to discourage livestock from entering the creek and, at least as his common sense told him, filter out waste runoff. It was a closed loop system that his mother had seen work well in Tennessee years past and was gentle on the land and surrounding waters. He really didn't want too many more of the critters for fear of over grazing or fertilizing.

And then there was Tiny Taylor, who fancied himself as sort of a village idiot and was diligent in his efforts live up to expectations. No one knew from whence he came, nor cared much about it. He spent most days lounging on the porch of Gas's Trading Post hurling insults to all who entered.

"Jeb Snarkle, you are as ugly as an unwashed cow udder."

"Erasmus Henry, you aren't black enough to be a slave."

"Sam, you are too old to have sex with anyone, let alone a goat."

"Injun Chief, you don't have a name because your mammy couldn't spell."

"Mama Mia, Sophia Pompassie, you have a derriere large enough to host a rodeo."

And on, and on, and on. Most laughed at Tiny's crudity and bizarre attempts at humor. Others ignored him. When Rubert Gas once asked him to loiter somewhere other than his front porch, customer visits declined, so he quickly invited him back in the interest of commerce.

But, then there was the time Bear Snarkle almost killed Tiny.

Bear was introduced to sex by one of Rubert Gas's visiting ladies. In fact it became more than that after a time or two. Bear began to feel genuine affection for "Fanny" as he called her.

He was first introduced to Fannibelle Cloisters by Rubert, who figured it was about time for Bear to grow up. Jeb didn't seem to have any interest in taking responsibility for the boy's development. He was too busy attending to Sophia Pompassie. So Rubert took it on himself to fill the void. He knew that Fannibelle was kind and gentle despite her broad experience. She was also relatively young, and would likely be attractive to young Bear. He wouldn't even charge the lad, a community service of sort.

Fannibelle laughed out loud when the young man introduced himself, with Rubert's encouragement, as Bear Snarkle, then quickly apologized and smothered him in an embrace, before leading him to one of Rubert's back rooms. She kept him for more than the usual allotted time, later explaining to Rubert that it took him a while to get the hang of things, but once engaged, he was tireless. "The glory of youth," Rubert had coyly observed.

Bear was back to see Fannibelle the next day, and though she was scheduled to depart, she stayed around to extend into the next. She left, promising Bear that she would come back again soon.

And when she did, Bear was back as well. Theirs became more relationship than transactional, a first for Fannibelle Cloisters. Bear was smitten with Fanny, and she was becoming attached to him in a strange, for her, kind of way.

One afternoon as Bear walked up the porch stairs to visit recently arrived Miss Fanny, Tiny asked him if he was ever gonna get tired of that Franco whore who fornicated for money with most in town. Just because she didn't charge Bear…

Bear was on Tiny like his namesake, wrapping his large strong hands around Tiny's neck, and demanding that Tiny apologize not only to him, but also to Fanny. Tiny, of course, could not answer because his windpipe was crushed closed, which Bear took as a rejection of his request and squeezed tighter. When Rubert finally pulled Bear off Tiny with the help of several other customers, Tiny was red faced and gasping for breath. Bear kicked him hard in the groin, which sent him into a death struggle to breathe.

Fortunately one of Rubert's other girls was close by. She bent over and placed her mouth on his, breathing heavily in and out, and finally got air to his lungs. Tiny, who had lost consciousness after the second assault, awoke to a beautiful if slightly aging lady breathing in and out of his mouth, and quickly began to remove her dress, ripping buttons and grabbing underneath for anything he could get a handle on. This earned him a solid slap from his benefactor, and a request for compensation if he wished to explore further.

Fannibelle had watched from the door as Bear defended her honor, and ran to throw herself into his arms.

Rubert could only shake his head in wonder and take pride in the community service he had initiated.

"Fanny, you are coming home with me tonight," Bear said.

Fanny looked at Rubert for a 'what do I do next?'

Rubert nodded his approval and said "OK, Bear."

Fanny never returned to the service of Rubert and Erasmus.

And so it was that despite exceedingly varied pedigrees, everyone seemed readily welcomed into the community originally staked out by Jeb and Sunshine, Polly and Sam, Feral and Randy, and the good Rev himself, a polyglot of diversity in the heart of the Ozarks.

Which led Rev. Divine to propose a name for the home of his flock. His ecumenical approach to religious grounding set the tone for the settlement's open armed welcome, unusual for this place and time.

And one Sunday as he expounded on his Jesus, Alien series, which had been running for close to two decades, it came to him.

"Jesus, Alien, came to me in a dream last night and asked that I share his and God Almighty's congratulations for being such an open and welcoming community. He further suggested a name for the settlement we share. Welcome. Welcome, Arkansas. Does anyone have any questions before we vote?"

Per usual, Jeb, Sophia Pompassie, and Tiny Taylor, were the only souls in attendance, so their support was crucial to the outcome.

Throughout the years, no one else in the village could stand to sit through Rev. Divine's inane sermons and revelations about God being the Lead Alien, and as such sending other inspirational aliens like Jesus Christ, Buddha, and Krishna to save his creation from destruction. First of all no one knew who the others were, secondly, it made no sense, and thirdly it hadn't worked. The neighborhood seemed to become more violent year by year.

Jeb attended every Sunday simply because Sophia, as a guilt-ridden, Italian-bred Roman Catholic, felt obligated to do so, and it was the only time he could get next to her. Tiny Taylor tagged along to poke fun and insults at the two wannabe lovers who couldn't quite pull the trigger. Jeb was still missing Sunshine after all the years, and had been beyond faithful. Sophia was not allowed by her father to talk to any man in public. So it was that their platonic interaction could occur only under the watchful eye of Rev. Divine. Tiny sat in the pew behind and whispered every sexual innuendo he could dream up, always inquiring of Jeb if he had gotten lucky the previous night.

So the vote on Welcome, Arkansas, came down to these three.

"Does that make those of us who live here 'Welcomers'?" Jeb asked.

"Sounds better than 'Welcomians' or 'Welcomites' I guess," acknowledge Rev. Divine. "Well said, Brother Jeb. I presume that this means you will vote in support of the new community name?"

Jeb nodded his approval. Sophia followed in suit. Tiny raised his hand to flip Jeb's ear from behind, which Rev. Divine counted as a yes as well.

"Very well, Brother Jeb, will you please spread the word to all of our residents about the unanimous vote in favor of Welcome, Arkansas, while I ring the church bell in celebration?"

"Yes sir, Rev Divine. Yes sir."

It seemed that everyone made love on Sunday mornings, except the four churchgoers.

Jeb's first stop was at Polly and Sam's. Both were walking around stark naked having been interrupted by the church bell. This was not a particularly pretty site at their advanced age.

"What in the hell is going on?" an angry Sam spat out. "Is something on fire?" The years had not been kind to Sam, and even Polly was tiring of his ill humor, despite the deep love she carried for him and her continued attempts to keep him engaged in intimacies.

Jeb laughed out loud. Said he had once heard of some guy up north near Skunk Creek, Ol' Dill or something like that, who was still going at it in his mid-eighties. With a female Tiny Taylor nonetheless. He had heard it from a passer-through who claimed to know and admire both.

"I ain't doing nothing with that idiot Tiny Taylor, I can assure you," Sam growled. "Leave us be, Jeb."

"Important news, Sam, sorry to interrupt."

Jeb informed them that the settlement, the village, the community that they resided in, now had a name, as unanimously decreed in Rev. Divine's church this very morning. Welcome, Arkansas.

"How stupid can we get," Sam asked pulling his pants up.

Next up were Feral and Randy, and they were caught by surprise as well. "Can't anybody have any privacy on Sunday morning?" asked a frustrated Feral, peeking from behind his front door.

"We're now known as "Welcome, Arkansas," an embarrassed Jeb hollered over his shoulder in departing.

And so it was at most stops along the way with his message of good news.

Rubert Gas and Erasmus Henry both had naked women with them when they answered their respective doors. Both women winked at Jeb, which caused him to blush.

The Daniels were fully clothed but smiling broadly which implied something.

The Pompassies sent Sophia to the door, which was a mistake. Jeb could not contain himself at this point and swept her into his arms in a swirl. His kiss was hard and fast. She responded in kind. It couldn't have been a better time for the two of them to interact as the senior Pompassies were doing the same in the privacy of their back bedroom.

"I will be back for you, Sophia," Jeb whispered as he sat her back on ground and continued his rounds.

Only Tiny Taylor was alone.

Jeb went running back to the Pompassies hoping to still find Sophia by herself. He did, and she slipped away with him to their hay barn.

For Jeb, it was his first time in twenty years. For Sophia, it was her second.

As they lay basking in the pleasure and joy they had shared, Jeb confessed to have thought about Sunshine as they loved one another. And Sophia confessed that Jeb had not been the first, which was the reason for her father's strict code about men.

True confessions behind them, Jeb asked if Sophia would consider moving in with him. He had loved her deeply from afar for many years and wanted to be with her always. Sophia acknowledged similar feelings and yearnings, but warned that her father would likely insist on a marriage proposal before consenting to such an arrangement. Actually, a wedding. Jeb said he would have no problem committing to anything if it meant spending the rest of his days and years with Sophia. In fact, he was prepared to make the offer right at this moment.

Sophia smiled her acceptance of Jeb's offer, rose and reclothed, shaking the hay out of her hair.

Jeb led her by the hand to the Pompassies front door and knocked loudly.

They had finished their frolicking by now and seemed in a genuinely good mood, until Jeb announced his intention to wed their daughter, and was there to ask Mr. Pompassie's approval. The latter lunged at him, screaming something in Italian, while Mrs. Pompassie clung to his arm and urged him to calm down.

Sophia smiled at Jeb and suggested that he return after she had an opportunity to discuss their deep love with her father.

She reached up to Jeb to pull a piece of hay from his hair, which sent Mr. Pompassie into another rage. "What have you been doing in my barn?" he demanded.

This was a prompt to take leave that even one so lovestruck as Jeb Snarkle could not ignore.

Ironically, Jeb's first foray into intimacy with Sophia produced the same result that his initial contact with Sunshine had. A baby bump.

Sunday morning was clearly the witching hour in newly declared Welcome, Arkansas, and all were simply welcome to join in.

Chapter 11

War (1861-62)

Time passed, and more bullets than usual began to fly. It was a time of war, one that stretched even into the river valley.

There were two battles that took place early in the War Between the States that hit home. One was at Wilson's Creek, outside of Springfield, Missouri, to the north, the other at Pea Ridge, Arkansas, even closer. The rebs won the first, the Yankees the second, and most poor souls in the middle didn't give a hoot.

Welcome didn't believe in war anyway. How can a community that welcomes everyone fight over some. Erasmus was black. He was part of Welcome, Arkansas, neither slave nor free. Rubert Gas was white. He was part of Welcome, Arkansas, as well, neither Johnny Reb nor Yankee. Feral Feester was a homosexual. He and his favorite lad were part of Welcome, Arkansas. The unnamed indian and his family were just that. Unnamed, and loved by all.

Where Welcome, Arkansas got in trouble was inviting soldiers from both sides in, treating them with respect, and expecting them to sit down at the table together, beyond the war that raged around them.

Sadly, Welcomers got burned in that process.

Rubert Gas had opened a saloon from the proceeds of his trading post. And that's when the profits really began to flow. Rubert made his own stuff. It was strong and nasty. And, soldiers on both sides loved it. They were also partial to his visiting women. Most Welcomers welcomed all, as was their tradition, and just looked the other way.

Sophia and Jeb's baby son was the first to be born in Welcome. And what a celebratory occasion it was. Even old man Pompassie was on board. That Jeb named the young lad Luigi, after Pompassie himself sealed the deal.

Sophia had foreseen correctly. When he found out that Sophia was with child, he quickly embraced the father as son-in-law, requiring nuptials the week thereof. He reasoned that daughter with child and husband was much preferred to daughter with child, and should be celebrated not mourned.

Rev. Divine presided as always, subject to his promises not to mention Jesus, Alien, and to read the entire text from the Pompassie's Roman Catholic Practitioners Handbook. Word for word.

Jeb's son Bear and Fannibelle were not far behind in the production line. They had enjoyed the Catholic wedding version so much that they insisted on a similar ritual. Neither had a clue of what Catholic meant or required, but felt blessed by God in the end.

When Fannibelle's time came, they settled on Bear Jr. for the baby boy who emerged. Both found grounding in the name. The indian blood coursing through Bear's veins would be honored in a further diluted state in son and name.

Rev. Divine finally decided that his divine revelation about Jesus, Alien was in fact not so divine after all, and began to bend his ecumenical reach back toward traditional messaging. It was all about the consumer, and what made him, or her, happy and holy.

The small cabin that Jeb and Sunshine had settled in twenty years earlier was soon filled with energy and baby coos and cries, as Jeb, Sophia, Bear, Fannibelle, and their two baby boys got to know one another quite well, despite the spare room that had been quickly added.

It was a strangely conceived and delivered family unit, but it worked so well that Bear gave up thoughts of his own cabin for the time being.

Jeb and Bear would work the livestock and fields, hunt, and fish most days. Sophia and Fannibelle would share mothering with Polly, providing all with moments of affection, respite, and reflection.

When both sets of newlyweds got back to normal romantic pursuits, they would slip off to Sam and Polly's cabin, running Sam out of his home for as long as they carried on, and further adding to his increasingly bad humor.

All of this love, happiness, and good will within shouting distance of each other. To hell with Sam, most agreed.

The veil was pierced early one crisp morning when Jeb headed up to Rubert's trading post for some goods and saw Erasmus Henry dangling from a rope attached to a front porch beam. He had been bloodied and beaten prior to the lynching.

Jeb screamed in horror, which brought Rubert forth, pulling up his pants, damsel at his side. They screamed as well. Others soon joined in sharing shock, then grief.

Erasmus was known as a kind-hearted soul, neither black nor white except in appearance, with a fondness for white women, who were happy to love him back. He generally kept to himself except when helping others. His brutal murder was inconceivable.

Rubert stepped forward, wiping tears from his eyes.

"I know who done it," he somberly reported. "It was the two Johnny Rebs who shut down my tavern last night. They had earlier been chased out of the saltpeter operation upstream by a Yankee raiding party, and yet had shared a comfortable whiskey pull with some blue coats earlier in the evening. Their behavior deteriorated with time and libation. It was them alright."

One point of conflict between Union and Confederate forces in the river valley during the war was located outside the settlement upstream, the largest in the area. Several caves were loaded with bat guano, a principle source of saltpeter, or nitre, which was used to manufacture gun powder. It was this source of product that spawned intermittent battles between sides, and in this case had led both blue and gray to Welcome for a drink amidst hostilities.

What had ultimately set the rebs off that night was the sight of Erasmus squiring around a pretty young white lady. He and she had settled at a table at the back of the room. Erasmus learned long before to always have his back to the wall, and tonight was no different. One of the Reb soldiers ambled up and asked the young lady if he could buy her a drink. When she pointed out that she already had one, he reached in front of her, grabbed her glass, and drained what remained.

"Looks like an empty glass to me," he observed with a crooked smile.

"I believe the lady said she didn't need a drink from you," Erasmus noted.

"Why not let the young lady speak for herself black boy?"

Erasmus rose, pulling a gun from beneath the table, and pointed it toward the offending presence. Rubert, sensing the confrontation, stepped from behind the bar with his shotgun pointed toward the other.

"Time to go home, boys," he ordered.

Both had staggered out.

"I know it was them," Rubert repeated.

By now the two Union soldiers who had shared drinks with the prime suspects had stumbled out of beds in Rubert's back rooms, with their charges for the evening. They were incensed at the lynching and bid their ladies goodbye, before mounting up and heading back to Union camp. They promised to return to bring justice to the murderers.

Since Welcome had never needed a sheriff before, townsfolk generally took turns. Rubert said he would cut down the body of his friend Erasmus and have the girls prepare him for burial. Jeb said he would gather a small search party to scour the immediate surrounds in hope of finding the culprits. He noted in passing that Erasmus's woman was missing as well and might have been kidnapped by them.

Bear and Mr. Pompassie would join him. Their womenfolk would prepare a feast to celebrate the life of Erasmus Henry. Polly would watch the young ones.

The search party didn't have to wander far to strike pay dirt. Just outside of the village their horses almost stumbled and fell on two bodies in a ditch. The two Reb suspects were still drunk from the night before, and literally incoherent. Jeb asked straight up if that had lynched a black man before passing out in the ditch. Both looked confused at the charges, then at each other.

"We didn't kill no one, now did we?"

"Not that I'm aware of."

"Have you seen the pretty lady that was with him?" Jeb followed. "The blonde one with blue eyes that you was fixing to fight him over last night?"

They looked at each other in confusion again.

"Last time I saw her was with a barrel of a gun pointed at my gullet," said one. The other nodded blankly.

"So, who killed our neighbor and friend, assholes?" screamed Mr. Pompassie.

Bear tied the two together with a rope looped ominously around a tree and promised to return. They fanned out looking for the young lady.

Jeb found her gagged and bound to a tree not far away. She was unconscious and had no clothes on. He assumed rape given the contusions on her body.

He hollered for his fellow searchers, not wanting to tackle this one on his own, which awakened the young victim. She began sobbing and shaking uncontrollably. When Bear arrived, Jeb sent him straight to bring one of the women to help. He untied the young lady and wrapped her in his shirt, handing water to her to drink. All he could think of was who could have treated such a beautiful young thing so horribly.

He sat with her until Polly arrived with a blanket, which she gently wrapped her in.

"Who did this to you, young lady?" Jeb finally asked. "Was it the two Rebel creeps who came on to you at Rubert's?"

She shook her head in the negative.

This set Jeb Snarkle's head to spinning. Two drunk Confederate soldiers, one lynched black man, and one brutally raped young white lady, and no connection between any of them?

Polly took the young lady, whose name was Star, in with her and Sam to care for her. Rubert wanted to hang the two suspects on the spot but backed down when the victim said they didn't do it. So he stuck them in one of his visiting ladies quarters with the door bound shut until he could figure out what to do next.

Jeb stepped in sheriff-like and interviewed each of the participants separately in this unfurling drama.

Soldier one knew he was a prime suspect in a lynching and was scared to death. All he could do was apologize for making such an ass of himself the night before, blame it on Rubert's homemade corn whiskey, and swear that he passed out cold in the ditch they found him in without knowing or doing anything else.

Soldier two couldn't quite grasp the severity of the charges being considered against him and railed on about the black boy and the white girl hanging out together and getting him in trouble. It just wasn't right, this mixing of sex and race, and it caused him such anxiety that he got drunk and didn't remember much else. His testimony left much to the imagination.

The victim, Star, was severely shaken, not only by the physical abuse that had been leveled on her, but the loss of her dear friend, Erasmus.

They were really more than friends and lovers, they were soul mates, who lived their own lives, and reunited as desired.

Star only remembered Erasmus awakening during the night and saying he was going to check a strange noise outside near the horses. "I never saw him again."

But a huge man with a bandana covering his face had ripped her covers back, pointed a gun at her head, and told her to spread 'em wide. He then proceeded to pummel her as she had never been forced on before. He finished once, then dragged her outside and took her again before tying her to the tree where they found her. She recognized nothing about the coarse man who had raped her, though she remembered his gloved hands being the size of axe heads and a bushy beard pushing out beneath the bandana. She assumed he had hung Erasmus as well, though he would have had to beat him unconscious first to pull that off. Erasmus would never have allowed a rope around his neck, no matter what.

"And you're sure it wasn't the Johnny Rebs, Star?"

"I'm positive," Star replied.

Jeb shared all this with Sophia later that night, seeking her opinion as to who was lying.

"No one," replied Sophia. "I believe them all."

"How can that be? They're all suspect. Two Rebel drunks, a black man, and a whore. There has never been anyone in these parts that even remotely resembles the description Star provided."

"Vagabonds are wandering in and out all the time. Could have been a bushwhacker or a total stranger."

"Doesn't make sense why he would go to Erasmus. Random man, random victims, random acts of violence? Out of the blue? Doesn't make any sense."

Rubert took over the questioning next day and got the same answers. Rev. Divine tried next with no difference in result. They finally pulled in Sam to try and piss them off with his sour humor and break apart their respective tales. No success.

All gathered to discuss next steps. The worst charge anyone could come up with was public drunkenness, which hardly made the two Rebel soldiers unique.

Unbeknownst to the grieving conveners, matters were about to get out of hand.

Jeb awoke early the next morning and looked out over his field and creek below. What he saw appeared as a dream. A group of union regulars was erecting a scaffold on a facing hill. A group of three soldiers crossed the creek and headed toward Jeb under cover of a white flag and a number of soldiers kneeling in firing position.

"What the heck, honey," Jeb hollered at Sophia who came out in her gown to see what was going on. They were upon them before Sophia had time to retreat to the cover of cabin so she covered herself with her arms for privacy. Polly was doing the same on her front porch while Sam fetched his shotgun.

"Are you Jeb Snarkle?" the ranking officer asked.

"Yes, what can I do for you."

"I demand that you immediately turn over the two prisoners who hung a black man and brutally raped his white partner. We intend to hang them across the river to set an example for others who might harbor violent ambitions."

"I can't do it, sir," Jeb responded. "They are not guilty."

"I demand it," said the officer drawing his pistol.

"I refuse, sir."

Shots rang out from the woods behind Jeb sending the union emissaries scrambling back down the hill toward the river. Jeb looked behind to see a line of confederate soldiers advancing and firing at the retreating blue coats.

"What the hell," muttered Jeb. His pig farm was clearly at risk as the unsuspecting porkers wandered around aimlessly below.

He looked on in disbelief as battle lines appeared alongside tiny Welcome, Arkansas. The Battle of Large Creek loomed in front of their very eyes. How had this come to be?

The morning of the lynching, the two Union soldiers who had "slept over" set out for their unit to fetch help in dispensing justice for the lynching. They figured that the two Rebel drunks wouldn't make it very far before the townsfolk apprehended them. They wanted the Union Army to make a strong statement in support of justice, law, and order for the residents of the river valley, who were split down the middle when it came to sympathies for north and south. Hanging the lynchers in Welcome, Arkansas, would do just that.

Shortly thereafter, Tiny Taylor, who had close personal ties with several in the company of Confederate soldiers who were routed at the Battle of Pea Ridge, and heard the blue coats muttering about delivering justice, headed off to find his compatriots and warn them that two of their soldiers were about to be hung in Welcome, Arkansas for a crime they did not commit. That both sides showed up on the same day at about the same time spoke to the spontaneity of most major Civil War battles.

With lines and weapons drawn, a strange spectacle ensued.

Sam told Polly to take his shotgun up to Jeb. As she headed off, Sam bent down to her and said, "Thanks, Hon, I'm tired."

Polly assumed that meant he was headed back to bed despite the drama unfolding below, and took off running to Jeb and Sophia, who had been joined by Bear and Fanny. Star followed close behind.

Out of the corner of his eye, Jeb saw Polly and Star headed his way, and then had to double take in disbelief at what was transpiring behind them. Sam was stripping off all of his clothing. When finished, he walked off his front porch, buck naked, holding a wooden walking stick for support, and strolled between the battle drawn lines. All firing ceased as commanders tried to assess whether this was a ploy, a secret way to infiltrate their ranks, a lethal armament disguised as a cane, or just a crazy old man.

Polly gasped when Jeb pointed her naked husband out to her and started to run toward him. Jeb grabbed her arm and ordered her to sit tight.

Sam made his way down to the creek slowly, stopping occasionally to lean on the cane and look skyward, then resuming his measured pace. He crossed the creek where the Union soldiers had done so just minutes before, and headed up the hill toward the scaffold, which by now had been rigged with a hanging rope.

Certainly no one, regardless of age or experience had ever seen anything like this before in their lives.

Sam walked up to the commanding officer, causing all around to point their weapons at him.

"I done it. String me up," Sam said simply and directly, extending his hands so that they could be bound.

Polly could barely see what was going on, but knew it wasn't good, at least for Sam.

The union commander suddenly raised his arm in salute to his southern counterpart, and ordered his soldiers to lay their arms down. The Rebels followed suit.

As Sam ascended steps to the noose, Polly spoke of the peace that awaited him, the escape from depression, senility and resultant anger that had dogged him the past decade. She whispered words of love and gratitude to and for him, then sobbed as he dangled silently in the breeze.

After it was all over, Sam's body reclaimed for burial next to his cabin, and the two Johnny Reb suspects released with the admonition to never come back to Welcome, Arkansas, again, Jeb sought out Polly and Star.

"I'm sorry to have to ask this, Polly, but he didn't really do it did he?"

"Are you kidding?" Polly shot back. "Star, you said the rapist took you at least two times, did you not?" Star nodded yes.

"Sam couldn't have done that if I held a gun to his head," Polly explained. "He was just fed up with life, his loss of the humor and the joy he had once found in it."

As he had told Polly, Sam was just 'tired.'

Polly smiled through her tears and added, "He also said, 'Thanks, hon,' which I took to mean 'I love you.'"

The Battle of Large Creek was thus averted, Jeb Snarkle's pig farm spared, and Welcome, Arkansas, was not so welcoming anymore.

They buried Erasmus Henry on the other side of Sunshine Snarkle, the community's first citizens of color.

And still a killer wandered free.

Chapter 12

LEARNING (1877)

Polly's death at age 89 saddened the community at large. She remained a vibrant part of everything to the end. Her passing, at the same age as Sam did not go unnoticed by Jeb.

One of her endearing legacies was getting Star hooked up with Rev. Divine, who was in his 60s at the time.

Over time, Rev had tired of the radical takes on religion that had intrigued him as the young minister who had taken Jeb Snarkle and his crew as flock. He in fact had become more of a cheerleader than a preacher, and spent most of his time making congregants feel good about themselves. He had even finally come to believe in God and accept the mysteries that went with that.

He also began to fancy a woman for the first time in his life.

Rev had rejected anything to do with the opposite sex as part of his original ministerial vows. He had been a relatively handsome youth and attracted female attention easily. There had been something obscenely powerful in rejecting it. And, if there was one thing that excited Rev, it was power. Shunting aside the temptations that reduced all men, not most, but all, to lesser humans fed his ego and soothed his soul. What no living person knew was that he had never kissed a woman, never held one's hand, never engaged in sex or even allowed the desire to do so to enter his mind. Rev was unusual that way.

At least until he made the mistake of looking into Star's deep blue eyes leaking tears as she spoke of the years she had wasted passing herself among men, only to lose the one she cared for most to murder, and herself to brutal rape. She considered her life nothing more than a blur, and if it hadn't been for Polly stepping in to love her as a daughter, she probably would have killed herself.

Long after Star had left him hanging onto her tragic story, those blue eyes stayed with him, looking in to find places that had never felt before, never once been touched.

He began to stare into Star's eyes every time he ran into her, which by intention, increased in frequency. Star finally asked him what he was looking at.

"The most beautiful eyes I have ever seen," Reverend Chester Divine finally spat out in spite of himself. This made Star blush and exit quickly. She went straight to mama Polly.

"Reverend Divine is treating me strangely." Star confessed to feeling confused, flattered, frightened, even excited. "He made me blush by calling my eyes the most beautiful he has ever seen. And believe me, it takes a lot to make me blush after what I've experienced in life. What's going on Mama Polly?"

Polly smiled and said that Reverend Divine may have fallen in love with Star, not an easy thing for a celibate man of the cloth to disclose. When Star asked what celibate meant, Polly explained that many ministers, preachers, and the like were called to swear eternal love to God, and no one else. Including sex. She laughed when she added that she had never known one to keep the vow.

"What should I do?" Star asked.

"If it were me I would probably flirt a little with the old guy to see what kind of reaction I might get, before deciding whether he was serious and if his intentions were worthy of further response."

The next morning Star called on Rev at his church as he was taking morning prayers. He was serious in his machinations and she watched him for a bit before announcing her presence. She thought he was going to faint when she did. She apologized for startling him and asked if they could visit for a moment.

"Reverend Divine, I behaved quite rudely when you complimented me on my eyes yesterday and want to apologize." She reached out and touched his arm. "I am so grateful for your kind words." Rev blushed, swooned, and stumbled to a pew to sit down before he fell. He invited Star to join him.

He then began his confession. Despite being twice Star's age, he believed that he was in love with her. He wasn't even sure what that meant, but knew it felt different than anything in his life to date. He had tried to bury his newfound emotions but found them leaking out every time he saw her. And she did have the most beautiful eyes he had ever looked into.

"Do you know how many men I have been with, Reverend Divine?"

"No. How many?"

"I don't know for sure, but a lot."

"Do you know how many women I've been with, Star?"

"No, how many?"

"None, Star, not even one. Zero. I wouldn't even know where or how to begin."

Star hesitated, then began to tremble slightly. She found Rev's naiveté and inexperience stimulating. And his admiration of an overused young woman with blue eyes inspiring.

"What if I taught you how, Rev. Divine? What if I taught you how to make love from beginning to end, and back to start again? Would you think less of me if I showed you how to pleasure a woman while finding your own?"

Star leaned into kiss Rev softly when he said or did nothing other than blush, then with more authority. He reacted with surprise, then tenderness. She reached over to undo his collar, then began to unbutton her own dress. About half way down she lifted his hand and placed in on her bare breast.

"None," "not even one," "zero," quickly became a part of Reverend Divine's past.

Star had never been loved by a man for her eyes. It was always for her body and the pleasure she provided.

Reverend Divine had never been loved by a woman. Period. Maybe his mother, but she had passed early in his life and he didn't remember much about her. What he did know is that he finally understood the meaning of his last name, in the context of love and pleasure.

It didn't take long for Reverend Chester Divine to propose to Star. They began to meet at his church during off hours to continue his training in the art of love making. Star was an experienced teacher, and Rev was a willing and fast learner. Their shared joy exploded around and within them.

Polly knew something was going on between the two, but kept it to herself. Star came to her with Rev's proposal.

"He said he knew he was old, but promised he would love me with all that was left in him for as long as he could, Mama Polly."

"Do you feel love for him, dear?"

"I think so, but I'm not sure what that really means."

"Then you do. You would know if you didn't."

"Do you think I should marry him, Mama Polly?"

"Does he make you feel whole, does he make you feel valued, does he make you feel good?"

"All of the above."

"It's totally up to you, Star. I can tell you from experience that marrying a man who is considerably older than you has its downside with age. Sam and I shared little at the end but memories. At the same time I wouldn't have had them without him."

"I guess it comes down to whether I want the rest of my life to just be a blur like it has until now. Or whether I choose to pursue a deeper meaning with what remains."

As they laid Polly to rest, Star recalled their conversation fondly. Her new husband did a masterful job of making everyone feel good about Polly, even in losing her. Star knew that she would never have become who she was, with a man whom she loved, and whose baby she was carrying, if it had not been for Mama Polly. She also knew that Welcome, Arkansas, was covered with Polly Snarkle's fingerprints, and filled with a healthy dose of her good will.

As Jeb and his son Bear lowered his mother's hand-hewn box into the ground next to Sam, just above the log cabin they had built nearly forty years earlier, Star rose, grabbed husband Rev. Chester Divine's hand, and led a small procession in picking up a handful of dirt and sprinkling a loving and grateful goodbye on her casket.

"Dad, I don't want to be a farmer," Bear Jr. pleaded. "I don't want to tend the land or raise animals. I admire what you and grandpa do, but I simply don't want to spend my life doing it."

"So, what do you want to do, Bear Jr.?"

"I want to go to school, Dad. I want to study and learn. I want a real education, so I can be whatever it is I choose to become."

"I've heard of this college up north," Bear replied, "recently founded by a group of religious folks, Congregants or something like that, who actually recruit indians to their school. It's in Springfield, Missouri. Maybe you should find your way up there. You can catch a train and I can get you to there. I don't think they will charge you for schooling since you are an indian, and no indian could afford it. We will miss you, but your mother and I want you to have an opportunity to be yourself. We hope you will come back home, but can accept if home is somewhere else. This is all the money I can afford to give you for now."

Bear Snarkle, Jr. did not return to Welcome, Arkansas, for over a decade.

⁂

Shortly after Bear Jr. left, a new pig farmer came to town. Jeb didn't much like the way he treated his pigs.

For one, he put a whole lot of them in a single pen, never moving them around, and confining them in their own waste and excrement until sold or butchered.

Jeb didn't mind the competition, as Jamon Hensbell accused him of when he complained. He just felt Hensbell was being cruel to his animals and the land they were confined to. He didn't like what washed from his pen into the creek either.

⁂

Young Jamon was loud and brash, and didn't appreciate being told what to do. He took pride in his Spanish roots, including his given name, which came from a renowned cured ham in the old country's wine-making region of Aragon.

He had run away from his first generation parents' home in Texas at war's end, and headed north. He stole pigs along the way until he had accumulated a respectable herd and drove them into the wilds of the Ozarks. He had stumbled on Welcome by accident, but was nonetheless, welcomed, pigs and all.

Jamon carved out a small corner of a field near the creek, cut down all the trees bordering the water, and constructed a pigsty. He knew nothing about raising pigs, but thought his kin had in the old country. He figured if he stayed to himself and tended his pigs as simply as possible, he could carve out a living in a wild place, maybe even find a local to bed down with and make some babies.

Turned out he picked the wrong local.

⁂

Welcomers were fruitful and had multiplied over the decades.

Jeb, even at his old age, had another with Sophia, this one a girl, another precious Italian-American, Ferderiko, a beautiful bookend to the sturdy Luigi.

Son Bear had two more with wife Fannibelle. She had told Bear when he swirled her away that she had never been a one-man woman, and she wasn't sure she could be. He promised her that she would be. And she had, with babies Sunshine and Moonbeam to join Bear Jr. and seal the deal.

Even Feral Feester and Randy got into the act, adopting a menagerie of orphaned animals to keep in and around their cabin.

And it didn't take long for Star to prove that Reverend Chester Divine could still deliver the goods, even at his advanced age. They named their daughter Glory, Glory Divine, and a son soon thereafter, Luke.

The Welcome, Arkansas, census of 1880 counted nine Snarkles, four Divines, three indians with no names, two Feesters, two Pompassies, two Daniels, one Gas, one Taylor, and one Hensbell. Twenty-five in all from the original four in 1838.

The small cemetery atop the mountain showed gravestones with "Polly Snarkle," "Sunshine Snarkle," "Erasmus Henry" and "Sam" chiseled roughly in rock.

All told, with gives and takes and comes and goes, a net gain of twenty-one hardy Welcomers.

Bear, unlike Bear Jr., did as his father did. He raised the pigs Jeb had passed along to him, farmed the land, and hunted and fished.

He earned a name for himself when a panther decided to feast on his pigs. First one, then another. Bear knew because he kept count. Jeb's rule of thumb had been fifty porkers, give or take a snout. It made so much simple sense. Whether it was fifty, or forty-five, or fifty-five, the land could comfortably absorb only so much traffic or waste. Bear kept to the formula.

That summer—the one of son Bear Jr.'s departure—when numbers began to dwindle to forty, despite a roughly even correlation between births, deaths, and feasts, Bear took notice. It wasn't that he heard anything at night, or saw anything during day. The herd was just shrinking.

One night he thought that he heard a muffled death cry, which awakened him from a light sleep. He grabbed his shotgun and ran down the hill to the herd.

There was a mighty commotion to the side of the field, and in the moonlight he saw a sleek, light brown shape drag a squealing bundle in its mouth into the creek. Bear ordered the panther to stop, which earned him no more than a disdainful look. Bear ran after and squeezed the trigger when he got into range. But nothing happened. He threw the shotgun to the ground and charged into the waist-deep water.

The panther finally dropped its prey and lunged at Bear. He grabbed it around the neck and submerged its mighty head. It lunged again, raking claws across Bear's rib cage, before Bear forced it under water again.

By this time several others had been awakened by the ruckus and rushed to help. He didn't need any.

They looked on in wonder as Bear took the fight to a finish, and dragged the lifeless panther's body to dry ground before collapsing.

Fanny rushed to his side, fearing the worst. Instead it was a smile that greeted her, along with the blood leaking out from the wounds to his side.

As Bear recovered, tensions began to rise between the Snarkles and Hensbell.

Jeb was increasingly critical of Jamon's destruction of his livestock plot, which took on the appearance and smell of, well, a pile of shit. He kept cramming more pigs and more pigs, some purchased from neighbors, some stolen from strangers, into his enclosure. Every time it rained heavily, Jamon smiled, because his sty was rinsed relatively clean. Because he had cut down the tree line protection to the creek, pig waste flowed in raw and unfiltered. He even allowed his herd to wander in and out of the creek at will. Downstream took on a green and pungent character.

Neighbors complained to Jeb and Bear. They first tried to appease Hensbell by offering him some of their land to rotate his herd on, if he would leave the creek tree buffer untouched. He laughed at them. They then threatened to have him expelled from the community. He laughed at them again. It was his land, his herd of pigs, and his profits he was protecting. He threatened to shoot them or any others who infringed on his rights.

The conflict escalated quickly to a near family feud between the Snarkles and Hensbell.

In the meantime Hensbell had seduced the indian family with no name's youngest daughter, who also had no name. She was a pretty, dark-skinned young lady, who was tiring of being the only one left at home with her aging parents. Her sisters had slipped out of Welcome in various stages with an assortment of suitors, never to return. She began to flirt with anyone who would notice, vagrant or homeboy, married or not.

Jamon noticed. He got her drunk on some of Rubert's home brew and took advantage of her in an unconscious state. When she showed up pregnant shortly thereafter, Jamon took her as his wife and gave her a Spanish name,

Dulcetta. He also acquired some more land up the hill to give her a proper home, which he began constructing without any help from his neighbors.

Sadly, no one ever figured out who had murdered Erasmus Henry and raped Star 15 years earlier. And most had stopped worrying about it. Until it happened again.

This time it was Jamon who got the rope, and Dulcetta who suffered through the rest.

Chapter 13

Suspects

This time around the shock was still real, the grieving was mixed, and there were lots of suspects.

The community at large breathed a "good riddance" kind of exhale for Hensbell. His self-serving and combative ways had not endeared him to many. Hanging was a brutal way to die, though, and none thought he deserved that. Most wished that he had just taken his pigs and moved on, and that they didn't have to deal with another murder.

Dulcetta, on the other hand, was grieved roundly for the indignities she suffered.

Her indian family with no name was so frightened that they fled for the deep woods immediately.

Bear and Fannibelle took Dulcetta in, cleaned her up, and provided a place to sleep and stay. They were terribly worried about her baby after learning what had been done to her.

They took some comfort that there was no blood issuing from her birth hole, just swelling and bruising both front and back. She had been brutalized. It would be wait and see with the baby.

It again was Jeb who had wandered up to Rubert's and found Jamon hanging in exactly the same place he had found Erasmus. Which made him the prime suspect up front. No one really thought that Jeb had a mean bone in his body, but the feuding neighbors had become more vocal and confrontational with every passing day. Maybe Jeb just couldn't take any more.

Rubert Gas promised Jeb leniency if he would just tell the truth.

"I don't know what you are talking about, Rubert," Jeb responded in disbelief.

"You had every reason to do it, Jeb," Rubert continued. "You just gave the boy what he kept asking for." The small crowd that had gathered nodded in unison.

"I didn't do anything," Jeb countered, "let alone hang someone."

Rubert asked Jeb to accompany him to one of his back rooms for the moment, at least until they could question him properly. Besides they needed to see where the indian lady was. Maybe she could tell them more.

Fannibelle had headed to their cabin as soon as it became apparent that Jamon was dead. Her screams from Jamon and Dulcetta's front door were heard by most everyone. Dulcetta was barely conscious and in a state of shock.

It was days later that Fannibelle was finally able to coax out the details of Dulcetta's ordeal.

Dulcetta recalled that Jamon had heard something messing with his pigs in the middle of the night and had grabbed his gun before heading out. She heard nothing for a while, and finally dozed off.

She was awakened by her covers being ripped back and a deep voice demanding that she remove her clothes and submit. She had pointed to her belly and tried to say baby, but he was on and in her before she could get it out. He had stuffed a sock in her mouth, tied her arms to the bedposts, and had his way with her until dawn, threatening her with a knife if she made any noise. It was the roughest treatment she had ever received in her short life. He left her tied and gagged when he finally could go no more, and left. She didn't hear a horse.

Jeb Snarkle had been released from Rubert's back room on the strength of Sophia's promise that he would go nowhere. She added that he had done nothing, but many were unconvinced at the moment.

Some were even grateful that he had done what he said he hadn't done.

When Jeb heard from Bear Dulcetta's account of the attack, he asked if he might raise a few more questions. Fannibelle said no, that the girl was still too fragile. Jeb asked Fannibelle if she would ask his questions. She agreed to that.

"Dulcetta, do you remember anything else about your attacker? Did he have a beard?"

Dulcetta couldn't be sure because he had been wearing a bandana, but she thought she remembered whiskers sticking out from around it.

"Was he big, Dulcetta? Did he have huge hands?"

"Yes, I'll never forget his weight pressed on me. Nor the knife that barely protruded from his large gloved hand," she sobbed. "I'm so sorry, Fannibelle, you have been so nice to me, but I just can't go on."

Bear promptly reported Dulcetta's answers back to Jeb, who immediately called a meeting of town elders.

"I told you I didn't hang Jamon Hensbell or rape…" Jeb stopped mid-sentence because it was so hard to say. "… or rape his wife Dulcetta. In fact it could have been any number of you, including my own son Bear. We could all be suspects in this horrible atrocity, but we're not.

"Think back to Erasmus and Star. Remember Star's sad tale of a horrible big man, wearing a bandana over his beard, with hands the size of axe blades, who repeatedly ravaged her?

"No, none of us committed this heinous crime. He did. Again, for no obvious reason. A random act of violence on random victims. Fifteen years later. And until we find out who 'he' is, all of our families are at risk."

Dulcetta slowly recovered her senses. And her baby seemed to be okay. No warnings of blood or damage. In fact, she soon felt subtle movement.

How ironic, thought Bear, that the baby of the man he had grown to hate was percolating in his very own house. Strange world indeed.

The indian family with no name finally returned from the shadows and asked Dulcetta to return home to have her baby. She reluctantly agreed, choosing family over the kind neighbors who had taken her in.

She was vaguely aware of her deceased husband's feud with the Snarkles, and in the end didn't understand the rift. But family was family, and she would be with hers. She didn't know how she would get along with a baby and no man to support her. They would have to do until she could find another one. For now, she would keep her husband's names, both his last, and the one he had bestowed on her. She would be Dulcetta Hensbell until that man came along, and would pass the last name to her baby, boy or girl, to carry for life in honor of Jamon. He had been pretty good to her despite his reputation and conflict within the community.

Dulcetta sensed that she was carrying a boy, although she wasn't sure why. If it was a he, she would call him Tyson. She could wait if a girl's name was required.

The head of the indian family with no name came to personally thank Bear and Fannibelle for their kindness to his daughter during their absence. He apologized for fleeing but said he feared for his whole family.

He then repeated in broken English a legend his grandfather had shared with him when he was a young man. He had never told a soul because of the terror it caused in his heart, but felt Bear should know given the mixed blood in his veins. He asked Bear to share it only with his father Jeb, lest all the neighbors think the old indian was crazy. Bear nodded his promise.

In the earliest of days, before the white man came, the tribes had paradise all to themselves. All of the game, fish, and water was theirs and provided them with a way of life he longed for yet today. The tribes lived in comfort, plenty, peace and harmony.

One day a strange-looking and strange-acting white man was brought in front of the elders. A scouting party had found him badly wounded from an encounter with a beast and presented him to the village for healing. The elders approved of helping him, and placed him with a young couple for care and feeding. They shared their lodge with him and slowly nursed him back to health.

One day while the brave was out hunting, the white man raped his wife. He assured her that if she ever told anyone, he would cut out her tongue and that of her husband. He also claimed a right to take the young lady whenever he wanted her, boasting that his white skin afforded him such privilege and assuring her that she was blessed to have the opportunity of sharing his attentions. This went on for weeks, with him feigning continued injury to prolong his position in the young couple's lodge.

One day the brave returned early from hunting to change out a horse that had gone lame for a healthy one. He found the naked white man attacking his wife as she lay frightened beneath him. The brave dragged him to the corner of the lodge and sliced his throat enough to make him bleed but not die. He then cut off his penis, and removed his testicles one by one. He flipped the wailing white man on his stomach, and jammed his reproductive organs into and up his back side.

As the white man lost and regained consciousness, gasping for what he hoped would be his last breath, the brave scalped him and stuffed his bloody hair down his throat until he could finally breathe no more.

The brave wrapped his wife in a blanket and forgave her, her honor having been redeemed with the slow humiliation of her unrepentant abuser. He then removed the hulking carcass, bleeding now from several extremities, and tied it by the neck from a limb in the center of the village.

Tribal elders approved given the nature of the offense.

When the wife began showing with baby several weeks later, the brave wondered if it was his or that of the evil white monster. His question would not be answered until she died in child birth, issuing forth from between her legs a badger. Badgers were known to the tribes as the meanest of all critters, feared for their bite and aggressiveness. This one was particularly frightful in that it could morph into a huge angry white man, and back to animal again.

The evil reincarnation would occasionally come out of hiding over the decades to rape and murder a young woman, then retreat into its animal state. Tribesmen killed every badger they encountered, but there always seemed to be one more.

"This was the story told me by my grandfather," the indian with no name concluded, soft voice trembling. "I thought you should know."

He feared that this was what was at play in Welcome, Arkansas, and felt compelled to run from it. He and his wife would be moving on as soon as his daughter delivered. Dulcetta was vowing to stay, and the old man hoped that Jeb would keep an eye on her.

Most Welcomers began tying their doors shut at night, and a dark cloud lurked above.

Even crazy Tiny Taylor seemed subdued, and went for weeks without insulting anyone.

Chapter 14

Going Large on Large Creek (2011)

"Get this, L.T. They will work with us to bring 10,000 pigs up to our farm! Not 500, but twenty times that many. Ten thousand pigs. Think how much money we can make on them!"

L.T. was one Lester Tyson Hensbell, IV, great-great-grandson of the original, Jamon Hensbell. Jimbo was his friend and keeper, as we jump forward in time a century and change to retain focus.

"OK, Jimbo, how in the hell can they cram 10,000 pigs on our little family farm? Where will they sleep, what can they eat, what do we do with their shit?"

"It's easy, L.T. They build big confinement houses. It will probably take three or four of them. Who knows? They jam the pigs inside, with slats to allow their waste to drop through to an underground slurry run, and ultimately drain into a big sewage lagoon, which we can spray on our fields, and sell to others in the area, for fertilizer. They'll sell us feed to fatten them up, antibiotics to keep them healthy, and help us secure a loan for the infrastructure. Finally, they will assure market pricing for all we can deliver to their specs. They just process and sell to other countries with insatiable appetites for pork. Did you know that China consumes half the pork in the world? Didn't think so. And China controls their prices to keep their citizens happy. It's as close to a risk-free deal as I've ever seen, L.T. We just have to keep the little porkers alive and well."

"Who is 'they,' Jimbo? Just sounds too good to be true."

"Does, doesn't it? But it is, true, that is. They've been doing it in other parts of the country for decades. Why not here in our own backyard, where we can feed the world and get rich doing it? 'They' is a giant international food conglomerate, one of several that control world markets for pork, chicken, turkey, beef, and the like. They know what they are doing, L.T. Believe me, they know what they are doing."

"It's almost like they're paying us to borrow their pigs, Jimbo. To fatten them up for market."

"That's exactly what it is, L.T. We just have to return them in good health and weight, and they support us in that as well. We don't even have to prove that we have the financial wherewithal to survive a big spill or economic downturn. And we can structure the deal to protect us from any contingent liability."

"So, just what do we have to do?"

"Not much really. They're pretty tapped in to the state government folks, and say they can get most anything approved. The only thing they worry about is that damn National River designation, and how close we are to the river, both physically and along the tributary we'll be spraying around. That's why they've never tried one here before. But they have us, well-respected local family farmers with a sizable plot of land and pig experience. And dammit, it is our land. Well, your land, and your family has controlled it for better than a century. We, you, can do what we want with it."

"Do we have to put any money in up front?"

"Not really, maybe a little equity. We borrow the rest long term, pledge the farm as collateral, build the factory, I'll call it, all after we cut a long-term deal with big guys. They call it a CAFO, short for confined animal feeding operation. The state even has special CAFO rules, though not many, and our folks know their way around them. I actually like industrial piggery better. Sounds quaint."

L.T. laughed. "What next?"

"Well, we have to keep it quiet, you know, because of it being close to a National River and all. Not only will all the weirdos in the Ozarks come out to raise hell, but water crazies from around the country will make it their cause. Kind of like they did with the National River bullshit. I guess we try and reach some long-term agreement with the powers that be and let them take it from there. Let's just keep raising our 500 pigs and act normal. We can meet with them next week if you want to see for yourself."

"No, I trust you, Jimbo. I'm having too much fun just living the good life. In fact, I've got a little lady coming in from Fayetteville for the weekend and I need to get the house a little cleaned up. College student. Met her in a bar and started talking pigs to her. Made her excited so I promised her a weekend on a real working pig farm."

"Sounds good, L.T. Oh, and one more thing to think about. If we go forward with this CAFO deal, you'll probably need to move. We'll no doubt need the property your house sits on to accommodate our space requirements. I would suggest we just tear your place down. Hell, it's a hundred years old anyway. With all the money you are going to make you can afford a frickin' mansion anywhere. Besides, the stench from 10,000 pigs is going to be disgusting."

"Sounds good to me, Jimbo. And, I'm sure you're right about the smells. Just hope the folks in town don't get too worked up."

"Don't worry. They like you and what your family has meant to the town over the decades. Good will goes a long way. And, we'll be able to hand out a few jobs from time to time. Preferably to somebody who can't smell shit if it's smeared on their upper lip. Besides, we'll be up and running before they get a first whiff."

"Thanks as always for looking out for me, Jimbo. Granddad Tyson Jr. was right about you. I know he would be proud, and probably the original Hensbell in the valley, old Jamon, would as well. They were always pushing to grow the herd, from what stories say that have been handed down over the years. They would approve of this, beyond either of their wildest imaginations. Just keep me posted on what I need to be doing along the way. What do you think in terms of time frame?"

"I really don't know, L.T. Reckon I'll know more after our meeting, which I will try and schedule for next week. We'll get back together then. You will be the one who has to sign any papers, since the land has been handed down to you. And, don't have too much fun with your college coed this weekend. I'm a little suspect of any young lady who gets excited by pigs. But then again, she is a Razorback, isn't she?"

Chapter 15

Welcome, Home (1887)

"They even spell Indian with a capital 'I', dad! That was the first thing I learned at the school you sent me to."

Bear Snarkle, Jr. was home in Welcome, Arkansas, for the first time in ten years. And, he didn't come home alone.

At his side was a beautiful Negro woman named Sadie, a young son with coffee and cream colored skin, Bear III, and tiny Polly Snarkle, named after her great-great grandmother. She was dark and beautiful like her mother.

The intervening ten years had been hard on Welcomers. And yet the population continued to grow, to nearly twice what it was in the last census.

The violence begat nationally by the uncivil Civil War was focused and brutal in the river valley, and that of its principal tributaries. The end of war did not bring the beginning of peace. Families were split, communities divided, inside, and against other settlements. Lingering resentments against both Blue and Gray festered, and burst forth in occasional violence and death.

Welcome, Arkansas, was not immune. When the war had ended over twenty years earlier, the community divide had been subtle, almost nonpartisan. The Battle of Large Creek, which didn't happen, had shown a humane streak in both spheres of combatants, if hanging a naked, very old, white man under false pretenses to bring justice could be seen as humane.

Sam, Polly's husband of no last name, had tired of life and the burden of age. He became less and less of the gentle soul whom Polly had embraced with all her heart, and more of a prick in her side. He had nothing to lose, and no more to give, other than his life to avert a full shooting battle which would have resulted in many deaths, likely including innocent Welcomers. In the end it was a brave and noble, if somewhat selfish, gesture. And it worked. Welcome remained welcoming and somewhat above the fray though the latter war years.

It was when all was said and done, treaties executed, and soldiers returned home, that life in Welcome became more challenging.

Many of these soldiers didn't head home but wandered, sometimes raping and pillaging, some marrying and settling down on occasion, even if they had left pre-war wives and children behind. They were both victims and perpetrators of violence and cruelty. Bushwhackers, they had called them during the war. Over time, some landed in Welcome. One of them was Posey Cornwall after a decade on the roam.

It didn't take Posey long to find a woman in Welcome, unlike other settlements he had stopped in along the way. She was an Indian and had a boy named Tyson, but was desperate for a home after the brutal murder of her husband years earlier. She had found no one to take her in because of her Indian blood, had no pride left, and would offer up anything a suitor might require of her. Posey was a willing mark given his lonely wanderings, and even built her a rudimentary hovel to provide shelter after they wed.

Posey Cornwall had an explosive temper when fueled by memories of war and corn whiskey. Rubert Gas provided the latter and Dulcetta paid the price. He beat Dulcetta with increasing frequency and wasn't especially patient with Tyson Hensbell either. He particularly resented the fact that Dulcetta would not permit Tyson to accept the Cornwall name. "The little bastard is just too good for that?" he asked nearly daily, and took it out on poor Dulcetta.

It also didn't take long for Posey Cornwall to end up hanging by the neck from Rubert Gas's general store, and Dulcetta to be brutally raped. Again. Per her account, by the same horrid creature who had done her earlier when she was with Jamon. A big man with big hands and a bandana covering bushy whiskers. And either he or Posey had gotten Dulcetta with child again, neither providing much hope for a positive outcome.

The reoccurrence of another heinous lynching and rape, the third in two and a half decades, put the village on edge again.

All Jeb and Bear Snarkle could think of was the old Indian's legend, and wonder why it might be happening in Welcome, of all places. They continued to honor his confidentiality, but worried about when it might come again.

Most passed it off to another random attack on a random victim, likely by a random wanderer. It was the random part that perplexed Jeb the most. He just couldn't wrap his mind around it.

Dulcetta, after recovering from the brutal rape and beating, decided she had had enough of men, and began finding comfort in Moonbeam (Snarkle) Biddle's arms. Moonbeam had stepped up, like Bear and Fannibelle had the first time, to tend to Dulcetta in her time of need. This time one thing led to another. And, then another.

After a couple of weeks of sneaking around—after all Moonbeam was still married to a former Yankee soldier name of Biddle, who was never present—Moonbeam invited Dulcetta and Tyson to move in with her. She didn't know if she would ever see her husband again, and didn't really care, but was prepared to defend her new love and lifestyle with whatever it took. Moonbeam would help Dulcetta raise Tyson, and birth whatever might issue forth from the sorry choice of gene pool.

The notion of two women living together in the post-Civil War Ozarks was an anathema to most. In fact, most didn't talk about it unless they were sitting around in Rubert Gas's saloon in a philosophical mood.

On most occasions it was Rubert who posed the provocative question of the evening, and his customers who sought answers.

"So, what about these two women all of a sudden living together like partners, right here in the heart of Welcome?" he asked on one such occasion. "Anybody think it's more wrong than right, or maybe even lands somewhere in between?"

"Well, you got Feral Feester and Randy sitting over there holding hands like they have for the last fifty years."

"Yep, but they're men. These is women. Everybody knows that men have more natural rights than women, and any colored folks either."

"Well, we don't have none of them around now, do we?"

"Not yet."

"So, who chops the firewood?"

"And, who butchers the hog?"

"Come to think of it, who cooks?"

"Or tends the young'un?"

"How do they even do it, you know the sex part?"

"Ask Feral."

"Don't think I want to know, but not sure what's wrong with it. At least until Moonbeam's wandering Yankee husband stumbles back in. Guessing someone will get shot. Think I'm rooting for Moonbeam and Dulcetta on this one."

Reverend Chester Divine, who had been quietly sipping his "drippings," which is what Rubert called his prime stuff, had a different take all together.

He confessed that Star had told him before they wed that she had once slept with a woman. She felt that she needed to get her whole past out on the table if they were to have the open and honest relationship she craved.

Once Rev had gotten over the shock, his curiosity had gotten the best of him.

"So what was it like?" he had haltingly asked.

"Warm and comfortable. And pleasurable as well."

"And, you didn't feel one bit guilty?"

"No."

"Only once?"

"Yes."

"Why?"

"Guess I just like men better for such things."

The simplicity and finality of her reasoning buried any doubts he might have had about proceeding with marriage. And, after a brief perusal of his Bible, hoping that he would find no specific prohibition in the sin sections, put his mind and heart to rest. He hadn't even thought about it again until the current conversation.

"So, Rev, you would be willing to marry Moonbeam Snarkle Biddle and Dulcetta Hensbell Cornwall if they asked?"

Why not, he mused to himself, before nodding slightly. After all he had done Feral and Randy decades earlier, and they were a most happily married couple.

And so it was that Welcome, Arkansas, welcomed yet another take on life in the Ozarks, as most called it now.

Bear Jr. and his young family settled in nicely. The story of his ten-year adventure was shared widely around the community.

College had been right and good for Bear Jr. He was curious and smart. Neither father nor grandfather took credit for that. But then again both had been brave enough to found and survive in Welcome, Arkansas. Maybe there was curiosity and brilliance in that?

Bear Jr. had sailed through course work, but more importantly excelled in establishing respectful personal relationships with professors. One in particular convinced Bear Jr. that he should continue his education and become an attorney, a lawyer, a judge, or something that dealt with justice and fairness. He was also the one who convinced Bear Jr. that Indian was not lower case.

He arranged for Bear Jr. to attend a prestigious law school, and soon had him on the train to St. Louis, Missouri, with the support of a wealthy benefactor.

It was there that Bear Jr. encountered and fell for beautiful Sadie, the daughter of a slave who had fled after war's end to escape the travails of a single black mother during Reconstruction in the south.

They met at a party at the law school Bear Jr. was attending. He was a student guest and she was a servant. He wore used dress clothes, she, a white uniform that fit quite tightly. Bear Snarkle Jr. had never seen anything so stunning and sexy.

One of the older guests was quite drunk and began to make passes at Sadie. She tried to stay clear of him, but he was always tracking her down, pawing at her, slobbering her name loudly. Bear Jr. kept waiting for the party host or another adult to rein in the perpetrator. No one did. So Sadie finally dropped a glass of red wine on his stiff white cummerbund. This sent him into a frenzy.

He screamed at the host to fire the "uppity nigger, immediately," or better yet, send her home with him so he could teach her some manners. The host was sympathetic with his servant, but did not want to alienate one of his major donors to the law school. So he simply slinked in the background. Other adults tried to intervene, but to no avail. The drunken white mega-giver wanted some of Sadie, and he was damn sure going to get it.

He grabbed Sadie by the arm and pulled her toward the front door, host still slinking about.

Bear Jr. could take no more. He grabbed the sorry prick and laid several punches on him before his fellow students could rein him in. Sadie ran for the kitchen and the donor exited, shouting to the host that he would have to find another naming gift for the new law library.

Bear Jr. broke free and ran into the kitchen to find Sadie huddled under a table. He knelt down and pulled her trembling body to his, whispering, "Everything is all right. I'm so sorry. Everything is all right."

It felt strange. Sadie had never been held by a white man before. She had been abused by one at a younger age, but that had involved mounting, not holding. She didn't know what to think or do next, as she carried great resentment for anything white, most recently the humiliating tight white uniform the host had made her squeeze into, and then the jerk who wanted to remove it.

So she just sat still in Bear Jr.'s arms, shakes subsiding, finding safety and warmth. Bear Jr. was awash in feelings of fear that his intervention could cost him his scholarship, embarrassment at being white himself, and sexual electricity that was fueling a bulge in his britches. So he just sat still as well.

When Bear Jr. regained his composure, he led Sadie from under the table and out the front door without acknowledging the host or those who stared on. He asked Sadie if he could help her get home. She nodded toward a streetcar and he stepped on with her.

When they reached her modest row house, she nodded for him to enter with her. Sadie's mother was waiting up for her and looked at the young white man with distrust.

"He saved me, Mama, the white boy saved me, and I am grateful to him."

The courtship of Bear Jr. Snarkle and Sadie Mays was long and tortuous.

Bear Jr. had correctly surmised that his scholarship was at risk. He had insulted and embarrassed a major donor, and potentially lost the law school a substantial naming gift. And he had done it because of a simple "misunderstanding" between the donor and an uppity colored girl.

"Where was his common sense, his prioritization of outcomes, his willingness to sacrifice his impulses for the common good? Could he effectively understand, interpret, or adjudicate the law with such deficiencies in judgment?" the dean of the law school had asked. "Where is your sense of justice, of right and wrong, of common respect and decency?" Bear Jr. had angrily responded.

It was finally decided that Bear Jr. would be put on probation, and that any more misjudgments would be fatal. Bear Jr. accepted his sentence. He knew he had to if any of his dreams were to come true. He also knew that he needed to see Sadie Mays again soon. They had parted under her watchful mother's gaze with locked-in eye contact, which did not go unnoticed by any.

Bear Jr. returned to Sadie's home and was told by her mother that Sadie was out with a long-time male friend, "of her own race," she had added. Mr. Bear would be wise to move on. Bear Jr. asked if he could wait until they returned. Sadie's mother refused. Bear Jr. left and waited around the corner. When Sadie and her friend walked up, Bear Jr. asked quietly if he could have a short word with Miss Sadie. Her escort took offense and slugged Bear Jr. in the face, knocking him to the ground. Sadie dropped to her knees and ordered the young black man to leave. When he refused, Sadie screamed for her mother, finally driving him away, head shaking in anger and confusion.

"Help me, Mama," Sadie instructed. "Bear Jr. is hurt."

An hour later Bear Jr. lay with his throbbing head on Sadie's lap while she gently wiped a wet rag over the gaping slice beneath his eye, before applying a sticky salve that was her mother's own home brew.

"Where does anyone get a name like Bear?" Sadie's mother laughed, "let alone Junior, implying that there is an original one as well?"

This was the beginning of a long and sobering conversation about coloreds and Indians that carried on through most of the night and into the weeks to come. Bear Jr. and Sadie had more in common than Sadie's mother was anxious to admit, but her sense of the sparks that were flying was accurate.

Bear Jr. and Sadie were finally married by a justice of the peace after the births of two children and his graduation from law school with honors. They had lived with Sadie's mother as they had nowhere else to go, and she begrudgingly accepted it all—out-of-wedlock conception, Sadie working two jobs so they could afford food, and helping raise the young infants. Even the couple's plans to move back to Welcome, Arkansas, to raise their family after graduation. All, except the notion that her grandson would carry the name, Bear III. This absurdity made her laugh out loud. As did Bear Jr.'s frequent retelling the story of the dropped glass of red wine on an old white asshole's white cummerbund that had brought them together.

Bear Jr. Snarkle was proud to bring his new family home to Welcome, Arkansas.

Chapter 16

Justice, Pigs, Mares, and Mules

Bear Jr. announced to his father that he wanted to become Welcome, Arkansas's lawyer and judge.

"You don't want to take over my pig farm, Junior?" the elder Bear asked in disbelief.

"No, Dad. I've been trained to administer the law, not slop pigs," Junior responded with a grateful smile.

"But we've never had any of those things before, Junior. Come to think of it, we don't really have any laws to speak of. Most disputes over land, borrowing things, even women, are talked out. Your grandfather Jeb is a particularly good listener. When parties to a dispute get angry and start yelling at one another, he comes to them as quickly as possible. Word gets to him before a respondent even has time to raise his voice. He drops everything and mosies over. Then, he just sits there and listens. Occasionally he will ask a question. Just last week I seen him work magic."

"Could your dead mule have just died of excitement, Henry," Jeb Snarkle asked, "trying to mount Doberman's beautiful mare?"

"No, I'm sure Doberman killed him. He owes me a new one."

"Did you find any wounds on your dead mule, Henry? Bullet holes, smash marks, knife cuts?"

"No, but he did have kind of a far off look in his eyes, like maybe he had been hit upside the head?"

"So, Henry, when do you get most excited these days?"

Henry thought a minute, then blushed and smiled softly. "Well, I guess when me and the missus is fixing to, you know …" Henry trailed off.

"Do you ever get a far off look in your eyes at those times, Henry?"

"I suppose so."

"Before or after?"

"Mostly after, I guess."

"Did it ever dawn on you, Henry, that your mule got every wish fulfilled with Doberman's mare? And as he reveled in the moment, simply had a heart attack from the joy of it all?"

"Well, no."

"Do you remember the odd couple that was traveling through a couple of months ago and pitched a tent beside Rubert's saloon? They stayed several days enjoying Rubert's freshest 'drippings', and apparently each other. Claimed they had met up on the trail some time back, took a shine to one another, and were literally inseparable."

"Some of the noises issuing from that tent seemed to confirm their story."

"And then late one night a different sound was heard. It was a scream of fright, of shock, of sadness. Rubert, and a couple of his remaining customers ran to the tent, threw open the flap, and saw the lady with tears streaming down her face, hollering for help. A naked carcass of a man, backside up, lay atop her."

"Rubert pulled the dead man off, threw a blanket to the lady to cover up in, and rolled him over. Rubert's first thought was that she had murdered the old guy. There wasn't no blood or cuts or bruises, but it was a natural inclination to reach about two naked strangers that no one knew, one of whom was suddenly dead."

"Rubert called for someone to fetch me, and I came staggering from a deep sleep. I examined the body of the old white man, and then the young lady. I found nothing amiss with either, though the latter was considerably easier to examine than the former. I then just sat on the tent floor and listened."

"The lady quickly explained that they were doing just what they did most nights, and had done ever since they had joined up. He was old, but had some money and liked a good time."

"'So, did you kill him for his money, lady?' Rubert had asked in an accusing voice."

"She started crying again as I shushed Rubert. 'Let her explain Rubert,' I had ordered."

"'No I could never do that,' she sobbed. 'He was too kind and gentle. No, he had just, you know, pleasured out, and collapsed on me with a far off look in his eyes. I knew something was wrong when he didn't close them like he always did.'"

"I arose and knelt next to the naked dead old man, looked him in the eye, and seen that look she described."

"'Rubert, she's innocent of everything except loving the old goat. Take a look for yourself. That look in his eyes is about as far off as one can vision,' I had reported."

"'What's your name young lady?' I then asked."

"'Henie,' she had replied."

"I asked Rubert if Henni could occupy one of his women's rooms out back until she sorted through her feelings and decided what to do next. With no conditions attached."

"'Okay, okay,' Rubert had responded. 'I reckon I can double one the girls up and they can take turns using the facilities when business calls. And, no Miss Henni, no business requirements of you. Unless, of course, you want to pitch in?'"

"I shot a stern look at Rubert, then said softly to Henni, 'so sorry' for your loss. You are welcome to stay in Welcome as long as you wish, no conditions attached.'"

"Henry, you seen that same look in your mule's eyes. I think he found everything on this earth that he was looking for. Doberman, I suggest that any offspring that might result from this moment of shared happiness be contributed to Henry in honor of his loss, and in gratitude for making the earth a happier place, if only for a moment."

"Bear Jr., I share this story in such great detail to illustrate that we already have a system in place to bring honesty and fairness to most disputes."

"You are correct, Dad, my grandfather served admirably as attorney, judge, and jury in the case of Henry v. Doberman, in an informal way. All I am saying is that in most places, justice is more than informal, and a system is in place to assure fair and impartial resolution. I have been trained in all matters of the law, and have returned to Welcome, Arkansas, to institutionalize the process. And, relieve the burden of responsibility on Grandpa."

Bear could only nod proudly in agreement.

"But who is gonna take over my pig farm?" Bear asked almost to himself. "I've got nearly eighty of them porkers running around, needing to be fattened up, and then herded and driven to market at the new county seat. It's too many and we need to cull down."

"How about Sunshine and her new fellow from upstream?" Bear Jr. asked.

Sunshine Snarkle had recently married a Casey from the village where the same family had once cared for Polly's husband-to-be Sam, long ago in the founding days. They had been in the upper valley since the earliest of days and had run out of neighbors to intermarry with. So the youngest of the direct descendants of he who had built the original gristmill set out to find him a life partner in surrounding communities. His eye had finally settled on young Sunshine and he had moved quickly. She was hitched and gone upstream before the family knew it. Bear and Fannibelle were pleased about their oldest daughter finding happiness, especially with a man. That could only mean more grandbabies.

"No, I don't think your sister and her new family will want to slop around with pigs when they can live a happy and respectable life beyond. Kind of like you," Bear poked with a smile.

"So, maybe Moonbeam and Dulcetta?" Bear Jr. responded.

Chapter 17

Nunnehi

"Turn your black ass over bitch, and get ready for something you will never forget."

Sadie thought she was in the midst of a nightmare. Her covers were gone. The beast was ripping her gown off. He was huge and white, with a bandana covering a beard. She reached for Bear Jr. but found only emptiness in their bed. He hit her with the back of a monstrous hand, choked her neck, and she went dark. But not before seeing another pair of oversized hands grab her attacker's neck from behind. The last thing she heard was a loud crack.

The commotion from Rubert's store drew Jeb's attention and he ran up the hill as fast as he could.

"Oh no," he muttered to himself, "not another one."

This time it was Tiny Taylor who was hanging by his neck, which was stretched at such an angle Jeb wondered if it was still attached.

"Oh no," he repeated, now to Rubert, "not old Tiny Taylor. He's been with us from nearly the beginning.

And then they heard a wailing from in the woods, toward Bear Jr.'s cabin. Jeb took off running again, leaving Rubert and the other Welcomers who had gathered to lower Tiny's body from the rafters.

Jeb found Sadie cradling Bear Jr.'s bound and gagged body. From a distance his grandson looked dead. "Junior!" he screamed as loud as he could, drawing still more Welcomers his way. Most stumbled about in shock that it had happened again.

Sadie was struggling desperately to pull the dirty sock from Bear Jr.'s mouth. Jeb breathed a sigh of relief that his grandson's eyes were open. He pulled out a knife and began to saw away at the heavy rope that was wrapped tightly around Bear Jr.'s neck.

It was only when both had completed their tasks that Jeb noticed Sadie's soft brown skin exposed beneath the ruins of her ripped up gown. She used what was left to try and cover her breasts to little effect. Jeb quickly removed his shirt and wrapped her in it, urging her to go inside and reclothe, assuring her that everything was going to be okay.

But was she okay? Had she been violated? Junior was breathing, but beyond that? Tiny Taylor was hanging from a beam in front of Rubert Gas's saloon. "What could possibly be okay about all of this?" he wondered aloud.

In the chaos that followed as Jeb untied Bear Jr., a cluttered story emerged.

Bear Jr. remembered hearing a noise outside the house, throwing on pants, and closing the door behind him. That was it. Nothing else. The large lump on the back of his head explained his lack of memory and spoke to a blunt instrument. The rope burns around his neck foretold what was planned. Beyond that, Bear Jr. was okay.

A finally clothed Sadie remembered the beginnings of a brutal attack from a large, ugly, bandana-covered white face and man, gown ripped apart before blacking out from a blow to the face. That was it. Nothing else. No, there was something else, but she couldn't put the haze to words just then. She would concentrate on it. She could confirm, after close personal inspection, that she had not been violated, not raped, nor hurt apart from the initial hit.

"Thank God," muttered Jeb, grateful for both exceptions to past incidents.

Comfortable with at least their immediate safety, Jeb strode back up the hill with fellow Welcomers to examine the rest of the story. Tiny Taylor had been released from his rope perch and lay spread-eagle on Rubert's front porch. His neck was so twisted it seemed to rest more comfortably facing rear than forward. Jeb had not seen many hangings, but no rope he encountered had done the damage of this one.

Again, it all seemed so random. Random attacks, random victims, random outcomes. Same sordid story all over again. And yet, that just didn't make sense. And as always his mind drifted back to the tall tale, the legend of the badger and the angry white man, that the old indian with no name had shared. Could there be a supernatural piece to the puzzle? And if so, what could they ever begin to do to neutralize the evil spirit that seemed to drive it all?

Several of Rubert's ladies began to clean poor Tiny's body in preparation for burial. He had shat and urinated himself, and was a stinking mess.

Sophia urged Jeb to go to Tiny's cabin, located in a remote corner of the Large Creek valley, and find a decent set of clothes to dress him in. Several grabbed shovels and began to dig a hole in what had become the Welcome, Arkansas, cemetery, with assorted gravestones scattered around Polly's, Sam's, and Sunshine's, with open space next to the latter to accommodate Jeb and Sophia when their time came. Jeb headed back into the woods.

After half an hour he approached what he believed to be Tiny's cabin, deep in dark woods. It dawned on him that he had been here only once before in his nearly fifty years of living barely half mile away. That simply wasn't the Welcome way, he mused. Welcomers welcomed all strangers into their midst with open arms and without judgment. But a Welcomer's home was their own, to share or hide in at their own discretion. Tiny was one of several who had chosen the latter.

Jeb found the front door tied shut. He broke a darkly draped window, the only one in the dwelling, to gain access. Tiny Taylor's cabin was as dark as a cave. But strangely clean, almost scrubbed sterile. What a weird contraction, thought Jeb, as he waited for his eyes to adjust to the black surroundings. He was finally able to make it to the door and throw it open to let in a little light. So strange, thought Jeb. Dark house in dark woods with only a tiny bit of a sunny morning leaking in.

Tiny always had been a touch weird.

Jeb was finally able to make out a lantern on what appeared to be the kitchen table. He lit it carefully and scanned the room around him. He found a potbelly stove, a bucket filled with water, the aforementioned kitchen table, and—the shock of his life.

Laid out carefully on a single bed in the corner was a tale of terror. An oversized woolen jacket with towels stuffed in to fill it up. Large gloves, again stuffed with something to make them appear bigger that the hands that might have filled them. A filthy bandana. A fake beard. A sharp Bowie knife. Individual coils of heavy rope, each knotted with a hangman's noose at the end.

Finally, stacks of written filth, in Tiny's own hand, railing against people of color, their interminglings with the purity of whites, particularly hateful references to women and their conniving ways to seduce white men, one racist tirade after another. And then the pictures, grainy and obtained from God knows who, of obscene sexual acts. White on black, white on indian, all photographed from a position of dominance, graphic, no secrets here.

Tiny Taylor hated all people of color, chocolate dark, creamed coffee brown, even deeply tanned. He didn't much like women either and seemed to blame them for every interracial interaction.

Jeb sat down on the bed, then rose quickly. This was no place to try and figure complex things out. So he wandered out the open door and sat on a large rock, streaks of sunlight providing some comfort in a dark hour.

Jeb began to process the mess that was in his mind. He was looking for reason and order. He talked out loud to himself.

"Tiny Taylor, you hated all people of color, and most, if not all, women as facilitators of immoral interactions."

"You hung black Erasmus Henry and raped the young white lady who was his friend and lover. Several times over."

"You hung Jamon Hensbell for consorting with an indian woman, a woman of color, who you raped over and over again."

"You hung Posey Cornwall for marrying that same woman of color, and raped her once again. Over and over again."

"You sought to hang my grandson, Bear Snarkle Jr., and rape his wife of color, because of their immoral union."

"Tiny Taylor, you disguised yourself as an oversized white bushwhacker, inflating your actual spare frame and small hands with fillers of all kinds, covering your fake bearded face with a smelly bandana."

"Tiny Taylor, you did it all in the name of hatred, racially driven, femininely derived."

As Jeb pondered the horror of it all, he heard bushes rustle and saw son Bear and his son, Bear Jr. emerge into the clearing where he sat.

"We worried about you dad, it took so long for you to simply retrieve Tiny Taylor's clothing."

"There is nothing simple about what greeted me," whispered Jeb Snarkle. He then proceeded to share it all with the men of his lineage.

All sat in shared shock for a time after.

"How was I spared?" asked Bear Jr. "How did I survive?"

"Nunnehi," suddenly stated Jeb with authority. "Nunnehi," he repeated.

Both Bears looked confused.

Jeb Snarkle went back in time to his promise to bring his first wife's father a bearskin as marriage offering, his tracking of and attack by a great black bear which left him grievously wounded, and the amazing intervention that saved his life and presented him with the bear skin that had earned him the special woman that birthed the first Bear Snarkle.

He recalled that when Sunshine had asked him about the near death experience, he vaguely recalled, between bouts of consciousness, an elderly indian of regal bearing with long gray braids walking toward him with a sense of peace and purpose.

She had whispered to him "Nunnehi," mystic traveler who comes to the aid of the Cherokee through time in moments of great need.

"Bear Jr., it was Nunnehi who saved you and Sadie from evil, son, Nunnehi who will be there for you and yours whenever and forever. It was Nunnehi who strangled Tiny Taylor while he was attempting to rape Sadie, and left him dangling from the beam at Rubert Gas's saloon. It was Nunnehi who loosened the noose around your neck so you could breathe. It was Nunnehi who even laid out the evidence of Tiny Taylor's deception, in his cabin and for all to see and piece together. It was Nunnehi who ended the cycle of racist violence."

"How did the name the 'Bear' come to be?" asked Jeb's son. He had never raised the question before, just accepting it as fate.

"Your mother, Sunshine, insisted that we name you, if you were a male, in honor of brother bear, even though one almost killed me. 'He was only protecting his family as he was raised to do. And, as you will do. The bear is a hero to all Cherokee,' she had reasoned."

"I, too, am honored to carry his name," observed Bear Jr., "in tribute to my Cherokee grandmother. And, to have passed it on to my first son."

The three generations hugged in gratitude and relief, and a sense of timelessness. One Jebediah, and two Bears.

"Oh yeah, Sadie found the lost memory she was chasing. Just before she passed out with the beast atop her and his hands around her neck, another set of hands encircled his and she heard a sharp crack."

"Nunnehi," whispered Jeb. "Nunnehi."

As they turned to head home and shed truth on the plague of murders that had haunted Welcome, a critter skittered across the path ahead. Bear looked at his father in disbelief. "A badger?" asked an astounded son. Jeb nodded. Neither would ever utter another word about it.

They burned Tiny Taylor in the pig grazing field, far below the cemetery where the hole they had dug lay empty. It would welcome the next Welcomer to pass on.

Chapter 18

A Meeting (2011)

Jimbo sat down with several men in suits over an expensive dinner. One was a corporate executive, one was an attorney for his company, one was on the governor's staff, and one was the director of the state agency charged with protecting natural resources. The corporate guy was buying, and clearly running the show.

The conversation ranged from the agricultural permitting process, to environmental rules and regulations, to reviewing a draft agreement, to timing, to what kind of obstacles might have to be overcome at the state level. All agreed that none were insurmountable.

The attorney pulled out a legal looking document with DRAFT in bold across the front. He explained that it laid out the terms and conditions of an agreement between L.T. Hensbell, as owner of a large parcel of land that ran adjacent to Large Creek, and his company, to construct and manage a confined animal feeding operation with capacity for ten thousand pigs. It covered everything from provision of the livestock, to feed, to antibiotics for prevention of disease, to buy-back weights and prices. One appendix was a formal partnership agreement. A second provided for a corporate guarantee of long-term debt to construct four enclosures to house the pigs, feed silos, and a lagoon system for their waste. A third addressed the need for seasonal working capital, which would also be guaranteed by the corporation. And yet another laid out in more detail a long-term inventory purchase agreement between the "family farmer," as they referred to Hensbell, and the company.

The attorney then presented a separate legal document that established a corporate cover for the "family farmer" in the form of a limited liability company. This would protect Hensbell from personal risk in the case something went wrong such as, God forbid, a breach in or overflow of the sewage lagoon system that could spill thousands and thousands of gallons of pig waste into a major tributary to a national river, and ultimately that river itself. This was very unlikely to happen, the lawyer explained, due to the twenty-five year flood plain specifications included in the original design. It would have to rain really, really hard and that would statistically happen only once in twenty-five years.

"When was the last one?" Jimbo inquired.

"Not sure," the attorney responded, "but that's why we're wrapping your boss up in an impenetrable veil of protection."

"I see, thank you, sir. I'm sure he will be very grateful," Jimbo confirmed.

"We don't have to worry about any of the gunk leaking into the local water table because it will be difficult to prove that it came from your place. So no liability there."

"Again, thank you, sir. You sure do look after your partners."

"We try to. So what do you think he would like to name his new enterprise?"

"How about using his initials, L.T.H, in some form or fashion?"

"Something like L.T.H. Farms?"

"Beautiful. He'll love it," Jimbo responded.

"L.T.H. Farms, LLC, of course," added the attorney.

"And one more thing, and this is important," cautioned the attorney, a serious look shadowing his smiling face. "It is vitally important that all of us maintain strict confidentially about our plans until your department approves everything, Mr. Director."

"We are required to post a notice inviting public comment, but I can bury that where the sun don't shine," the Director assured. "We'll have you permitted before anyone has time to raise any questions."

"In fact, once we execute final documentation, I see no reason why you and your boss can't begin construction. We'll provide up-front funding to allow the banking system to catch up and repay ourselves from their advances. Again, it is imperative that we all keep this quiet until we get all of our ducks, or pigs in this case, in a row. There may be a little complaining after the fact, but no one can do much about it once we are up and running. We can make this work if you and your boss are all in and wearing your best suit of thick skin," the corporate attorney concluded.

The final toast of the evening was to a new limited liability company, L.T.H. Farms, LLC. The attorney would provide all the paperwork in final form for execution by Mr. Hensbell.

"It shouldn't take more than a couple of weeks," he added, "at which time we will need to meet the young lad and obtain his signature."

"You name the time and place and I'll get him there," promised Jimbo. "It is a sincere pleasure doing business with someone who knows what they are doing and why, as well as has the best interests of their partners, and even community, at heart."

A deal had been struck behind closed doors, and that very community would likely pay a stiff price.

Chapter 19

Closer to Heaven (1890s)

Resolution of Welcome, Arkansas's string of unsolved murders was followed by several years of severe drought. It was almost as if one dead travesty had birthed another. No one in fifty-plus years of the settlement's existence had ever seen it so dry.

Even Large Creek became small, and the river it ran into barely trickled in shallow spots. All the small settlements along the river that had grown and survived migrations, periodically in and out, as well as a great war and the residual violence and division it had spawned, tried to cling to their respective ways of life. It wasn't easy.

On Bear Snarkle's advice, Moonbeam and Dulcetta began to reduce the size of his pig herd to accommodate the sparse grazing resources and reduce waste runoff into the creek. And, most in Welcome found novel ways to conserve water.

Drinking water was rationed by family, with priority given to the youngest and oldest members of the community. Many moved to community bathing upstream in Large Creek, and stopped drawing scarce water from wells. Most went from weekly baths to monthly to minimize the impact on the creek, and fewer took notice of the odor emanating from the shrinking livestock herd. Rubert Gas even reduced the liquid composition of his famous "drippings," rendering it more chewable than potable. Few complained about the hardships imposed by drought. Strangers were still welcomed to Welcome, but were required to abide by the new water conservation guidelines.

Bear Jr. ran for the position of county judge, and was elected with an overwhelming mandate, in that he was the only candidate who had ever been educated in the law. This stamped him as "elite" in a few corners of the community, but most appreciated the expertise he brought, and the continuation of the humane approach to resolving disputes that his grandfather Jeb Snarkle had instituted.

The first legal matter he was called on to adjudicate involved Moonbeam Snarkle, her new partner Dulcetta Hensbell, and surnames.

Dulcetta had delivered another boy, whom she reluctantly named Cornwall to at least acknowledge the latter's role in the creation. She and Moonbeam had been relieved to confirm that it was his offspring as opposed to Tiny Taylor's rape. There was no mistaking a big hairy ball of baby for anything but her crass second husband. They would call him "Corny" for short.

In a shared decision, Moonbeam and Dulcetta wished to merge all last names (Snarkle, Biddle, Cornwall) into one, Hensbell, to reduce the natural confusion that accompanied one woman married to a man who was never around, one woman with two children from different sires, and two women cohabitating, as well as honor Dulcetta's promise to herself to perpetuate the Hensbell name.

Judge Bear Jr. formally affirmed their right to do so in his inaugural ruling.

His next case involved the new water conservation efforts. While everything was voluntary, as were most rules in Welcome, the informal bathing guidelines came into conflict soon after a young couple moved in from Texas. It took on the nature of sort of a class action suit, brought by most women in the community, to cease communal bathing.

Welcome's newest citizens were an unusual couple. When Reverend Divine asked if they were married, both replied "sort of." When he couldn't get a clearer answer after further interrogation, he advised them of his rule that one needed to be married to engage in sexual activities, a stipulation that they agreed to and enacted on the spot. They even paid in cash for the privilege of officially sanctioned sex.

James was short and spindly, and hardly ever spoke. Ruth, on the other hand, was beautiful, buxom and bawdy. When it was time for what had become the monthly community bath, the creek was packed. As Ruth began to disrobe all eyes wandered in her direction. Most wives soon diverted their gaze back to the remaining waters of Large Creek or the baby blue sky. Most husbands remained fixated on the most perfect body any had ever seen. Ruth obviously enjoyed the attention and took her own sweet time dipping in the water before emerging to bask on a flat ledge of rock. James sat down beside her and began covering as much of her as he could with the dirty shirt he had been wearing, but little was left to the imagination.

This particular shared bath time dragged on well beyond the established norm.

It didn't take long for a move from monthly to weekly communal bathing to surface as a community agenda item, particularly among the gentlemen. When pressed as to "why" by Fannibelle, Bear could only shrug and claim "good hygiene." Fannibelle couldn't imagine where such a big word had popped up from, but figured that their son, Judge Bear Jr., and his big city education had something to do with it.

The real legal and philosophical problem was that weekly bathing ran counter to the discipline imposed by shared monthly baths, and threatened to degrade Large Creek. In short, gawking was legal, but fouling water was not.

In the end, Judge Bear Jr. recused himself from the case and asked Reverend Divine to increase his pleadings for rain.

It did so happen that Ruth and James, last name of Farmer, had actually been happily married for some time and had no intention of stirring up matters of conscience and impropriety in the community. Ruth was just a bit of an exhibitionist, and reasoned, with James' consent, that she might as well show it while she had it. Babies and age would soon add padding and sag. After a while she finally gained most ladies' trust as to her lack of negative intentions, and the couple began to meld into the fabric of the village.

Neither was James a real farmer. He had been a banker in Texas, which is why he had cash to pay for the reaffirmation of their marriage vows. No one asked as to why he had left banking in Texas or why he seemed to always have plenty around to pay for things. They just assumed the best, which was the Welcomer way. And, as he began to pay for things in his way, more cash found its way into virgin hands.

When James needed help building a cabin for him and Ruth, he paid young men with coins and bills, who in turn paid Rubert Gas for his "drippings" in same. When he wanted a mess of fish to fry up for him and the missus, he paid Luigi Snarkle to catch and clean them. In cash. When it was pork he and Ruth craved, he gave a wad of bills to Moonbeam and Dulcetta for a half side. He even began to drop a coin or two in a bowl at Reverend Divine's Sunday service and pass it around, occasionally drawing another.

Having seeded the beginning of a cash economy in Welcome, James approached the village elders with a unique idea.

"Has anyone ever thought about starting a bank in Welcome, Arkansas?"

"No."

"Are there any other banks in the county?"

"No."

"Is there much currency in the county?"

"No."

"Wouldn't it be nice to draw it to Welcome and serve as banker to the region? To accept deposits, keep the money locked up safe, lend it back to someone to build a house or buy a couple of cows, and repay it from the operation or sale of same?"

Heads were starting to nod all around. Why couldn't Welcome, Arkansas become the banking capital of the valley?

That might even lead to a post office, one concluded. Or help draw a real doctor to town, another added. Or help fund a school, a third chimed in.

"Banking can be the key to a healthy and vibrant community," James Farmer concluded with a flourish.

Deep thoughts from such a wimpy guy, wondered Jeb, but even he found himself caught up in the moment. As Welcome's founding father, he reveled in its progress.

It was the fourth summer of the great drought that Glory Divine and Tyson Hensbell got together. They were too young for such things, but skinny dipping in the creek to stay at least partially cool provided a playground for exploration.

For Glory it was a natural extension of her mother Star's approach to sex education. That Star had been somewhat of a lady of the night in her younger years influenced Glory in her thinking.

Star harbored no regrets. It was what had brought her to Welcome, Arkansas, to begin with, seeking love and adventure in the wild frontier. She also needed to earn her survival, and became a regular at Rubert Gas's, slipping off from time to time with some drifter or cowboy before always returning to Erasmus Henry, who kept her happy and fulfilled, until his tragic demise.

But, then again, Glory Divine was also the precious daughter of a good Reverend, who preached abstinence until marriage. There were several solid reasons for his views on sex, as juxtaposed to those of wife Star. First and foremost, he had been a virgin when Star introduced him to the pleasures of the flesh. A very, very, very old virgin, but a fast learner. Second, other's marriages were a primary source of food and drink for his family. Whether it was a jar of honey, a tin of goat's milk, a dram of Rubert's drippings, a couple of still warm eggs, or on one occasion, a genuine half of a pork belly, and lately in the case of James and Ruth, cash money, weddings were vital to the survival of his personal flock.

People came from the far reaches of the hills to be joined by Reverend Divine. Did it matter that they had to swear on his Bible to God himself that they had never had sex before to qualify for his services? No, for it was well worth a bevy of lies to be blessed with one of his poetic, romantic, even graphic on occasion, one-hour sermons.

In actual fact, Reverend Divine was very much in favor of sex after marriage, an almost righteous belief grounded in the pleasure and good health it had brought him. He often spoke in sensual terms to promote it, invoking the "beauty of a heaving breast," or "the silkiness of a smooth thigh," and even on occasion "the heavenly joy of mutual release," to stir the spirit and prime the pump.

More than a few of his client couples had to interrupt their ceremony to rent one of Rubert Gas's back rooms for a "reflective rest period" before continuing to the "I now pronounce you..." In fact the good Reverend encouraged it. It was important to be sure that one wanted to go through with the whole thing before sealing the deal, even if it violated his "sex only after marriage" dictum. What the heck? They had started the process, he was always paid up front, and it was stimulating for the local economy.

No, Reverend Divine was not against sex. In fact, it had saved him, even in a premarital sort of way, but that was no one's business but his and Star's. He had come a long way from his early "Jesus, Alien" ramblings that had confused so many of his congregants.

Contradictions in his message still abounded, but were lost in the aura of good will that accompanied it.

Despite the mixed messaging Glory Divine was raised with, she was a very well-educated teenager compared to most. Several of the local boys had their eye on her as she frolicked in Large Creek, displaying her prematurely developed assets, and she teased them accordingly. That said, Tyson Hensbell would be her first real student, though he hadn't a clue.

Glory started slowly, not wanting to scare him away. He was shy, naive, almost reclusive, but a handsome devil in a heavenly sort of way. An underwater touch here, a passing brush up there, and Tyson had to start hiding under the surface to avoid embarrassment. He just couldn't understand what was happening to his body in moments of proximity to Glory Divine. Until she explained it to him in private.

Tyson had lingered in the spring fed waters of Large Creek one late afternoon after the others had left. He could finally relax after hiding his bottom half from others for most of the day. He crawled out and lay on a flat rock like a big lizard, to just soak it all in.

He was half asleep when a soft touch snapped him to attention. He started to scream, but Glory stilled him with her mouth on his. She raised his hand to her breast. Tyson was feeling things he had never felt before, from top to bottom, and in between. Glory finally pulled back and scooted over beside him.

"This is what is going to happen, Tyson. Just do exactly as I say. You have to trust me on this one. We are going to have sex, Tyson, you and me, first time for either of us. You know like our parents and the animals do. But we need to be very careful, or we'll have a baby, just like our parents and the animals do." She then explained in intimate detail what was about to happen.

"My mother first had sex at about my age, and it didn't mess up her life. She told me about it and shared that like me, her body developed early. She said she wished that I would wait, not quite as long as my father, but that if I chose not to, there were several rules that should be followed at all cost."

"Rule 1 - Never let a man force you. Kick, slug, or even shoot him in the privates if need be, but remember that it is your body and choice, not his. I have picked you, Tyson. You are my choice."

"Rule 2 - Never let the man stay inside you. He, you in this instance, shoots stuff that sparks life when joined with what I have inside, and we don't want a baby at this point, now do we, Tyson? So, I have to trust you to pull it out when you start to feel too good. Always pull your bushwhacker out when you think you're going to heaven."

Tyson looked confused. "Bushwhacker? Heaven? What's it all mean?"

"You'll figure it out soon enough, Tyson."

It didn't take long to leave Tyson Hensbell limp and swooning, and longing for more.

"See, it's simple, Tyson, you and me, fun and feel good. And you pulled out just right."

The whole river valley, including beyond Large Creek, was becoming a dry tinderbox. One could wade back and forth across the river itself in more places that anyone could ever recall. As such, communities along the river interacted more. Interdependence became a new fact of life, and was embraced by most.

Livestock herds were reduced throughout the region by sharing meat and produce to reduce pressure on the waters. Some settlers even moved on in search of wetter and more fertile lands. Times were harder than any time since the great war.

Tyson and Glory continued their fun and feel good explorations throughout the summer, meeting and greeting in some very unusual places, but continuing to keep it their secret. Like the several times they both feigned sickness during church time. While both sets of parents were engaged in praying for them among other things, they wrestled about in those same adults' respective beds in unholy connectivity. And then there was the new treehouse Tyson had thrown together back in the deepest, darkest woods. They could hoot and holler at their loudest and never draw attention. And on, and on, and all around they went.

As luck would have it, Tyson began to get a little closer to heaven before pulling out. Heaven seemed to last longer the more he put off a timely withdrawal. Glory didn't much notice, lost in her own celestial glow. Until she missed one of her monthlies. And then another. And the small bump on her belly began to grow.

When she went to Tyson with the news he shrugged. Wasn't his fault was it?

"That's not the point, Tyson," Glory responded. "We simply can't tell a soul. My father would kill me. My mother would want to keep me home to raise the baby. Neither outcome appeals to me. I have no idea how Moonbeam and Dulcetta would respond."

Their mention triggered an idea in the back of Tyson's mind.

He knew from his mother Dulcetta of an old lady who lived far back in the hills. Most had heard of her. Few had seen her. She lived very, very alone.

Dulcetta's indian family with no name had used her to acquire herbs, herbs for healing, herbs for feeling good, herbs for taste, herbs for livestock, ancient remedy herbs that one had to know where to look for in far removed corners of the river valley. Dulcetta had continued the practice and knew where to find her.

"Maybe she could help us," wondered Tyson. "Maybe she could make the baby go away or grow up somewhere else?"

"Yes," responded Glory. "Maybe she could even raise the baby for us until we are old enough to want it? See if you can learn from your mom how to find her. Tell her you have a friend who is desperate for relief from a stomach condition. In the meantime, I will stay covered up with the loosest clothing I can find. We can't let anyone in on this secret of ours."

"Do we still get to play 'fun and feel good?'" Tyson asked in a halting voice.

Glory's answer confirmed his worst fears.

"Probably better not until the baby has safely arrived."

Tyson Hensbell was clearly going to have to find some new playmates.

Several weeks later, Glory and Tyson were headed southwest out of Welcome in search of a strange old lady.

Dulcetta had found it hopeful that Tyson had asked in the first place. He had never seemed to care about others or how to help them much before. He said he had a friend who was real sick.

What had really confused Dulcetta was the secrecy of it all. No names, no locations, no hint of who was in need. Just directions to his mother's old friend's house so deep in the Ozarkian woods that even Dulcetta had trouble finding it on occasion. She described the intersecting trails that reduced to a narrow path at the end, and the cave with spring water issuing forth where the old lady lived as best she could.

It took Glory and Tyson close to a week to find the place. And when they finally stumbled onto a small stream of water and traced it to its source at the mouth of a cave, they were staring straight down the barrel of a gun.

Tyson thrust his hands in the air and screamed "Please don't shoot, I am Dulcetta's son, and my friend and I need your help."

"Prove it."

"OK. My mom has been married three times. First to a pig farmer named Jamon who was my father, then to a drifter named Cornwall who is my brother's dad, and now to a lady who comes from the Snarkle line, though this last one has never been consummated. She was raped twice by …"

"Okay, okay. What do you need?"

"I am Tyson Hensbell and this is my friend, Glory Divine, daughter of Reverend Chester and Star Divine, and we need help with what she is toting around in her belly."

Glory raised her shirt to display the ever-growing baby bump.

"Stupid kids. What do you suppose I can do?"

"Well for one, can you let us sit down for a minute and catch our breath? It's been a long walk, especially for my friend here."

Glory was touched by Tyson's concern. When the old lady didn't respond, Tyson helped her settle on a large rock.

"What do you want from me?"

"We need your help in figuring out how to deal with this baby. Can we make it go away? Can you keep it for us until we grow up? What can two kids do with a baby they're not ready for?"

"Well, first of all you can stop fornicating."

Tyson looked confused at such a big word. Glory smiled weakly and whispered to him, "fun and feel good."

"Oh, we've already done that."

"Good," grunted the old lady. "I mean after as well, until you are really ready to have one of these."

Tyson and Glory nodded, without much enthusiasm.

"I reckon I could make the baby go away, but it would cause your friend here pain and guilt. Anyway, it's my friend Dulcetta's grandbaby living in there, her first one I'm a guessin', so I could never do that. Here's what I can do."

The old lady then described what would be coming to pass. Glory would be getting larger and larger, and start feeling the baby move about in her belly. She guessed that from their description of when they started noticing the belly bump that such would happen over the next several months. It would be hard to hide the baby, but if Glory was successful, she would feel pains in her stomach toward the end of the ordeal. They should return to the cave at the first indication of such discomfort.

"I will help you deliver your baby, and raise it here in my cave until you return for it, no more than two years later. If you do not return by then, I will deliver Dulcetta's grandchild to her, and share the whole story. I will take good care of your baby. It will be up to you to give it a proper home and raising after that. I've never intervened like this before, though I've had several of my own over the years. I do it only in honor of my dear friend Dulcetta, and in no way as a favor for you silly children. That is my offer."

Feeling meek and somewhat chastised, Tyson uttered a soft "Thank you," and Glory hugged the old lady. She fed them and allowed them a spot to sleep by her fire, before sending them packing with directions for a shorter and more direct trip home.

"It should take you no longer than two days. Don't forget the way because you will not have much time when your friend starts to deliver."

"Do you have a name, sister?" Glory asked in parting.

"Yes I do, and don't call me sister … mom."

Time passed slowly for Glory, but not for Tyson Hensbell. He had found a new preoccupation, and wasted little time spreading the Hensbell brand far and wide. If Glory suspected, she didn't pass judgment. After all, she was the one who had freed the beast.

First, it was a young lady from the large settlement upstream who had accompanied her father to a livestock auction at the county seat. Tyson had helped Moonbeam and Dulcetta drive a herd of pigs there.

She caught him looking at her with a sly smile and thought him exceptionally good looking. She had just stopped seeing her childhood boyfriend and was in need of a good time. She figured that this guy might just be the one to provide it. He was.

Tyson had also made a decision. To hell with this pulling out just before heaven. Henceforth he was riding the glory, so to speak, to pleasure's end. They were able to sneak off behind a nearby cabin at the height of the auctioneer's performance.

It didn't take long for his new friend to brag to her friends about the exciting new boy in her life, and several decided to sample on their own, finding excuses to accompany parents to and near Welcome. Tyson Hensbell was always available.

And then there was Ruth, beautiful, irresistible Ruth Farmer. While James was busy organizing Welcome's new bank, Ruth was busy watching young Tyson Hensbell from afar.

She had really never cheated on James, despite her show off nature, and she had been offered many opportunities. She just said no. But now, she was getting concerned that James was not going to be able to provide her with the baby she craved. It was not for lack of trying, but simply a fact of nature. She guessed that she was going to have to try something new if she was to become a mother. So, she did.

Tyson had noticed Ruth from the days of the first community bath. He found everything about her intimidating—her randy spirit, her openness, her body, which was unlike anything he had ever seen. And he had seen quite a few most recently. When she came on to him he shied away at first, unsure exactly what was going on. This was not his style as he was very much into his fun and feel good beyond dear Glory. But, he finally succumbed to temptation. Again, and again. And, again.

At first, Tyson, really thought he really was in Heaven. Gone and died. Ruth didn't even pretend that he needed to pull out. He guessed that she was taking something to keep from having babies, but he didn't dare ask for fear of reminding her.

After a while Tyson began to wonder if he was being used, given the frequency and perfunctory nature of their interactions. Still, he stepped up as best he could.

It hurt his feelings when Ruth announced that she would not be seeing him in this way again, but freed him to resume expanding his horizons.

What Ruth didn't tell Tyson was that she had missed her cycle and that he was probably the father of her baby to be. Ruth couldn't be certain because she had continued her efforts with James, but it surely had been fun to introduce young Tyson to things he had yet to learn from the younger set of partners. In her heart she knew that she was carrying Tyson Hensbell's baby.

And time would tell a story that several others in the neighborhood were as well. The Hensbell line was alive and well.

When Glory's time came, Tyson dutifully led her back into the woods toward the old lady's cave. Unfortunately they didn't make it before a baby popped forth, a little baby boy. Neither Tyson nor Glory had a clue as to what to do, so Tyson wrapped the periodically screaming new born in his shirt and carried it behind Glory, still attached to her privates, as she waddled slowly toward their destination.

The old lady could only shake her head in disgust when they appeared. She quickly grabbed the tiny bundle, severed its connection to his mother, heated water from the spring to clean him, and slapped the hungry, thirsty infant on Glory's breast. They would need to remain with her until she could be sure that the little boy could live without mother's milk. Glory felt a motherly tinge of regret when that time arrived, but knew in her heart that this was best. She promised to "return for Tyson Hensbell Jr. as soon as she felt comfortable caring for him," failing to add "with or without Tyson Sr.," who was frankly ready to get back to making his rounds.

They parted, mother and father, from baby Tyson Jr., without further attention. The old lady gathered the baby to her bosom. She milked her goat with one hand, and sprinkled in a touch of butterfly weed, to provide nurture and love to the charge she had accepted. It brought back warm memories of her own, and left her smiling.

A dangling irony from the last days of Welcome, Arkansas, not one totally lost on most Welcomers, was that two of Welcome's most faithful and loyal wives had emerged from Rubert Gas's "stable of beauties," as it was called in the early years.

Fannibelle had given Bear Snarkle Bear Jr., Sunshine, and Moonbeam, the latter two aptly named for the attributes they lent to life in Welcome.

Star had brought joy to old bachelor Reverend Chester Divine's life with Glory and Luke, and added lady of the night context to the historical underpinnings of the community.

Both ladies were courageous, honest and true.

Chapter 20

Hellfire and Mountaineers

The lightning bolt scored a direct middle of the night hit on a huge pile of dry brush in the woods atop the hill. Flames erupted and leapt to the parched and brittle tree line along the ridge in a rush. Wind surged and pushed it down the hill. All of Welcome, Arkansas lay in its path.

As a wall of fire roared down and around the hillside, Welcomers began to awaken and scream. Most didn't have time to dress before heading to the creek or flanking ridges, trying to outrace the inferno.

Bear Snarkle screamed at Moonshine and Dulcetta to run his pig herd into the creek. They turned their dogs on the squealing mass and got most of them headed the right way.

The squirming scrum of pigs and humanity huddled in Large Creek looked at one another in confusion and terror. When the tree line that Jeb Snarkle had planted decades before to help filter livestock waste and protect against stream bank erosion caught fire, large sycamores began to explode with heat and topple into the creek, fortunately landing mostly on pigs, with a few exceptions, and fueling the fire line leap across waters and up the facing hill. Smells of burning flesh, animal and otherwise, fouled the air beyond smoke. Cries of pain mingled with squeals of death all round.

As dawn shown through the morning haze, what remained of Welcome, Arkansas, began to emerge from the creek and the hills around. It was a deadly and tragic site.

And that didn't include new parents Glory Divine and Tyson Hensbell.

They had been cavorting in Tyson's rudimentary treehouse when the lightning strike exploded. Right next to them. They were burned to a crisp before they had time to uncouple.

Welcome, Arkansas, was no more. It had ceased to exist. More than half a century after Jebediah and Sunshine Snarkle, Polly Snarkle and Sam set foot on the creek-banded mountainside, roughly three decades after Reverend Chester Divine named it.

The "Big Lightning Fire," as it was soon known, wiped out Welcome from top, where it hit, to bottom where even Large Creek had been unable to contain its fury. It burned down the entire mountainside and surroundings, including every structure, from Jeb Snarkle's original homestead, to Rubert Gas's Saloon and back rooms of ill repute, to Moonbeam and Dulcetta's pig barn, to Chester Divine's church, to Bear Jr. and Sadie's newly constructed log cabin. Nothing but ashes remained, beyond a few bones and pieces of metal, and the headstones in the Welcome cemetery, honoring among others the founders.

The human toll had been tragic.

Nothing was ever found of Tyson Hensbell and Glory Divine. Unknown to any, they had been making love in the vortex of the conflagration, and went out in a blaze of "Heaven."

Reverend Chester and Star were heartbroken. Glory Divine had been the star of their constellation, the joy of their union. That they were spared the details of her sexual proclivities and out of wedlock child was the only blessing to emerge from their loss. Star would have understood. Rev. Divine wouldn't have. Luke would carry on, but not fill the hole in their hearts.

Dulcetta mourned once again. Her friend and lover Moonbeam Snarkle was gone as well. When the fire began they had rushed to herd the pigs into the creek, and were actually successful in rescuing most. But when the wall of fire reached the trees at water's edge, exploding on them with heat and flame, one had fallen directly on Moonbeam standing waist deep in the creek amongst the porkers. She had mercifully died immediately.

When Dulcetta took stock of her life looking back, she could only wonder why. Persecuted for her indian heritage, two worthless husbands, multiple rapes, two at the hands of the same sick perpetrator, two clueless boy children, one now missing forever, one lost genuine lover, and her house and livelihood destroyed by fire.

She would carry on with son Corny, but where and how she wasn't sure. With whom, a man, or a woman, was the first question she would have to answer. She wasn't sure about that either.

Rubert Gas was gone, as were several of his ladies of the night and the clients they had been in the process of entertaining. Distracted until it was too late to flee.

The Pompassie family and farm. Toast.

All told, the human toll exceeded ten lives lost or missing, nearly a quarter of Welcome's known population or visitation.

When the ashes settled, village elders gathered to assess and contemplate the future. Their assessment was bleak. They would have to start over from scratch. Not unlike 1838, town founder Jebediah Snarkle had observed. He was particularly aggrieved. Not only had he lost a granddaughter in the disaster, but also his "most beautiful place on earth."

Some wanted to rebuild on the spot. Everyone's property lines preserved as before. Post conflagration status quo.

Others weren't so comfortable with that approach. First of all Welcome, Arkansas, was nothing but ashes and ruin. At least they had started with some fertile land and beautiful water half a century earlier. A core group was more philosophical. Several viewed it as sacred space which should not be desecrated by new human intrusion. Others were frankly spooked by rebuilding on the ashes of those the community had lost.

As usual, James Farmer had a novel idea that combined elements of all angles of view, including his previous vision for Welcome. He envisioned a new town, a new name, a new beginning. Several ridges up and over, currently unencumbered with people, unsettled, not as scenic or near the water, but flat, practical, and suitable for a new community layout. And, that bank thing again, a new community bank to drive it all.

Citizens would pool all of their currency and he would contribute what was left of his to start the bank. They would evolve from a barter economy to a cash one, with deposits growing as their economy and in-migration did. And the bank would lend these funds out for construction and other forms of community development. He would be happy to organize and manage the bank, as he had in Texas.

This concept began to gain favor among most of what remained of Welcomers. Even Jebediah Snarkle saw merit in starting anew and leaving the old site and cemetery as a shrine to founders and lost loved ones.

Only Dulcetta Hensbell balked at the idea. She wanted to rebuild on the site of Bear Snarkle's destroyed pig barn, graze those who had survived in the creek, and replenish the herd. She could make a suitable living doing what she and Moonbeam had done with Bear's stock if she could buy it from him, and memorialize the woman and lifestyle she had come to love.

After some discussion it was agreed that the community would deed over the entire property that was once Welcome, Arkansas, to Dulcetta at no cost in recognition of the land's sorry condition and her status as an impoverished widow. Bear Snarkle would also contribute the remains of his herd to Dulcetta to help launch her new venture, and in honor his lost daughter, Moonbeam.

Perhaps Corny would grow into a lad who could contribute to her efforts, though based on everything she had seen from him to date, Dulcetta was skeptical. He looked and acted like his worthless father more each day. That said, Dulcetta had never had problems attracting partners, and she surely would have her eye out for one of either gender moving forward.

Most agreed that a new community would need a new name. Welcome would remain where Welcome was. But agreeing on what was to become on the new site was more challenging. Finally, Reverend Chester Divine proposed a Biblical name, maybe something to do with a mountain in sacred text, since they would be building atop a mountain. Many were initially neutral to the idea, but budged his way when he proposed that residents would thereafter be known as "Mountaineers." It had a rugged manly feel to it, certainly more so than "Welcomers." He scoured the scriptures for options. Star suggested that he needed to come up with something to make the women feel comfortable a well. His eyes lit up when he found a sort of ladylike name to go with Mountain. Star approved, and the community quickly concurred as well. They would simply cut the mountain to Mt. and add a feminine touch.

She smelled the tragedy before she learned of it. Prevailing winds had moved the remains of a smoke plume across the Ozarks toward her cave. She sensed disaster and pulled the baby to her chest.

Weeks later word reached her of the Welcome disaster, the loss of life, and more specifically, the name of Reverend Chester Divine's beloved daughter Glory. The lady had always harbored doubts that Glory would return for her child, but this secured that outcome. She would take her friend Dulcetta's new grandson to her.

With help from several in the community, Dulcetta had erected a temporary lean-to shelter at the bottom of the hill that was once Welcome, near the fenced in area where her pigs were corralled. The charred remains of a potbelly stove kept her and her son warm, and water from the spring quenched their thirst.

Across the mountain, activity was at a fever pitch as most former Welcomers pitched in to build a new town. Mountaineers they were now, and strangers from around the area joined them in creating and broadening the community footprint. Cash money flowed in with the newcomers who were drawn to the opportunities that were blossoming, including the 2% interest on their money paid by the newly sanctioned Mt. Bank.

It hadn't taken long for James Farmer to construct a safe room for any who wished to protect their money from theft or natural disaster, and grow it for future investment. He even appointed a board of directors, a new concept to most, to help him manage the operations of Mt. Bank. He chose a mixed lot that included denizens like Jeb Snarkle and Feral Feester, as well as several new to town, whom he seemed to have known from a previous life. Curious, thought Jeb, but he said nothing as he was enjoying the trust that was being placed in him. James' wife Ruth was the token female on the board, and a wise addition when it came to building confidence among community women. That she was showing more pregnant every week just added credibility. No one could have imagined it was Tyson Hensbell's spawn.

What could be simpler that keeping one's money safe, growing it, and lending it out at a rate of interest that would further strengthen the community, the bank, and its assets?

Moreover, there was more talk of applying for a formal post office designation and establishing a one-room school house, again led by James Farmer, who seemed to have his fingerprints on every new and creative idea.

Even Reverend Chester Divine got caught up in the energy in the wake of his devastating loss, and began to raise money for a new church, depositing it all in Mt. Bank until he could begin construction.

Mountaineers were moving forward at a rapid pace to replace and better the lifestyle that had been theirs for the last half century.

This was the sense of purpose and excitement that the old lady walked into with a small baby in her arms, inquiring as to how to find Dulcetta. A few eyes rolled before she was referred to the old Welcome, and made her way there. Dulcetta was running her pigs into the creek when she arrived.

"Mother May,"—that was what Dulcetta had always called her—"it is so good to see you. I need your comfort for I am heartbroken. I have lost the woman I loved most in the world, as well as my older boy in a great fire, and am trying to start over with these pigs and this land. It is so hard."

The old lady smiled and handed the baby to Dulcetta, who responded with a confused look.

"Meet your new grandson, Tyson Hensbell, Jr., son of your boy Tyson and his girlfriend, Glory Divine. You are all he has in this world."

Dulcetta sobbed in confusion, then joy, then wonder, and clasped the baby close to her chest. "How? What? When? Why?" The questions just rolled on.

They set down at the rudimentary table in the lean-to and the old lady shared the entire story, including Tyson's coming to her for help because of his mother. Neither Tyson nor Glory had felt they could tell their respective parents for fear of embarrassing them in the community. She didn't reveal her concern that neither of the young parents would ever return for the baby or her threats to tell Dulcetta if they didn't. That part was irrelevant now. She added that in parting Glory had asked her to care for the baby until they could, and to call him Tyson Hensbell, Jr.

Dulcetta was overwhelmed with emotion. Her own grandson, named after her son who had been named after his father in a loosely translated way. A generational lineage of Hensbells and pig farmers spawned by a young indian maiden from a family with no name.

She was also afraid. How could she do this on her own? How could she raise a young one and a baby, and care for her source of livelihood, a herd of pigs, by herself. She begged Mother May to stay with her for a while, at least until she could find a man or a woman to take her on. She was still young and attractive, and with all these folks moving into the new town, surely someone would want to have her.

Mother May agreed with her assessment and strategy, and could stay for a couple of weeks to help Dulcetta implement it. Dulcetta began that very evening at the newly erected Mountain Saloon on Main Street.

Finally, after a few wasted sleep arounds while Mother May helped care for her children and her pigs, Dulcetta settled on a prospect for her new pig-farming, child-raising partner. In this case it was a "he."

Leonard Weiner, pronounced "weener, as in sausage," as he introduced himself, was a young, strapping, nearly handsome guy who came across as simple and naive and loved music. He had wandered into town alone from one of several possible locales back east, depending on whom he was sharing his story with, and immediately started entertaining. First, it was at the Mountain Saloon, followed shortly thereafter with Reverend Divine at his Sunday service. Sometimes it was a banjo, others a fiddle. Some of his songs were raunchy, others romantic, still others divine. His voice could range from holy to sexy, and his pitch from tenor to bass.

Dulcetta first seduced him between sets at the Mountain Saloon, and again the next day after church. In that Reverend Divine was operating in a large tent until he could afford and build a real place of worship, there hadn't been much privacy or time for their second encounter, but Dulcetta had snuck it in. While Dulcetta had not had much luck with males over the years, she had never had trouble attracting them. She had a good feeling about this one.

After a week, he was hooked. And, then it was time for her to share her vision of their future together.

She discussed her plans with Star, who agreed to take in Mother May and the two young ones for a couple of nights while Dulcetta introduced her new man to what would come to be for him. Dulcetta also mentioned in confidence that the arrangement would offer Star an opportunity to meet her new grandson. She promised more details later. Star was stunned, confused, and excited.

Between bouts of pleasure, Dulcetta painted a picture of a new beautiful cabin just up the hill from her expanded pig operation, which would pay for the whole thing. She failed to mention her two young children until Leonard was starry eyed in love. When she got around to that part, Leonard shrugged and confessed that he knew nothing about either, pigs or children, but it would surely give him some new material for songs.

"Will you marry me, Leonard Weiner?" Dulcetta had finally asked with some trepidation.

"Sure," Leonard responded without hesitation.

A week later, Reverend Chester Divine pronounced Dulcetta Hensbell and Leonard Weiner husband and wife, and allowed that they might begin their sexual lives together as well. This brought a chuckle from the assembled friends and neighbors, which Reverend Divine simply wrote off as expressions of joy. Mother May attended, with babies in tow, and even introduced young Tyson to the Reverend, after the service, as his new grandson, Tyson Hensbell, Jr. She met the Reverend's dull stare with the promise that Star would explain, before rushing forward to hug the newlyweds.

Dulcetta insisted that she, and her children, keep her first ever last name, Hensbell, in honor of establishing a solid history amidst the chaos that had been her life, and in honor of her scoundrel first husband Jamon. Leonard did not object. He was enjoying his new wife and the pleasures she provided too much to quibble about historical relevance. Besides Weiner, pronounced "weener," was far from worth fighting over.

The months passed quickly, a new town began to emerge where there had been none, the population of newcomers grew, as did Ruth's belly and

Mt. Bank's deposits. Reverend Chester Divine finally forgave his beloved Glory for having a child out of wedlock. It took a series of sermons on sin, rationalization, and equivocation for him to get there, but arrive he did. Star had already embraced Tyson Jr. as their own, and began to help care for him.

When Ruth's time finally came, she delivered a handsome, healthy, young boy whom she proudly named Tyson. James didn't really like the name or the fact that the lad looked nothing like him, but figured he would grow into a familial resemblance. He was just happy to have finally delivered the goods. So he thought.

Another phenomena began to occur across the broader region during that time. A lot of young unwed daughters started showing as pregnant. More than the occasional one who was generally hidden away or had their pregnancy cut short. This seemed almost an epidemic, or even an infestation.

Funny thing. As moms and dads began pressing expectant mothers as to who was responsible for their condition, the name Tyson surfaced time and time again.

"But, he was so cute."

"The guy was so handsome."

"He tricked me into it."

"I thought he was protected."

"I didn't know what he was doing."

The excuses were as varied and ill-conceived as the results of Tyson's efforts. And, it was always just Tyson, no last name, just good-looking, smooth-talking Tyson.

As parents began acknowledging their daughters' conditions among themselves, instead of hiding it as usual, it became clear that a young man named Tyson had unleashed a torrent of new life during a very short period of time. Most agreed that they needed to find this young man and hold him responsible, at least financially. He obviously couldn't marry all of the young ladies, but he surely could contribute to the cost of raising babies in challenging times.

A small group of fathers, almost a vigilante band, went from village to village calling out any Tyson they could find, without much success. One Tyson was 87 years old and far from handsome. It could not have been him. Another was in his mid-50s, the father of eight, and grandfather of twelve. He looked tired not handsome. And finally, a baby named Tyson in the new mountain named town whose father was named James.

One of the dads was more cynical that the others, and began to probe. A baby named Tyson? Born during the same cycle of propagation? "Do you know anyone named Tyson?" he had asked Ruth when he had her alone for a moment. Her instant blush told him all he needed to know. The Tyson he was seeking was right here in the midst of this new community and he would root the lad out.

He followed up with Ruth like a dog on a bone.

"So, you do know a Tyson, and I'm not talking your son? Is this correct Ms. Farmer?"

Another blush, and the dad drilled down.

"Could this Tyson be the father of your boy child named Tyson?"

"No, he's dead, burned up in the "Big Lightning Fire."

"But not before he planted life in you and all these other young ladies who are carrying or delivering it as we speak? Ms. Farmer, I intend to share my theory with your husband unless you tell me the truth, right now."

"Go ask Dulcetta Hensbell," was Ruth's tired response. "She was the mother of the Tyson who died."

"So, where do I find this mother," he pushed.

"Go to old Welcome and follow the pigs."

The band of distressed dads descended on unsuspecting Dulcetta and Leonard. Dulcetta sobbed at the memory of her lost son, which calmed the crowd a bit. The persistent pursuer of truth was able to discern through subtle questioning that Dulcetta's lad was in his teens, was thought by some to be a very handsome young man, had traveled widely about the region helping Dulcetta and Moonbeam take pigs to market, was probably a virgin when it came to sex, and most certainly could not have impregnated a long line of innocent lassies and married women. Dulcetta was firm in her denial that son Tyson had ever sired a child, let alone a bunch of them. While lying was distasteful to her, the consequences of not doing so were incalculable in this situation.

The pack of fathers soon left, after Leonard entertained them with his new song about kids and pigs, most of them with a smile on their face. Except the one father, who was convinced that he had uncovered the mother lode of reproduction. Tyson Hensbell. He didn't know what to do other than name his new grandson Tyson, and encourage the others to follow suit when baby boys were involved. Or, he could seek revenge.

One fine Ozarkian morning alive with the raucous colors of fall, Reverend Chester Divine headed to Mt. Bank to discuss how he might finance a new church with James Farmer. He found the doors to the bank locked shut, and wondered if he was bit before opening time. The sign on the door said "Closed," so he grabbed a seat on the bench in front and settled in.

Several additional patrons wandered by and tried the door. Still no response. One glanced at his time piece and muttered something about "an hour late." Can't even get in to count my own money," which evidently he did every morning.

Reverend Divine finally headed over to Jeb Snarkle's new house on the edge of town closest to old Welcome, and asked whether he knew, as a member of the Mt. Bank's board, why the bank wasn't opening as usual on this particular beautiful morning? Jeb shrugged in ignorance, threw on his light coat, and headed back to the bank with Reverend Divine. His knocks went unanswered as well, and his face reflected concern for James Farmer and his family.

They lived in a comfortable house on the other side of town, which was where Jeb and his entourage headed next. Same scenario. Locked door and unanswered knocks. No sign of life anywhere.

They returned to Mt. Bank with the angry patron demanding that they break down the door so he could get in and count his cash money. Which is exactly what Jeb did.

It didn't take long to figure out that there was no money to count.

The door to the safe room was wide open. The room was empty. James Farmer's impenetrable fortress, as he described it to bank customers, was picked clean as a hound's tooth.

President Farmer's office was empty as well, except for the piece of paper on his desk with a single word scrawled across it. "SUCKERS." That was all it said, all that remained in the secure confines of Mt. Bank.

Jeb sent Reverend Divine to fetch the town's new sheriff, a loud rotund man, who had just been appointed over the objections of some who wanted a more dashing law enforcement official to serve and protect them. Sheriff Angus Perfidious was definitely not that.

Jeb then sat in James Farmer's presidential chair and began to piece together all the signs he had missed.

James Farmer had arrived from Texas claiming to have been a successful banker there. He had displayed ample supplies of cash money in a community that had little. James Farmer seeded a cash economy, as he called it, in an historically "bartering" community. He paid real money for services rendered, which in turn passed through hands to others for goods and services before ending up back in Mt. Bank. Where had he gotten his, Jeb had wondered from time to time, but didn't delve into it. He had worried a bit about the community's new dependence on currency, which from his perspective had little or no value.

James Farmer had a sexy young wife who seduced the community into trusting her and her strange looking husband. It was whispered around town that her seductions extended to other male citizens, but no one would come forward to confirm. Her pregnancy and choice of names for her young son fueled additional rumors, particularly in the wake of the many new Tysons all around, but Jeb Snarkle hadn't bought into any of it. And he certainly hadn't sampled the wares personally. Rumors carried about as much value as paper bills with famous faces on them, Jeb had concluded.

Several new faces began showing up to help develop and execute James Farmer's vision for a growing and dynamic community. Jeb had sensed an unusual bond of familiarity between them and James, but thought little of it. James placed them on his Mt. Bank board of directors, though locals knew little about them.

Customers flocked to Mt. Bank from around the region, to deposit what cash they didn't spend in the safety and security of a real bank, and earn a return as well. And, that which they did spread around eventually made its way back to James Farmer's safe room. After the loss of everything for so many, having a safe place to protect their cash and other valuables was a Godsend.

The funny thing about James Farmer's community development model—bring the money in, keep it safe, and lend it out to those who were contributing to the growth and prosperity of the community—was that the last piece of the equation was more talk than action. Come to think of it, most loans were to the president's cronies and were rarely invested in local projects.

A picture began to emerge in Jeb Snarkle's mind that made him sick to his stomach.

James Farmer was no more than a common thief, a swindler, a flimflam man, who talked big, accumulated what belonged to others, promised the impossible, and ran off with everything a community entrusted him with. He had a flamboyant accomplice and several others to pitch in on the charade.

He had surely done the same thing in Texas, and who knows where else. How had Jeb not seen through him and them? Why had his instincts failed him? These questions would haunt Jeb Snarkle to his grave, and probably hastened his journey thereto.

By the time Sheriff Perfidious arrived, James and Ruth Farmer, their bastard son, and his immoral buddies were well on their way to bilk another simple and unsuspecting group of innocent citizens, probably a state or two away. The good sheriff could only shrug, and agree with Jeb Snarkle's analysis. There was little to be done on his end.

The little mountain town with the feminine Biblical name would have to start over. Again. With lots of Snarkles and new Tysons soon to be vying for space.

Chapter 21

Loss and Lines (Turn of the Century)

Time passed. So did visionary founder Jebediah Snarkle, at about age 82. Despite his accomplishments, he died with a heavy heart. He had lost his beloved Sunshine far too early. Their son and grandchildren would have made her proud, as they did him. He trusted them to take his original dream and make it their own, to steward the land and water lovingly and diligently, and transition the legacy of Welcome, Arkansas, to whatever iteration came next. He stewed that he hadn't given them enough grounding in the history of it all to assure that. History was important to Jeb. So was water—precious, clean, clear water that brought and carried all life. He worried about that as well.

His marriage to Sophia was lackluster after a scorching start, but included two beautiful children with classic Italian names in honor of her family's roots in the old country. Both Luigi and Ferderiko had moved on to different parts of the country, never rooted in their father's vision and dream. Sophia and Jeb had slipped further apart, neither loving nor hating, just existing. She knew he could never give up the grief of losing his first love Sunshine. It was such a part of him that it weighed their own relationship down. She hadn't planned on being second fiddle for all time. He knew that, and regretted his inability to move beyond Sunshine. But, not really. His heart wasn't in that.

He also felt responsible for the Big Lightning Fire, though he wasn't quite sure why.

He knew why, and carried guilt, over the Mt. Bank fraud. He should have sniffed James Farmer out. His instincts screamed that something was wrong, convoluted, perverted. But, he neither shared nor acted on them. His passivity had cost the community dearly.

In the end, not even his precious children, grandchildren, and great-grandchildren could snap him out of the funk.

They buried him on the mountaintop that had revealed to him the most beautiful place on earth more than six decades earlier. Between his beloved Sunshine and mother Polly. They hoped that he would find peace there. They felt that he deserved it.

His line moved on. Bear had retired to hunting and fishing and loving Fannibelle with all of his heart. No more pigs.

Bear Jr. was adjudicating left and right, and gaining visibility on the state political scene. His Sadie had borne him three more baby Snarkles, including a late-in-marriage lad the very month great-grandfather Jeb passed. If they would have known that he was leaving, they would certainly have named the baby Jebediah Jr. in his honor. But they didn't, and had settled on Sam Snarkle, in honor of the boy's great-great-grandmother's husband well before, leaving the founding father of the line's name for another occasion. All agreed that the Juniors and Thirds and founding women's names passed down through generations were getting a little confusing anyway.

The other two were girls, Sally Snarkle and Adola Snarkle, born soon after Bear Jr. and Sadie had moved back to Welcome.

Bear Jr. and Sadie had birthed the makings of a family dynasty, of mixed race no less, somewhat of a novelty in the Ozarkian landscape.

Bear Jr.'s sister Sunshine had married a Casey from upstream and was raising a family of her own. More deep roots with Snarkle tentacles.

All missed dear Moonbeam.

Bear III and Polly both attended the same college their dad had, and were pursuing professional studies in the fields of medicine and journalism, respectively. Bear hoped they would be successful in all they did, but not forget their roots, and maybe even come home to roost someday. Neither had shown the slightest interest in marrying or adding to the lineage just yet.

It would seem that Jeb Snarkle could rest assured that his legacy was in good hands, if indeed he had found the lasting peace to do so.

All told, nine Snarkles in the community to carry on.

Over time, Dulcetta Hensbell's herd grew. As did little Tyson Jr., into a strapping lad with a strong resemblance to his father and grandfather. Dulcetta and Leonard even had one of their own, another boy they named Tunes, in honor of Leonard's true passion. Hensbell, of course, per her eternal vows. Dulcetta's life scorecard was decidedly male with three husbands, three boy children, one by each, and one male grandson. A mini male dynasty of Hensbells on her own. Except for the one true love of her crazy Indian life, Moonbeam Snarkle.

Dulcetta was particularly proud of her grandson, Tyson Jr. He stepped up to whatever responsibility she passed to him, despite his young age. He worked hard and did not shy away from any task, no matter how dirty or tedious. The only thing she didn't like was his occasional mean streak. Grandpa Jamon had possessed one as well, and Dulcetta remembered it getting and keeping him in trouble with others in the community. Particularly Snarkles.

In the meantime, Sunshine's oldest daughter Ella Casey had been matched up with an older man from a successful merchant family in a resort town up north on the big river. He had been too shy to engage in much courting, but between family connections a deal had been struck, and little Ella seemed quite happy.

Elmer St. Goody was neither saint, nor good. In fact he was now deranged. He was the dad who had pushed hardest to find the Tyson Hensbell who had impregnated his precious daughter, the one who had called out Ruth Farmer with similar accusations regarding her new son Tyson, the one who was sure that this Tyson Hensbell had knocked up a lot of innocent young women and left them to raise his spawn on their own. He knew that to be true, despite the protestations of the reckless lad's mother. How he wished that Tyson had survived the Big Lightning Fire so he and his fellow fathers could have presented a great big due bill. The other dads had let it go. He couldn't. So, he named his grandson Tyson.

Sarah, the daughter in question, had eventually committed suicide while her Tyson was in his early teens, leaving Elmer and his wife to raise the kid.

Elmer didn't know why Sarah had done it, but guessed that she had just given up. She had never found a man to love and live with to help with her Tyson, who was a true disaster of a young man if ever there was one. He was uncontrollable, unremorseful about all the bad things he did, and inconsolable when he found his mother hanging by a rope. He was the biggest "un" Elmer had ever encountered.

Elmer was also sure that getting stuck with Sarah's Tyson had also cost his wife her life, and now it was just him and the man-child-devil himself, Tyson St. Goody. If this wouldn't derange a fellow, nothing would.

So Elmer went back to what he had considered doing in the beginning. Seeking revenge for the lives of his daughter and wife who had died because of one Tyson Hensbell. He would kill the bastard's offspring with the Jr. attached to his name, as well as his own no good grandson, to even the ledger for those he had lost. He would spite the one who had started it all, whom he would also have killed if he could ever have gotten his hands on him. Elmer wasn't sure if the math worked out exactly to "equal," but knew he had to do something.

Elmer St. Goody shot his bastard grandson Tyson while he was sleeping. One down, one to go.

He then made his way over to the Hensbell pig farm under cover of darkness. Dulcetta and Leonard were snuggled under covers. Their Tyson was nowhere to be found. He, in fact, was in the county jail, some twenty miles away, sent there by Judge Bear Snarkle, Jr. after he had attacked a fellow drinker at the Mountain Saloon in a state of extreme drunkenness. It was his third such offense in less than a month, and Judge Bear Jr. was convinced that a lesson was warranted. Over Dulcetta's tearful objections, he had sentenced her grandson to thirty days.

As dogs began to bark, Elmer fired his shotgun into the air and demanded that Tyson Hensbell, Jr. come out and meet his maker.

Dulcetta was the first to exit the door, long gown flowing in the wind, having heard something in her deep sleep about her grandson. She was panicked about his wellbeing. Leonard stumbled out not far behind, carrying his own weapon As Elmer drew down on Leonard, thinking him to be Tyson, Dulcetta thrust herself between the two, taking the full load before falling to the ground. Leonard fell to his knees and hugged her to him, blood flowing all around. Their young son ran screaming to join in.

Dulcetta Hensbell was gone. The resilient Indian lady who had suffered so much in life, and in love, finally succumbed to the cards that had forever been stacked against her.

Elmer turned his weapon on himself, mission accomplished.

When word of his mother's demise while trying to protect her family reached Tyson Jr. in jail, he went temporarily insane, screaming, storming, banging his head against the stone walls, bleeding from self-imposed wounds. They let him rant until he lost consciousness.

When he awoke, an eerie calmness had overtaken him. He digested the facts he was told, shaking his head slowly in disbelief. He then asked to see Judge Bear Jr., who had already decided to grant him amnesty from the remainder of his sentence because of his heavy loss.

Tyson asked the judge to release him to attend to his mother's funeral and other personal matters, including the care of her pigs.

Judge Bear Jr. nodded his concurrence and offered his sympathies.

Tyson Hensbell, Jr. nodded back. He then asked the judge if he could be frank with him. Again Judge Bear Jr. agreed.

"Judge," he began, "you put me in here to teach me a lesson, a lesson I have learned well. Thank you."

"You're welcome."

"You took me away from my family at a time of great need. Because I was in jail, a man who wanted to kill me, because of something my own father did to his daughter, killed my mother instead." Tyson's voice was calm and level, and the judge was not sure where he was headed.

"Judge Bear Snarkle, Jr., the lesson I have learned from you is about revenge, and I will have mine and my family's on you and yours."

Over time, two lines had been drawn in the scruffy, stony topsoil of this remote Ozarkian county, one rooted in pigs, the other in history. Both were sourced in women of color, Indians, with a capital I, as Bear Jr. had been taught in college to spell it. Full-blooded Native American mothers of great beauty, wisdom, and resilience. Sunshine died birthing her line, Dulcetta defending hers.

Snarkles and Hensbells would feud and fuss, cuss and mistrust, murder and lust through generations in their Ozarkian paradise. Others became more like bit players in the unfolding drama and rival philosophies that would rattle about among these principals. Two lineages, one bastardized, the other co-opted by destiny, two towns, one gone, one new, competing forces in the ongoing battle for heart and soul. Their conflicting views would shape the waters of the Ozarks far into the future.

Chapter 22

Westward Ho? (1927)

"The most beautiful place on earth," as Jebediah Snarkle had called it when he first looked down on Large Creek and the bluffs, fields, and wooded hills surrounding her. Bear Jr. smiled at the memory. His grandfather began to refer to creeks and streams and rivers as "shes" and "hers" in his later years. He would never explain why, but Bear Jr. assumed that it had to do with love. Bear Jr. also recalled grandfather Jeb's prediction that the valley would regain its natural beauty after the Big Lightning Fire, "as nature usually does," was how he put it. His grandfather had been a wise man. Sadly, he had not survived to see it come to pass. But, it did.

World War I intervened across the globe, and in the Ozarks. Luke Divine wanted to enlist, even at his advanced age. He wanted to fight.

Over the objections of his mother Star and his long-deceased father, Reverend Chester, whom his mother was sure would also disapprove, he caught the train to St. Louis, Missouri, and signed up.

Luke's life had been a troubled one. He had always been number two in his pious old father's and young mother's life. Reverend Divine had doted over daughter Glory from the moment she was born, two years before Luke. When she died in the Big Lightning Fire he was devastated and found comfort only in talking to her in heaven. When he discovered that she had not only had sex before marriage, but had birthed an illegitimate child, he forgave her and talked to her some more.

With Luke it was always different. When he came home drunk, he was condemned rather than simply punished. When he impregnated a young lady he didn't want to marry, he was exiled, not counseled.

And on those occasions he returned from exile, including to his own father's funeral, he was scorned, even blamed. Luke Divine's life had not been a happy one.

He had passed recent years living with his mother and her second husband. It was an odd situation. The guy she had married not long after Reverend Divine's passing was not much older than Luke and enjoyed his company. They often ended up getting in trouble together, be it spirits or women or fights over both, as Glory looked the other way. He even supported Luke in his move to war.

Glory didn't know if she would ever see her troubled son again. She didn't.

Meanwhile, the little mountain town with the feminine Biblical name got its own doctor and newspaper. As Bear Jr. had hoped, his son completed his medical studies and returned to hang out his own shingle.

Bear III also brought a bride from back east, just as his father had. He had met the lovely Lucinda in school where she was studying to be a nurse. Their courtship had been passionate and swift, and had since produced two more Snarkle girls. The community felt blessed to be on the receiving end of a two-for-one deal. Nurse Lucinda provided medical support when she wasn't having babies, while Dr. Bear III handled primary care.

Polly had also returned home. She came alone. A long, drawn out love affair had come to an abrupt end when she had announced her intentions to return to her hometown and start a village newspaper.

Her big city lover wanted nothing to do with a life in the sticks with stinking hillbillies, corn liquor, and the animals they screwed for fun. At least that is how he put it their last night together. Polly was grateful that his true condescending colors had shown before she had gotten in too deep.

Polly launched the *Welcomer Press*, so named in honor of her deep local roots, with borrowed money from the newly-chartered community bank. This bank was a real one, regulated by state bank examiners, and despite previous experiences, was perfect to help support the growth that was occurring. Old timers had to admit that James Farmer's model for economic development and shared prosperity was a sound one in theory, because it was working. He was just a crook.

Amidst all this local peace and stability a strange phenomenon was coming to pass. Some Snarkles were getting bored.

Bear Jr. launched the discussion with idle speculation about what life might be like in other parts of the country. The Ozarks was beautiful, and had been good to the family. But what about Colorado, or California, or Washington state? Were they not the coming lands of opportunity as the

Ozarks had been fifty years earlier? And, what about this new road, Route 66, that would carry you all the way to Los Angeles, California? What if we took a road trip out west to check it out?

Bear Jr.'s musings were written off as those of an aging misfit, as the claptrap of a burned-out lawyer, the dribble of a used-up mind, by most everyone. Except his children.

Old Bear, the original, flat out told him they were crazy. How could they leave "the most beautiful place in the world?"

"How can we know that it is without seeing for ourselves?" was the response in unison.

Surprisingly, the women were okay with it.

Sadie knew from the beginning that she had fallen in love with an adventurer. She could help manage the grandkids for the three to four months they would be gone exploring. Maybe it would settle Bear Jr. down for what remained of his life.

The children were mostly in. Bear III saw it as an opportunity to expand his base of medical knowledge. In his absence, wife and nurse Lucinda could surely tend to the general medical needs of the community, and forward special cases on to a big city hospital.

His sister Polly didn't have anyone to leave behind and could write about the trip for possible national syndication.

Youngest brother Sam was more enthusiastic than anyone. He had privately conversed with his siblings about moving on anyway. He had the utmost respect for what his family had carved out in the wilderness over the past nearly one hundred years, but wondered what he could add to it. Just another Snarkle living the good life in a land of plenty and of many. He was all in.

Case in point was Sam's inability to focus on a career path. He tried college but didn't really like it. Too confining. His passions were the creek and the woods, fishing and hunting. And while he kept his kin in good supply of game and fish, it was hard to make a living out of it. He farmed a small plot near the old Welcome site with a few cattle, pigs, and goats, but still no wife or children. He had his choice of women along the way, but no one really lit a spark. He enjoyed their company and their love on occasion, but not enough to settle down.

Sadie worried about him. Bear Jr. didn't. After all it had taken him almost thirty years to settle down and bring a black woman and two mixed race children home to the Ozarks. Sam was only 27.

Beyond that, the family had lost Sally to the flu along the way, and Adola was recently married, and had moved away.

Plans for departure came about quickly. It would be Bears II and III, Polly, and Sam on the road trip of the century. They would buy a new Ford Model T, stack the bare necessities on top, drive north to intersect with the new great national highway, Route 66, and follow it to Los Angeles. If they liked what they saw, they would return to fetch their loved ones move west. If they didn't, they would accept the Ozarks as home for the remainder of their lives and careers. It was all that simple.

"You may never see me again," a hurt Bear Snarkle warned his heirs as they loaded up to leave.

Tyson Hensbell, Jr. had expanded his pig business. Like his grandfather and father before him, he cared little about how many critters roamed his land, left to him by grandmother Dulcetta, and more about how much money he could make. He envied the Snarkles for their prominence and wealth, in an Ozarkian way, and was bent on revenging his grandmother's death however he could. Money would provide a start.

One day as he was running his pigs into Large Creek, he noticed a stranger wandering down the hill. He drew his sidearm and asked what he wanted.

"I want to talk to Tyson Hensbell, Jr."

"That would be me. Who are you?"

"My name is Tyson Farmer, and I believe that I am sort of a relation of yours."

The name sounded familiar and Tyson Jr. invited him into his house.

"So, who are you and how are we related?"

"Do you remember James and Ruth Farmer?"

"Aren't they the ones who started a bank and ran off with everyone's money?"

"Yes, but there's more to the story. Your sixteen-year-old father was pokin' my mother and got her pregnant with me."

"How do you know?"

"My mother told me so."

"So, what does that make us?"

"Sons of Tyson Hensbell, kind of brothers, I guess."

"Tell me more."

"My mother left her husband long ago, and he has evidently landed in jail for yet another bank fraud he attempted. Mom was not implicated and has since moved on out west."

"How do you know we are sons of the same father?"

"Mom told me the whole story. Evidently our father was knockin' up young ladies all over the county before he was fried in a fire. Mom was convinced that the only way she was ever going to have a baby was to go beyond her husband. She picked Tyson Hensbell because he was young, good looking, kind of naive, and a likely stud horse. It took a while so mom began to question whether the problem was with her or James. But she kept at it. Our father was an energetic and willing partner who seemed to be ignorant about birth control."

"You know his antics eventually cost my mother her life, don't you?" said Hensbell. "A father of one of the young ladies he impregnated went nuts and set out to kill me since he couldn't get my father. He shot my mother dead, probably by accident, and then killed himself. I will forever hold Judge Bear Snarkle, Jr. responsible for her death because he had me locked in jail at the time, for no good reason at all. I will avenge her death."

"I'm sorry."

"I also know that there are an unusual number of 'Tysons' about my age running around the county with different last names. Several have approached me with a similar story. I guess old dad was packing a potent weapon," Tyson Jr. added with a smile.

"So, are you married? Any kids?"

"Nope. I tried it for a while but didn't like being tied down. I would like to have a son or two sometime, to carry on my business, and my grudge with the Snarkles. There are so damn many of them around."

"I'm betting if you lined up all the Tysons our age, their wives, and their children in a row, we would outnumber the bastards."

"Why are you here, Tyson Farmer?"

"I want to help you, Tyson Hensbell, Jr. I want to make some money. I want to find a wife and build a family. And I'm willing to help with your pigs as well as avenging the murder of your mother, if you will give me a chance."

The first week out on the road was a mess. It rained most of the time through Oklahoma. Flat tires were a regular occurrence. Pop off the offending flat, patch, and pump it back up. Time and time again.

The going was slow and generally uneventful, with a few exceptions. Like the small town in western Oklahoma where all the bags came flying off the vehicle when an anchor rope broke. Fortunately, only one bag popped open.

Unfortunately, it was Polly's, spewing her undergarments all over main street, to the delight of several lollygagging teens who gleefully helped her pick them up, one by one. Even Bear Jr. got a kick out of his daughter's embarrassment.

And, then there was the west Texas speakeasy where Bear III got wasted on a local rotgut concoction and threw up all over the interior of the Model T. Bear Jr. did not laugh at this and made him clean up every last drop of yuck, causing III to puke again, and costing the travelers two days before they could carry on in a vehicle without a sickly stench.

Days had turned slowly into weeks, and then rain turned into sleet as a winter storm crept into eastern New Mexico to welcome them crossing the state line.

"Maybe this wasn't such a good idea, Dad."

Chapter 23

NO!!!!

Bear the elder's screams of anguish pierced the countryside.

"NO! NO! NO!" he cried over and over again. Fannibelle rushed to try and comfort him, or at least find out what had set him off.

She saw a piece of paper at his feet and picked it up as he hugged himself and shivered. It was a wire.

"Mr. Snarkle,

I regret to inform you that there has been a tragic accident in eastern New Mexico, near Tucumcari. Three passengers in a Model T Ford have died, while a fourth clings to life under a doctor's care. The vehicle slid off the road in an ice storm as it climbed a tall hill after entering the state. The lone survivor moves in and out of consciousness and mentioned your name and location several times. I don't know how to call you, but you can try and ring me up at the number listed below. I apologize for being so direct. I know how hard it will be for you to read this, but I don't know any other way.

Sheriff, Quay County, New Mexico"

Fannibelle added her shrieks of despair to those of her husband. As she reached for Bear, he keeled over gasping for breath. She knelt beside him cradling his head in her lap. When he ceased to breathe, she fainted. By the time nurse Lucinda could reach his side, the attack on his heart had taken him away.

An entire family tree wiped out in a clock tick, depending on whom, or if the one hanging on in Tucumcari, survived.

Sadie drove to the nearest phone line and called the number at the bottom of the wire, as soon as she could control her sobs. She really didn't want to know who was alive if indeed they were. There were no winners in this outcome. Only losers.

The voice on the other end of the line crackled in the distance. She was able to confirm that she was speaking with the sheriff and that he was attempting to be professional as well as compassionate, and failing miserably at both.

He described in halting terms the scene and circumstances of the accident, how the car had slid down the steep side of the icy road, rolling at least three times before hammering into a tree which stopped its descent.

She hesitated, then plunged in.

"Is there still a survivor, Sheriff?"

"Yes, ma'am, but only one and barely. His condition has improved slightly overnight, and the doc thinks he has a fair chance of making it."

"He," processed Sadie. That means my dear Polly is gone, that I will never see her alive again. Sadie shivered and sobbed at the realization.

"So, Sheriff, what can you tell me about the survivor?"

"He's younger that the rest, and has muttered the name Sam during several moments of being conscious."

Sadie didn't know whether to be grateful or hateful. Her beloved husband was dead. Her special son, Dr. Bear III was dead. Polly was dead. How much death could one bear? She began crying uncontrollably.

Lucinda took the phone from her and began sobbing herself when it became obvious that she would never see her husband again. She asked through her tears if she could call back when they had regained their senses, and hung up without waiting for an answer.

"Good riddance," was all Tyson Hensbell, Jr. could mutter when he heard the news, evoking a crooked smile from Tyson Farmer. "Saves me the trouble of getting even."

Chapter 24

Coming Home

They laid the three Bears next to one another, directly in front of Sunshine and Jeb, plots interconnected. They placed Polly next to the other Polly, her great-great-grandmother and namesake. All just above the site of the former town of Welcome, Arkansas, now Tyson Hensbell, Jr.'s pig farm, the melding of old with new, history with commerce, two puddles of bad blood. An overnight near doubling of the settlers' place of rest.

Most of the new town came out to honor the three generations of founders and settlers, all felled with one swoop of Death's scythe. The sense of loss and history's grounding weighed on most shoulders and in most hearts. It hadn't been easy to get from first notice to commemoration.

Sadie was the logical choice to fetch the bodies—three lifeless, one broken in many places and ways. She worked out logistics with the Quay County sheriff, utilizing trains, vehicles, and the kindness of others to bridge gaps along the way. It took her two weeks to reach her injured son, and the loved ones she would bring home to bury.

Sam was in great pain and emotional distress. The one bright light in his haze was a young Navajo maiden named Mai who had tended to his every need since he regained consistent consciousness. Her name translated "Bright Flower," which indeed she was. He vaguely recalled the Cherokee strain in his own lineage, diluted with each successive generation, but honored with naming rights. Except now, there were no more Bears.

He tried to isolate from the loss of father and grandfather, unaware that Bear himself had also passed of a heart attack back home when learning of his own losses. And Aunt Polly, too. Try as he might to compartmentalize, it all jumbled together in too much grief to bear. Except when Mai smiled at him and took his hand in hers. That was what he awakened to when the fog lifted. That was what he looked forward to each morning as normal sleeping patterns returned. He was happy to see his mother, but she could not light him up like Mai. It didn't take Sadie long to figure this out.

Sadie learned that Mai had grown up on a reservation in the Navajo Nation, and migrated with her own mother to Tucumcari as a teenager to finish high school and seek employment. Mai and her mother resided with the local doctor and sat with patients in his small clinic to provide company and comfort. He provided them with lodging and food in return.

Sam had not spoken a full sentence since the wreck. Just his name. Mai's English was passable and she could elicit a nod or occasional smile from him with generic questions. She felt deep remorse for his hurt, even in her heart. She had never heard of nor experienced such loss herself, but bubbled with empathy in a way that lifted Sam up.

The doctor advised Sadie that Sam was probably okay to travel physically. It would not be painless, but there was little additional harm to do. He was more worried about the fragile emotional condition of his patient. Perhaps with drugs, Sam could make it. The three bodies had been embalmed and placed in simple caskets, also ready for returning home. It would be a difficult journey logistically, but "Sheriff can figure it out," the doctor assured Sadie.

Sadie approached Sam late one afternoon about whether he wanted to go home, while Mai gently stroked his hand. Sam nodded yes, but then looked at Mai and uttered his first real post-injury words.

"With her."

Sadie asked if that meant with Mai to her home or taking Mai to his own. He nodded yes vigorously to the latter.

"But Sam, you can't just drag a young lady home with you unless she wants to come, and even then ..."

Sam pointed to Mai who was nodding in the affirmative.

"You would seriously leave your mother and other family, leave with a man ten years your elder whom you only just met and who can't seem to remember how to speak, and go to a remote village in the heart of the Arkansas Ozarks?" Sadie asked in disbelief. "Why?"

"He's a good man. I want to care for him as he returns to health. I want to be with him and have his babies. This is a feeling lit deep in my soul by love and compassion."

The second thing Sam said since the wreck was, "I love you, Mai."

Sadie was overwhelmed with emotion.

Mai's Navajo mother was heartbroken and overjoyed at the same time. Mai was her only daughter, the one who had left her past and heritage behind to seek a brighter future than her reservation offered. And now she wanted to leave forever.

But Mai had seemed so happy since she first sat next to a strange man's bed and clasped his hand. It was as if the ancients had joined their hands together in love and purpose. Who was she to argue with their wisdom and power? "I want more than any hurt for her to be happy," her mother pondered.

She did insist that if Mai were to accompany Sadie and Sam back to the Ozarks it would be as a married woman. Suddenly Sam was speaking in full sentences. The doctor blamed his loss of words on the concussion he suffered and said a gradual return to fluency was normal.

The only words Sam needed for now were, "I do."

"I do, too," Mai laughed.

And so it was that Indian, with a capital I as Sam's dad used to love to say, blood re-entered the Snarkle flow, promising to stem Native American dilution and merge Navajo with Cherokee into future offspring.

Reverend Chester Divine's chosen successor as pastor to his flock had been a serial womanizer and had lasted less than a year. Putting the moves on the now deceased Polly Snarkle had been the "case closed" that sent him packing.

Reverend Staple Gunn, despite his unusual name, was a perfect fit in the community. Substantially older and wiser than his immediate predecessor, he quietly and slowly courted the widow Jones, subsequently married her, and settled comfortably into the little mountain town with the feminine Biblical name.

His handling of the Bear line memorial service, some two months after their demise, was exemplary. He touched on the unprecedented loss in the context of history, but focused on the extraordinary contributions of the lineage.

Bear Snarkle, of direct Cherokee Indian descent, beloved husband, proud father, and responsible pig farmer. Bear Snarkle Jr., the community's first lawyer, even-handed judge with a keen sense for dispensing justice, and like his father before him, beloved husband, and proud dad. Bear Snarkle, III, community doctor, yes, and beloved husband and proud father. Beyond founding contributions to a flourishing community, it was their shared sense of family that defined their time on earth.

And finally, Polly Snarkle, entrepreneur, writer, whose family was the entire community. Indeed, the legacy of the line was the village itself.

Chapter 25

L.T.H. Farms, LLC (2012)

Time passed. Large construction trucks passed as well, on their way to the newly named L.T.H. Farms, LLC. As with most things in the Ozarks, people generally tended to their own business, but a few whispers began to percolate.

"What in the world is going on over at the old Welcome, Arkansas town site?"

"Why all the traffic?"

In that the highway to old Welcome went straight through town, it was hard to miss. Several curious citizens drove down to see for themselves, but found the gravel road to the now named L.T.H. Farms, LLC place gated, with a padlock attached, and mini-security cameras mounted around. There was something happening down there. They couldn't see it. They couldn't hear it. And, they couldn't smell it. Yet.

Jimbo Whippet planted the rumor that L.T. had hit it big at a casino over in Oklahoma, and was building a mansion with the proceeds. He would welcome the community in to tour once completed.

In actual fact, four metal containment houses had been erected, one just yards below the old cemetery, and waste water sluices constructed under each, all pointed downhill toward an empty lake-size hole situated in a flat space above Large Creek. An elaborate pumping station was erected to move water from Large Creek to the top of the hill and flush it under the containment structures. A feed tower sat next to each one. An incinerator to dispose of dead pigs was stuck in the corner of the property.

Most of the heavy stuff had been trucked in under the cover of night.

A small cabin had been hastily assembled to accommodate Jimbo back in the woods, around a contiguous hill. It would serve as a caretaker's cottage once the pig CAFO was up and running.

Likewise a temporary dormitory structure provided shelter for a small but seasoned group of construction workers. They were allowed to return to their real homes over weekends if they drove out at night. Otherwise, they were confined on site.

The old Hensbell place and its contents had been totally demolished. L.T. was nowhere around, having relocated to Fayetteville for the time being in a rental unit he shared with his pig-farm-loving college coed.

"This must be one hell of a place he's building."

"Yep, ol' L.T. must have really struck it rich."

"Oh, well. I've always believed what's good for a citizen is good for the community."

The little mountain town with the feminine Biblical name—Mount Bathsheba, Arkansas—had no idea what was in store for it.

Chapter 26

Another Wedding (1927)

"My sister is coming to live with me for a while, Tyson. She is coming out of a tough marriage to a drunk in Oklahoma and needs a place to recover. She's a hard worker and will help with the pigs if you are willing."

"She's not our half-sister too, is she?"

"No," Tyson Farmer laughed. She had a real dad, not a teenage pimp."

"OK," responded Tyson Jr. "Maybe we can expand the herd with an extra set of hands. What's her name?"

"Honey."

"You've got to be shittin' me."

Tyson Hensbell, Jr. did indeed expand his pig count, further pressuring the land given to his grandmother long before, and adding waste to Large Creek. But running 150 pigs and marketing them all over the region padded his pocket and started him thinking about a large house, and maybe even a family. First he needed a wife.

Honey jumped right into the pig slop. Her brother had been right. She was a hard worker. What he hadn't said was that she was not hard to look at either. Like her mother Ruth, she was shapely and flirtatious, and genuinely pleasant to be around. Her escape from abuse fueled an energy and enthusiasm that was catching.

It didn't take long for Tyson Jr. to bed her, then transition her to his cabin. Her brother Tyson had hoped such might happen, for he had a serious girlfriend himself, a transplant from another village, who had moved in with him. He also detected a softening of his boss around the edges. Junior wasn't frowning all the time. He paid more attention to cleanliness. Honey could even make him laugh on occasion.

The two Tysons, Hensbell and Farmer, soon had a serious conversation. Tyson Jr. wasn't in love, far from it. But he enjoyed Honey's looks, attentions, and work ethic. He also had enough money to build a new and large house. Did her brother Tyson think she could have babies? Because extension of the Hensbell lineage was a prerequisite for a permanent relationship. A simple yes triggered the ask.

"Tyson Farmer, since Honey's dad is off in prison somewhere, would you agree to give your sister's hand in marriage to me?"

Tyson had never seen this side of his boss. Almost politely professional. Whatever his sister was doing to and for Tyson Jr. was changing him. For the better. Maybe it was because his chief antagonists, the Snarkles, were mostly dead and gone? Or maybe it was because his sister had tapped into a Hensbell account that had lain dormant?

"Yes, but you probably need to clear it with her first."

One more "yes" resulted in a call on Reverend Gunn, who officially sanctioned the deal. Just the three of them to witness. Work began on a new wood frame house in the heart of what was once Welcome, Arkansas, immediately thereafter. Tyson Jr. knew the community history all too well, and took great pride in filling the void. He knew he couldn't get rid of the old settler—mostly Snarkle—plot at the top of the hill, but he could sure as hell overshadow it. And, come to think of it, his grandfather Jamon was buried up there too. He might even be proud.

Just weeks later, the first dividend was paid. Honey was pregnant and Tyson Jr. would become a father at the ripe old age of 35, extension of the line of successful pig farmers assured, assuming they had a son. If not, they would simply keep going at it until they did.

They would name him Tyson Hensbell III, if and when. If the Snarkles could be so vain, so could he.

Chapter 27

Amends (1930s)

The Great Depression wreaked havoc on the valley.

Tyson Jr. was forced to reduce his herd to its lowest count since his mother's time. The market for pork shrunk in proportion with the financial hardships that emerged. He couldn't afford to feed them anyway. If he had not built his house before, he could never have paid for it now.

A nationally imposed "bank holiday" preserved some of the community's pot of savings, but also constrained liquidity. Barter returned as the currency of need.

Some along the river packed up and headed west in hopes of finding a way to survive. Sam Snarkle had experienced all of the "west" he could handle. He would stay put and start a new lineage of Snarkles from the depleted rootstock that preceded him.

From the nine blood Snarkles founder Jebediah had left behind in the village, only Sam remained. With the Bear line and Polly wiped out, Lucinda moving back east with her and Bear III's children, Sunshine settling far upstream with hers, and Adola marrying a Missouri man, the founding family had shrunk to one until he and Mai began replenishing it.

They named their first child, a boy, Nathaniel, trying to put the past behind them. All those Seniors, Juniors and Thirds, and Sunshines and Pollys had become confusing anyway. They were starting over in the shadow of their smiles, but on their own. A little girl followed. Sam wanted to add a traditional Navajo name to the line, but Mai declined. They opted for Matilda instead. They would call her Tillie, with love. They lost another little boy prior to birth. So it was Nathaniel and Tillie to carry forward.

Tyson Jr. and Honey, on the other hand, took on a decided feminine bent. Their first boy was a girl instead. As was their second. Honey was pleased but knew her husband wanted a boy, and vowed to keep trying to make him happy. Plus, she loved babies.

Sam Snarkle began to spend more and more time on the river. He fished daily, supplying his family and neighbors with fresh bass and bream to eat. He also started to noodle big catfish again, which could feed whole families for days at a time.

Sam couldn't remember who taught him where the big ones—ten, fifteen, even twenty pounds—would lay up in underwater ledge holes, but reckoned his grandfather Bear had something to do with it. He had always enjoyed stripping down naked and wading or swimming up to the rocks, feeling about underneath with his hands until he felt a giant tail or pectoral fin, working the beasts around to position his hands to grab their mouths or gills, and jerking them out of their aquatic dens and skyward with a guttural growl of glee. Torn flesh and random bites from different critters didn't dissuade him from the thrill of pursuit.

Noodling was even more rewarding when Mai would go with him. She didn't much like grabbing the large prehistoric critters, but enjoyed getting naked in the creek and seeing her man do manly things. They often celebrated Sam's successes with a frolic of their own on a nearby rock or gravel bar, which contributed to her being with child more often than not those early years together.

Sam also began percolating an idea for making a living around his love of the waters. He heard of a man named John up in southern Missouri who made fishing boats for floating Ozarks streams, and guiding wealthy customers from as far away St. Louis and even Chicago on multi-day "float trips" and providing them with the comforts of home in beautiful, remote settings on the great river along the Arkansas-Missouri border.

He called them "johnboats" in honor of his own creativity, and their wide shallow drafting provided stability in fast water, capability to slip through the leanest of riffles, and room to set up comfortable chairs for clients to fish from. It was gentlemanly "roughing it" of the highest order and if it worked up north it should certainly sell on his river, a place of unparalleled beauty and wonder, Sam reasoned. He would travel up to the big river and look into acquiring a few of these johnboats when times got better.

Tyson Jr. opened the front door to his big house, and a frown crossed his face.

"What do you want?"

"I have something for your wife," said Mai.

"What could you have that she could possible want?"

Mai held up a small packet of herbs.

"Honey, the Snarkle lady is here with something she wants to give you."

Honey greeted Mai with a hug, to Tyson Jr.'s surprise. He promptly walked out.

"You know how I feel about them Snarkles, don't you, Honey? How do you know the Indian one so well?

"Well, it's not them any more, Tyson Jr., just him when it comes to adults. And she is a sweet, nice, caring person. I met her in the store one day and we visited. We were drawn to each other and have visited often since. I usually go to her house because I don't want to upset you."

"So what was that bag of weeds she brought you today?"

"The son you've been clamoring for."

When Honey's time came again, she did have a boy. She and her husband were elated, and one of the first to call on her at home was Mai Snarkle. They shared tears of joy.

As Honey sat nursing the newly named Tyson Hensbell, III, dad asked her what Mai had to do with him.

"Probably nothing my love, but the herbs she shared with me, when we were trying to get pregnant again, were from her mother back in New Mexico. She is Navajo, you know? Navajo tradition places great importance on the role of women. In fact it is known as a matriarchal society."

"So what does this have to do with our son?"

"It is said that with all this wisdom and power, Navajo women can in fact influence birth outcomes to favor sex preference. Mai shared a third generational bundle of pickings from her ancestral reservation that leaned toward male conception. I made a kind of tea out of them and sipped it daily until I became pregnant. The rest is history, with or without the lore."

"You mean that Snarkle lady helped us conceive a boy?"

"I'm not saying yes or no, but who cares? I am grateful for the effort, and for our new son. So, thank you, Mai!"

"It's just one of those Indian legends, you know."

"How do you know, and what's not to be grateful for? This grudge you hold against the Snarkles should be a thing of the past anyway."

"I will always hold Sam Snarkle's father responsible for my mother's death. He locked me up while she was murdered. I could have stopped it."

"He might have locked you up, but he wasn't the one getting drunk and picking violent fights. That was you. And, he will always be dead. Sam Snarkle has nothing to do with it. Besides, he's part Indian, just like you. Doesn't that make you brothers of some kind or another?"

Sam Snarkle was slopping his small herd of pigs when he saw Tyson Hensbell Jr. striding swiftly toward him. He placed his hand on the small pistol he always carried on his hip.

"Snarkle. I'd like a word with your wife if I could?"

"She's inside," responded Sam, opening the door and motioning for Tyson Jr. to enter. Mai set sewing by the light of the sinking sun. Tyson Jr. strode up to her.

"Ms. Snarkle, I want to thank you for caring enough to try and help my wife and I have a son. I have no idea whether your herbs influenced the outcome, but you tried. For that I am thankful."

He turned toward Sam. "Sam, my wife Honey has set me to thinking about the long-running blood feud between our clans. The tragedy that has befallen yours is unfortunate. The success that has touched mine is something I'm grateful for. Somewhere in between is middle ground that you and I could seek to occupy. As Honey points out, we're sort of brothers, mixed breed brothers, me owing to my brave grandmother Dulcetta, you to your great-grandmother Sunshine. Our roots are different, but the Indian blood that runs through our veins has more in common than not."

Tyson Hensbell, Jr. extended his hand. Sam Snarkle reached out slowly to grasp it. Mai smiled softly in the background. Tyson Jr. nodded, and strode out into the evening.

A future crisis downstream would bring them closer over the coming years. They would come together to fight plans to dam their river. Float trip outfitter and family farmer.

Chapter 28

Damned (Mid-20th Century)

In 1958, the United States Congress passed an omnibus bill to dam Sam and Tyson Jr.'s river, among others. In two spots, no less. The first, just downstream of Large Creek, would flood the creek and surrounds with a lake covering the former site of Welcome, Arkansas, the settlers' graveyard, and most of Tyson Jr.'s family farm. It would also put Sam's float business out of business. The second would only add insult to injury. All in the name of flood control, energy generation, and economic development, in particular, tourism.

Sam went running to Tyson Jr.'s house the moment Mai shared the news report with him. They walked to the top of the hill in silence, stopping at the small cemetery of settler memorializations. They gazed across the valley, Tyson Jr.'s herd, and down to the creek.

"The most beautiful place on earth," Sam whispered to no one in particular.

"We can't let them do this, Sam. We gotta stop them."

Once clear of the Great Depression, the decades following Sam Snarkle's and Tyson Hensbell, Jr.'s handshake were the most prosperous in the river valley's history, from far upstream down to the confluence with the big river, all along the 125 miles of river course. It was good to the Snarkle and Hensbell families as well.

Recovery from the Depression had been steady throughout the valley for those who stuck it out. Most residents were used to hardship and scrapping by, which is exactly what they did early on. Several families even returned from California when their dreams did not materialize. The Second Great War largely passed most by but for a few who signed up, some of whom never came back.

By the time Nathaniel Snarkle and Tyson Hensbell III were old enough to enlist, the war was over. Their dads were deemed a bit too old to serve, and were more interested in raising family and doing business than being heroes anyway. Serving country either way, the oddly suited close friends reasoned.

Tyson Jr. began to expand his herd as demand and capacity to pay increased. He stopped at about two hundred head, eliciting praise from his friend Sam Snarkle, and many of his neighbors, for his efforts to protect his land and the creek below from degradation. He was actually able to gradually raise prices over time in his expanded regional market due to a healthy balance between supply and demand.

Sam contracted for a small fleet of johnboats to launch his float service. The boats were nimble enough to float stretches above and below the Large Creek confluence and comfortable enough to start attracting attention from wealthy patrons in regional cities who wanted an adventure in the wilds of northwest Arkansas. Beautiful gravel bars and leaping smallmouth bass were plentiful all about. It was a proven formula for success.

Both entrepreneurs were creating jobs for residents as they expanded, further aiding the regional recovery.

Time passed, children grew, and Nathaniel and Tyson III headed out to college. Both helped their fathers during the summer, though Tyson III was happiest when Sam's float trips were overbooked and he needed more hands on deck. Beat the heck out of slopping pigs.

The guys were buds. They drank beer together, skinny dipped with girlfriends in the creek together, went fishing together, and generally were inseparable. It was assumed that each would move into their father's businesses and be groomed for succession. They did, and were.

The United States Army Corp of Engineers built dams. Under the Flood Control Act of 1938, they were given that authority in the name of flood control, bringing electricity to poor rural communities, providing jobs, and lake-based recreation to the masses. Economic development, they called it.

Damming the nation's big rivers began earlier out west, with a broader mission that included water diversion and allocation. Natural desert communities like Los Angeles, Phoenix, and San Diego had an unquenchable thirst to slake with growth, and big agriculture needed water to support temperate growing seasons.

Hoover Dam, formerly Boulder, was constructed during the heart of the Great Depression.

In the Pacific Northwest, the Columbia River and tributaries were dammed as many as sixty times to provide hydroelectric power to a rapidly growing region.

The first major dam west of the Mississippi was constructed on the mighty White River near Branson, Missouri, in the early 1900s, and was followed by several more through the middle of the 20th century.

A series of lakes provided enormous economic development opportunity and growth to an underserved region in the nation called the Ozarks.

And, the Corp soon began working its way into the tributaries of the great river up north, as Sam called it, including the one that Sam and Tyson Jr. claimed as their own. The 1958 Omnibus Bill zeroed in on their river and put its existence at grave risk.

Ironically, it was at about this time of great dam building momentum that the opposition began to stir.

Case in point was a spectacular stretch of the Colorado River not far above the Grand Canyon, which had been spared from destruction by Hoover Dam. They called it Glen Canyon, and with its nearly two hundred miles of river course and feeder canyons, many considered it to be as beautiful and breathtaking as the Grand. Then, in the early 1950s, the surveyors began sneaking around, and low and behold a plan to dam the Colorado River near Page, Arizona, emerged. The Grand Canyon would be bookended by high dams, and the Colorado River's natural flow disrupted once again. Less than ten years later, Glen Canyon was buried under Lake Powell, paradise lost.

The protests that came from all corners of the southwest were to no avail. A reformed Hollywood starlet who was only the third woman and the 175th person to run the rapids of the Grand Canyon, was a leader in the opposition. Katie Lee took off all her clothes in protest photos. Her friend Edward Abbey wrote eco-terrorism fiction about blowing the whole concrete mess up. Even today, there is an active effort to decommission the Glen Canyon Dam. All to no avail to date.

And yet the "dam and destroy" mentality of the mid-20th century has virtually disappeared. The cost to build is exorbitant. Return on investment is impossible to calculate. As a nation we've run out of prime prospects for imprisonment. And maybe, just maybe, a sense of what has been lost percolates behind the collective conscience.

Dams deliver economic development. They control floods. They can generate hydroelectric power. But they also destroy special places of beauty, culture, history, and lore. And, in the end, they will lose, because nothing can stop water from finding its way over time. The great lakes will fill with silt. Floods will breach and erode man-made structures. Waters are not meant to be constrained by mankind through history. All rivers will flow free again. Someday. At least that's what Sam and Junior told each other over a glass of whiskey from time to time.

Sam Snarkle and Tyson Hensbell, Jr. began to organize to protect their river. They were joined by their children, their children's spouses, and countless neighbors and allies from around the region. They formed a River Protector Society (RPS), earned donations from many of the wealthy clients who had floated with Sam, and garnered national attention from high profile visitors and magazines featuring what would be lost.

Of course, there was opposition to the opposition. Some bought into the theory of prosperity promised from a big lake. It had certainly followed dam development on the big river up north, and in other parts of the country. Politicians loved talking about job creation and cheap and plentiful electricity in some places where there was none. They knew what was best for a backward corner of the nation and they were bound to help make it happen.

At one RPS meeting, Sam got so incensed he promised to blow up any dam placed on his river. Instead, he found his pick-up truck exploded during the middle of the night.

On another occasion as Sam and Nathaniel led a party of four wealthy oil men on a four-day, three-night float trip down the thirty-mile stretch above and below the mouth of Large Creek, they came around a sharp bend to find Cecil Shill, who was running ahead with the commissary boat, strung on a couple of strands of barbed wire. He was dangling above the water, whimpering in pain, with his johnboat capsized downstream against a large root wad. It took them nearly an hour to disengage Cecil, by which time their clients had seen enough and demanded to be taken in. Sam was incensed at this overt effort to put him out of business, and couldn't imagine who would stoop so low.

Neighbor began to mistrust longtime neighbor, and a pall settled over the few civilized discussions that took place.

Mixed constituent messages did begin to confuse some elected officials who waffled in the crosswinds of controversy. What had seemed in the beginning a simple economic development play had taken on an ugly local tenor. The two-dam project dragged forward through study periods and funding debates at an agonizingly deliberate pace, while tension and sporadic violence increased at home.

Finally, as much out of frustration as cause, Nathaniel Snarkle announced that he was going to run for the congressional seat held by one of the most fervent supporters of the Twin Dams Project, as it had come to be known. While the latter hid out in Washington, afraid to come home after a flashy promotional tour early in the discussions, Nathaniel went door to door in the district to gather support. His message was simple. The people we elected to represent us in Congress were precisely the ones who were trying to destroy our river. If elected, he would serve only as long as it took to defeat any damming of our river, then come home to resume floating it with his dad and their clients.

In that Nathaniel was clearly a one-issue candidate, with volatile opponents as well as supporters, he always carried a pistol. His wife, Layne, was homeschooling his two sons, Skeet and Solomon, to spare them the intrusions on their family life. She was proud of her husband's candidacy, but fearful of everything from local violence to living in Washington, DC, in the unlikely event that he won.

Tillie Snarkle was doing her part to fight the dam and elect her brother as well. Twice married and divorced, single mom of Sabrina, Tillie had recently returned home with a new boyfriend to reground and recharge. The timing for both could not have been better. The river valley was in an uproar, the river she was raised on was at risk, and the rebellious spirit which had cost her two marriages was perfect for the moment.

Tillie had most recently wintered in southern Utah, where a similar battle was being waged over preserving or losing a special place to the U.S. Army Corps of Engineers. An attractive young lady had developed a unique fundraising strategy to fund the protectionists' legal bills. Tillie would copycat it to raise money to save her river. She called it her Special Places Calendar, and she would sell it for $50 a pop. Her new boyfriend was a professional photographer and could handle production.

January's cover was a photo of Tillie on a trail across the face of the highest bluff on the river, leaning out over the edge in a welcoming pose, shot from the river below.

February featured Tillie behind the thin veil of the highest free-flowing waterfall between the Rocky and Appalachian mountains.

March was Tillie from a distance atop a short, stocky, smoothed rock face, with large chemical looking tears dripping down the face.

April caught Tillie peeking out from behind one of the Hensbell piglets; May, neck deep in crystal clear water as shot from the canoe immediately adjacent; June, jumping into the river from a large boulder; July, proudly hoisting a three-pound smallmouth bass toward the camera, and on and on and on.

The disarming part was that Tillie Snarkle did not have a stitch of clothing on in any of the photos, covered only in nature's finery, like her mentor in southern Utah had modeled for her. The calendar sold quickly and nationally, and in fact the newly-notorious *Playboy* magazine ran it in its entirety, with an editorial in support of the no-dam movement.

Nathaniel's opponent called it pure and simple pornography, to which Nathaniel responded that in the Ozarks he knew and grew up in, seeing a beautiful young lady "hanging out" in one of the most stunning places in the world was not only a natural wonder but a joy to behold. Even his sister.

Mai could only smile, while Sam blushed.

The river cause was now part of the national dialogue and environmental groups rallied to support opposition to the dam, as well as Nathaniel Snarkle's unlikely candidacy.

Nathanial Snarkle carried his district by a surprising margin. The recount demanded by his shocked opponent was no more than an embarrassment. As promised, Nathanial moved to an apartment in DC, and immediately began lobbying his fellow legislators to kill funding for a dam that would destroy one of our national treasures and was not needed or wanted by a majority of locals. He always had a spare copy of his sister's "Special Places Calendar" to leave behind. Washington, DC, which had always run on sex and money, was quick to embrace Nathaniel, his calendar, and his cause. Besides, de-funding was always easier than funding.

Nathaniel and Layne had decided that it was best for the family to stay behind in the little mountain town with the feminine Biblical name for the time being, as he was serious about serving only as long as it took to kill the Twin Dams Project.

Tillie enjoyed her newborn naked notoriety for a while, but finally tired of her photographer boyfriend. She did decide to stay with the family and lean on them to help raise her young daughter. She would help promote the family float business and even take a turn at guiding old rich men down the river from time to time.

It didn't complicate her decision that an old friend was showing interest in spending some time with her. Tyson Hensbell, III was exactly Tillie's age. Like Nathaniel, they had grown up together, fished and caught frogs together, skinny dipped and played doctor-nurse together. T3, as Tillie teased him, had not done well with marriage either. He had blown through the same number that Tillie had, but had no children to show for it.

The Hensbell clan contributed mightily to the Snarkle victory as well. Tyson Jr. hosted multiple pig roasts at his farm to allow Nathaniel to connect to even more potential constituents. That a Hensbell came out so strongly for a Snarkle was not lost on the old timers.

"He must be a damn good man if Tyson Hensbell, Jr. is fur him," was heard over and over again around the district. This drew in a number of votes from bastard Tysons and their family members.

At the election eve celebration, held at Hensbell Jr.'s house because it was the biggest one around, Sam Snarkle embraced Tyson Jr. and raised a glass to his family in gratitude. Tyson Jr. returned the toast in honor of the Snarkles he had once held in such contempt. After a century and a quarter there was finally peace in the valley, grounded in the hope that their great river would be spared.

It had started innocently enough.

"Tillie, let's hike down to the big waterfall for a picnic."

"That's a long and steep trek, T3. Can't we just find a spot down at the creek like we used to so long ago?"

"No, Tillie, I have a reason."

"OK, I'll bring some fried chicken and you bring the beer, just like we did so long ago."

"It wasn't that long ago."

"Well, we had to have Nathaniel buy us the beer, as I recall. That's a long time ago. And, let's hike up from the river. It's easier."

As they headed up the trail, T3 observed that he hadn't walked it for years. Tillie concurred, laughing at the memory of her photographer ex-boyfriend lugging his camera equipment up the half mile up from the river for their recent calendar photo shoot.

It took a half hour to round the bend to the creek that issued from atop the rock lip before drifting or crashing, depending on recent rains, some two hundred feet into a shallow pool, then cascading down to the river.

"It's still a breathtaking sight," whispered Tillie. Let's have one of those beers," answered T3.

They sat and reminisced over beers two and three.

"So what was your reason for traipsing up here today, T3?"

He took her hand and led her up the slick rock to the falls, which were flowing light this day, drifting in the wind.

"Can I see what it looks like in person, Tillie?"

"What, T3?"

"You know, the photo shot."

Tillie smiled and nodded. She slipped to the side and ducked behind the falling water, where she slowly and seductively removed her clothes. She then stepped to the back edge of the falling water, leaned forward with her hands on her hips, her chest thrust out and up, and smiled again.

"You've seen it all before, T3, pre-baby sag, prepubescent, pre-nonvirginal, or something like that!"

"My, how you've grown," exclaimed T3, as he strode directly through the falls to embrace his old friend.

As they sat in the afterglow, waist deep in the shallow pool, they heard a commotion below. Soon a couple of older men with their teen age sons came into view, staring in wonder at the stunning falls. Until one of the boys glimpsed what lay before them. Tillie waved and smiled without covering up. The boys wandered up looking for something to say, as the men hung back.

"Where are you all from," Tillie smiled.

"Texas," the oldest stammered.

"That's a big place," Tillie challenged. "I've lived there too. Can you get a little more specific young man?"

Tillie enjoyed the next five minutes of Q and A, until the old dads called out for the boys to go back to the river. They reluctantly and shyly bid the bathers farewell. Tilly laughed out loud when she heard in the distance, "Can you believe that?"

"So, Tillie, did you do it up here with your photographer friend, too?"

"Yep. But he wasn't nearly as comfortable dealing with nature as you are."

Fried chicken never tasted so good.

Chapter 29

Stench (2012)

The first truckloads of pigs rolled in under the cover of darkness. Only the town drunk, Chester Thurman, saw them, and he announced to anyone who would listen next morning that the circus had passed through town about midnight. Said he heard a whole lot of squealing going on. Well, it could also have been a traveling whorehouse with all them high-pitched noises, he added. As usual no one paid any attention to Chester Thurman.

Townsfolk did began noticing the smell in mid-summer, when most things began to stink a little anyway due to the heat. It seemed to waft over from the direction L.T.H. Farms, LLC. when the wind was just right, but one couldn't be sure. Any attempts to check things out were rebuffed by barbed wire and some non-familiar looking dudes in camos prowling the fence perimeter with assault weapons.

There had been an informational meeting posting, buried in the local newspaper, regarding operating permits being sought by L.T.H. Farms, LLC. But, the date had passed by the time most residents saw it. The few who did and tried to attend were told that the meeting would be rescheduled due to the low turnout, so as to give the entire community adequate opportunity for comment. It never was. Nor was it required to be.

Summer passed to early fall and the stench diminished with cooler weather. Chester Thurmond reported a few more midnight squealer trucks coming in, but was ignored. Again, as usual.

Chapter 30

Unraveling (1970s)

On March 1, 1972, the 37th President of the United States of America signed into law permanent protection of the beloved river, by declaring it America's first national river. Most locals celebrated far into the coming years, but not all. This was not like fighting dams, the latter argued.

The bill to dam the river was dropped at the end of young Nathaniel Snarkle's first term. But he wasn't ready to quit yet. He feared that the Corps would raise its ugly and powerful head again and began pushing for a more lasting solution. He had found a willing ear with the new administration, which had ushered in a more proactive approach to facing environmental challenges, especially the head of the Department of the Interior, who actually came up with the idea of a national river.

Nathaniel embraced it enthusiastically and rushed home to share the good news. He also announced that he would run for a second term to help shepherd the national river designation home. He was re-elected, but it was soon obvious that unexpected turbulence lay ahead.

The first opposition arose when it became clear that the United States government would have to acquire acreage adjoining the river in order to protect it. This amounted to extortion to some, no matter how much they were paid for their land. The Farm Bureau joined certain property owners in staging rallies against the plan, in the interest of protecting family farms. "First the government wanted to dam our waters, and now they want to take our land," was a common refrain heard in some corners.

Nathaniel represented their concerns in Washington as he was elected to do, and was able to add some "grandfathering" considerations for family farms, particularly upstream of Large Creek. The fact was that with all the bluffs and mountains lining the full river's course, fertile bottomlands along the river, which generally flooded out a time or two a year, were few and far between.

What surprised Nathaniel the most was the rabid opposition of Tyson Hensbell, Jr. None of his land along Big Creek would be impacted, as evidenced in the early designations of protected land. Nor would most landowner plots in rich valleys set back from the river. Still, opposition cloaked in the broader cause of individual property rights gained momentum.

Midway through his second term, Nathaniel declared his intention to retire at term's end. The Twin Dams Project was dead, and the fight for a national river would take a while because of political meandering.

In fact, Sam needed his son's help with his float business, which had grown and expanded its market reach on the wave of publicity attached to national river talk.

So Nathaniel came home, confident of a positive outcome, and grateful to his constituents for their trust in his crusade.

Tillie and T3 stayed together almost eight years. They never married because Tillie refused to drop her Snarkle last name, and T3 decided that he didn't want to be formally bound to "one of them women's libbers." Still their relationship sparkled with energy and affection, and ultimately with a baby girl as beautiful as her name—Miss Molly—in year seven.

They had spent a lot of time traveling together in the interim, even to Europe for nearly a year of bumming around from hostel to hostel, sharing love and weed, as was the nature of the times and their particular inclinations. They hadn't really planned to have out of wedlock children, but both agreed that Molly was a special surprise.

Sadly a less pleasant surprise began to surface about the same time.

There was a reason T3 hadn't survived either of his prior marriages.

Not that Tillie was a saint. She wasn't, and even had an affair on her second husband. She just hadn't chosen well and had only Sabrina to show from her past failures. She loved her first daughter to death and particularly enjoyed having her so close to her grandmother Mai. The two of them had bonded as one, and Tillie even thought her daughter resembled her Navajo granny more than she did herself. Her shaded skin and high cheekbones foretold a beautiful woman.

No, it wasn't Tillie or her last name that was the problem this time. T3 had once been a binge drinking alcoholic and wife-beater under the influence.

He had tamed the beast in the glow of his relationship with Tillie, but it began to leak out slowly and sporadically over time.

Tillie wrote off the first couple of rounds to alternative causes. Like, not enjoying helping his dad raise pigs, or lack of sleep when Sabrina, and later baby Molly, were restless during the night. But when he started in more frequently on Tillie, she stopped covering up for him and showed Mai her bruises. He was careful not to harm her face, which hinted to her that he knew what he was doing in some way, but her arms, stomach, and even buttocks carried certain proof. Finally, one dark night he threatened the baby in the midst of a drunken tirade. Tillie left his home and never returned.

With final approval of America's first National River exactly one hundred years after President Ulysses S. Grant's designation of Yellowstone as America's first National Park, and the sudden disintegration of Tillie and T3's close but informal relationship, the Snarkle-Hensbell truce of more than forty years unraveled at a furious pace.

When Sam approached Tyson Jr. with the news that his son had beaten Sam's only daughter and threatened their shared granddaughter Molly, Tyson Jr. exploded with denial. T3 had told him that Tillie had been sleeping around all over the valley and had recently infected him with a venereal disease.

"Hell, Sam, I would have beaten that hell out of Honey if she had done that to me."

"It's not true, friend, it's just not true. Did you check it out with a doctor? Your son is a drunk with a temper as bad as I recall you having as a young man, and he needs your help, not your ignorance."

"My son doesn't lie, Snarkle, and don't you ever call me friend again. And, as for that tree-hugging son of yours and the federal land grab that is threatening family farmers like me, I wish you would tell him how much I despise the harm he has rained down on our valley."

"So, Junior, you are willing to throw away our nearly half century of friendship, and return to the old days of feud and folly, because you won't face up to a lying son and the Farm Bureau?"

Tyson Jr. stepped toward Sam, leaned into his face, and spat the words out with venom, "Yes, Snarkle, yes I am. And you had better get out of here before I avenge my mother's death on you rather than your dead dad.

"And, one more thing, Snarkle, you had better recognize that the daughter of my son carries the noble name Hensbell proudly and visibly until she marries. I demand that your whoring daughter honor our name as well as share custody with my son."

"Neither you nor T3 will ever hold precious Molly, if I have any say in it," Sam shot back.

The Snarkle and Hensbell clans were clearly at each other's throats again.

Chapter 31

Turmoil

Turmoil returned to the valley, as it did to the nation.

Assassinations, war, government murders of student protestors, presidential resignations. There was no end to the cycles of violence.

The only thing that ran clear and free of contradiction was the river itself. America's first National River.

One of the newly-minted National Park Rangers found Tyson Hensbell, III shot dead not far from the river. There were at least five bullet holes in his head. Someone had apparently been very angry at T3.

Tyson Jr. was beside himself. His only male heir, the only worthy successor to his throne, was gone. And beyond that was the insulting nature of his demise.

He demanded that the sheriff immediately bring in his son's ex-girlfriend for intense interrogation. She had motive, as he had just left her because of her infidelity and promiscuity. She had anger and guilt enough to go beyond just killing, to killing viciously. And though she would surely have an alibi, the sheriff knew you just couldn't trust those Snarkles.

The sheriff could only shrug, and ask if Tyson Jr. knew of anyone else who might have harbored a severe grudge against his son.

Tillie was shocked and aggrieved. She had come to love T3 over the years for what he was in his many sober moments, a lively, funny, sexy playmate. She wished that she had figured out the alcohol part earlier. Maybe she could have helped him do something about it. She knew that his threats against young Molly were fueled by something beyond him, and that he had loved his only child with something close to adoration. She was also kind of shocked that the sheriff asked what she had been doing the night of the murder.

"You think I might have had something to do with this, Sheriff? I loved T3 when he was normal and sober. I left him only because he began to beat me with increasing frequency, and threatened our child when he was drunk."

"So, you left him rather than him kicking you out?"

"That is correct, Sheriff. Why would you think otherwise?"

"It's not important, Tillie."

When Sam and his family attended Tyson, III's funeral, Tyson Jr. demanded that they be removed. Reverend Gunn objected and tried to calm him. Sam and his family members bowed their heads toward the casket and left on their own.

"You killed my only heir, you bitch," Tyson Jr. screeched at Tillie as they left. Little did he know how wrong he was.

Tillie went to her mom with tears in her eyes.

"It's okay, dear," Mai had comforted.

"No, Mom, it's more than that. I missed my second period in a row. I think I'm pregnant, Mom."

"How could that be, Tillie? Have you been with someone else since leaving T3?"

"Of course not, Mom."

"But I thought you said that you hadn't been intimate for months?"

"We hadn't, but I think I know what happened. The night he ultimately threatened Molly, he was even more drunk than normal. He became enraged when I wouldn't submit to his advances. He threw me against the wall and I hit my head, blacking out briefly. When I came to he was atop and inside me. I'm pretty sure he closed the deal, but I can't be certain as I was in and out of consciousness. When I finally came to for good I saw him pacing the room with our sleeping child in his arms. It was then that I heard him threaten her, something about ending her life when he took his own. I leapt up and grabbed her, then ran for our lives as he staggered after us, flailing about, then falling. I never came, thought, or looked back, leaving that dark moment behind us, except for this, his parting gift. What do I do, Mom?"

Chapter 32

Junior (1980s)

Someone finally named their kid Jebediah Jr. almost 150 years after the original Jebediah Snarkle settled next to Large Creek and later founded Welcome, Arkansas. Eight generations of Snarkles in the valley in all, counting mother Polly. There had been all sorts of Juniors and Thirds and Bears and Pollys, even Sunshines in the line, but never one named after Jebediah himself.

Skeet Snarkle, first son of Nathaniel and Layne Snarkle, had delivered the honors. Skeet, and his brother Solomon, had kind of slipped under the local radar. Both were born as the battle against the Twin Dams Project was in full throttle. Layne homeschooled them to keep them out of the war zone, particularly when opposing sides got hot, and when Dad was elected to Congress, serving two terms in Washington, and helping win the dam wars as well as launch the national river initiative.

Skeet attended the state university, majoring in business, and finding a partner. Skeet was like that. He was all business. His wife was his partner, not his lover, though they managed plenty of that.

They hadn't been married long when Betty Sue popped up pregnant. Skeet had intended to wait a bit so they could get their financial matters on an even keel, but such was sex and life, he reasoned. They lived in Little Rock, where he worked for an accounting firm while he pursued his CPA designation.

Betty Sue delivered a strapping baby boy in perfect health. She and Skeet had already decided to bestow the ultimate family name on their first if it was a son. So it was that Jebediah Snarkle, Jr. came to be. As soon as the young man was able to travel, Skeet went with father and grandfather to the patriarch's grave, nestled between mother Polly and first wife's stones, touching the plots of the three Bears. It was emotional for all. Even the baby cried.

They looked out on Jebediah's "most beautiful spot," and tried to ignore the Hensbell pig farm and pompous residence that ate up much of the view. Sam also felt a pang of regret for the loss of his prior civil relationship with

Tyson Jr. Thankfully no one was home at the Hensbells or there probably would have been words, or worse.

Sam again thanked his son for finally bestowing the founder's name. Sam was once told by his mother Sadie that he would have been the first if they had known that Jebediah would pass soon after his birth. But Snarkle name confusion had been at epidemic proportions at the time and Sam sounded so much simpler.

Skeet and Betty Sue soon had another boy who they named Solomon.

The Snarkle line of males was back in business.

On the other side of the great divide, a newly-angered generation of Hensbells roiled the waters of Large Creek. Tyson Jr. expanded his herd in the interest of making money. And Large Creek became a bit more green.

The sheriff could never determine who had murdered T3. What was stranger was that more and more suspects emerged. T3 had increasingly alienated others toward the end his life's path, drunk, demeaning, and often violent. He had hurt others, both men and women, and someone had hurt him back.

Tyson Jr. was having nothing of this. He knew that the bitch Tillie had shot T3 once, and then again and again and again and again—in anger, in guilt of her whorish behavior.

And then there was Lester. Oh, how he hated the name that the bitch mother had bestowed on who was now his only heir. At least he had a male successor now. Even the Snarkles couldn't take that away from him.

Tyson Jr. did go to court seeking full custody and re-naming rights for baby Lester, who he knew would take his pig farm to new heights. The judge had granted partial custody and proclaimed that both parties could call the boy any damn thing they wanted. Tillie called the little one Lester Thomas Snarkle. Tyson Jr. settled on Tyson Hensbell, IV, honoring his long lineage and one-upping his historical rivals.

Thus, Lester/Tyson IV grew up in a state of great confusion and found it easier to answer to just about anything. He loved his mother and sisters, but could not escape the adoration of his grandfather. All Tyson Jr. was living for into his 90s was to hang on long enough to pass his pig farm and grand plans for expansion over time to his grandson. He was aided and abetted in this pursuit by his trusted aide Jimbo Whippet, who had basically run the farm for the past decade.

He was younger, wiser and perhaps even more greedy than the old man himself, which suited Tyson Jr. just fine. They both agreed that a five hundred head herd could be sustained on the farm, and that with Jimbo's help, Tyson IV could lead them there.

Moving a herd that size through to production would require a substantially larger distribution network. Sooner or later it would be time to reach out to some of the large, international agricultural corporations for partnering opportunities.

When Tyson Hensbell, Jr. finally passed at age 94, Lester/Tyson IV was 16 years old and quickly becoming a man. He had decided on his own to go by L.T. Hensbell, which had pleased his grandfather, and crushed his mother, even though he had hung on to the Lester part. Tillie began to turn her affections to daughter Molly.

L.T., not unlike his great-grandfather, the original Tyson, was extremely handsome, and no stranger to young ladies across the county.

They laid Tyson Jr. next to his granddad, Jamon, who had moved in from Texas with his herd of stolen pigs just after the Civil War, and was later brutally murdered by the local recluse Tiny Taylor, for no other reason than marrying an Indian, lovely Dulcetta, Junior's grandmother. It was she who was given the original deed to the whole Welcome property. Welcome, Arkansas had been devastated by the Big Lightning Fire of 1893, and the town relocated and renamed to escape the memory. Out of recognition of the incineration of her only son, Junior's father Tyson, and her desire to continue her husband's pig farm in the burned out valley, the community agreed to sign the entire property over to her in the Hensbell name, which she carried throughout her life and two subsequent marriages.

Despite their ownership of the land for nearly a century, as in life, the Hensbells were stuck on the fringes of the old Welcome cemetery, notwithstanding the farm and large house that laid out below it. As always, the Snarkles claimed the center ground.

What hadn't changed with death was the intense animosity that continued to fester between the Snarkles and the Hensbells. Everything from naming rights to land management, from water quality to herd size, from property rights to colorations of integrity, carried a battle line down the middle.

That Skeet Snarkle and the primary Snarkle heir, Jeb Jr., lived in another community diminished opportunities for direct conflict among the warring clans, but didn't lessen the underlying tensions.

Chapter 33

A Float Trip (1995)

Nathaniel Snarkle had promised his grandson Jeb Jr. early on that he would take him on a grand float trip down the entire river to its confluence with the big river from up north in his 12th year. Just like his father Sam, the great float trip entrepreneur, had promised and delivered for him at age 12. It would be just the two of them at the end of Jeb Jr.'s school year for as many days or weeks as were required. It had taken Sam and Nathaniel twelve nights out and had been worth every minute invested. To both.

Nathaniel, in fact, gave credit to his dad for providing a life-changing inspiration to a young boy, and Sam was certain that it led him into the float business as a career.

So it would be grandfather Nathaniel and his grandson Jeb Jr. on their own in the beautiful river valley, which, but for the Herculean efforts and passion of a strong cadre of locals, would have become a lake, a water graveyard, perhaps even a cesspool on occasions.

Instead they would float down free-flowing, late spring waters full of clarity, fish, and critters. They would live off the land as best they could and ask Skeet to re-provision them with the basics half way through.

Sam was dying to go, but at age 95 could only share vicariously. He and Skeet did put the adventurers in at the top of the river's navigable course. The weather was spring cool and the water high. Their first couple of days would be challenging with a fully loaded canoe, but without further rain they could likely settle in for a comfortable ride thereafter. Skeet worried a little as rain in the forecast was 50-50, and it wouldn't take much to raise the river quickly. But he knew that even in his mid-60s, Nathaniel was an experienced and competent stern man, and definitely knew when to bail out and get off the river. They could track him down if that came to pass. And still, his oldest boy?

Sam assured him that he had felt the same last-minute misgivings with Nathaniel so long ago, and that they would be okay.

"It's not like going for a walk in the park," Skeet observed.

"No it's not," Sam responded. "It's a long trip on a wild river without many people on it in some stretches. But Nathaniel has been there, and your boy Jeb Jr. has spent a fair share of his time on the river, too. He's a natural. But you're right, things can get crazy if the weather unloads."

It did, and they did.

The pack had been challenging. Ten to twelve days on a high, fast river, even with frequent re-provisioning, required a lot of food, drink and gear. Two coolers, stuck side-by-side length wise, and a plastic dry box angled across in front of the stern seat, with tent, fold up chairs, and camping gear piled atop, all secured with bungee cords. They were headed out in one fully-loaded canoe.

"Old Gray," Nathanial called it. It had been his first canoe as a youth, and though beaten with time and heavier than the newest models, it could hold more than any of them.

Skeet shoved them off mid-morning with a promise to leave a cooler full of replacement ice and provisions at the mouth of Large Creek, and then at several access sites below.

First night out was a joy. A chilly one, but a joy. A big campfire never felt so good to either, and driftwood was plentiful on the gravel bar they had set up camp on.

They celebrated with steaks. Sam even poured himself a glass of Cab Sauv from the plastic container he had stored it in. No glass allowed on a national river.

"So Grandpa, what do you dream about sleeping on a gravel bar on this river you call yours?"

"Well, let's get one thing straight. First of all it's not mine. It's ours because our forefathers helped settle it, and it's all of ours now because it belongs to the nation, a national river."

"As for dreams, we'll see what tonight brings. During my day dreams, I dream about you a lot, with the hope that you and your kids and theirs can grow up on this great river that is clean, and protected from pillage forever."

"What is pillage, Grandpa?"

"It's an ugly word, son. It means destruction. Intentionally harming. Serving self above others and taking all one can in the name of that end. With a river like this it means killing it with dams, polluting it with waste, animal or human, diverting it from its natural course to water fields, filling the valley with too many people, and on and on. Enough nightmare stuff on an incredibly beautiful evening. How about we bed down? Tomorrow we resume our quest."

As Jeb Jr. drifted off to sleep in the warmth of his sleeping bag, Nathaniel whispered a silent prayer of thanks for times like this. You just can't have conversations like these at home, in the presence of others.

Day two was similar to day one, with a warming sun lighting up the fish. Jeb Jr. even captured a couple frogs whose legs would fry up nicely with goggle-eye fillets.

As they sat eating dinner, a lone beaver appeared from under a root wad and made its way past them upstream with a sizable branch, only to return soon after to get another one.

"Building a den," Nathaniel confirmed.

"Don't get to see that much at home," Jeb Jr. laughed

And still not another living soul for two whole days.

It took them one more to pull up at the mouth of Large Creek. Skeet had left a cooler loaded with fresh ice, water, and perishables to swap out for their melting one. He would pick it up later, and do the same at an access point further downstream later in the week.

Nathaniel was pleased with their progress and the fact that high water was settling down. He could not be more proud of his young grandson, his river sense, his conservation ethic. He would grow into a passionate river keeper like those who had gone before him. Nathaniel was thankful for this.

Two more glorious days turned into a threatening night, then heavy rain and winds. Nathaniel had sensed it coming and found a gravel bar with elevation to set up camp. He taught Jeb Jr. how to stake the water level with sticks in gravel, so they could follow any rise during the night. About 2 a.m. Nathaniel awakened Jeb Jr. so they could move the sticks higher up the gravel bar, in that they were partially covered. By dawn they were gone, flushed downstream by a surge of brown water.

"Must have really rained upstream son. Think we will sit this one out up here, well above the current. When the river turns brown and begins to spin and roil, it's better to just let it have its way than fight it. We've got all the time in the world, and a safe perch from which to observe its power."

And still, the rain kept coming down, in surges of thunderstorms. Jeb Jr. leaned into his grandfather when a lightning bolt knocked down a tree directly across the river.

"I think we're going to be here a while, boy," Nathaniel whispered to his now frightened grandson.

~

Back home, Skeet was getting worried. He didn't show much to Betty Sue or Nathaniel's wife Layne, but they both could tell.

The cold front that had stalled just over the upper reaches of the river was producing record rainfall, and showing no sign of abating. And the flooded river was still rising and generating more force by the hour.

The family gathered for dinner on Sunday night at Sam and Mai's house as they usually did, with Skeet and Betty Sue and Layne. Sam said he had never witnessed such rain in a short time span in his 95 years on the river. This was not an observation any wanted to hear, but they knew it to be true.

"Don't worry," comforted Sam, "Nathaniel has them tucked in a tent high on a gravel bar well above the floods. He knows better that to set out on water like this."

"I just hope they have enough water to drink," worried Skeet. "I was supposed to resupply at a takeout that is surely just below them the day this hit. I was prepared to advise them to get off and let the weather pass through, before resuming their journey, given the forecast I had just heard. I have no idea what Dad would have done. "

"Anyone know when this is supposed to pass on through?" asked Betty Sue.

No one did.

~

After two days of lying in a tent, Nathaniel was getting restless. He had never seen rain like this during his years on the river, and it showed no sign of letting up. He wished it would have waited just one more day before unloading as Skeet was to leave a new cooler and water supply for them to swap out the very morning after the deluge hit. Apart from having to consistently move the canoe and coolers up closer to the tent, there was little to do but just wait.

Three days after it had all begun, the sun began to peek through, adding welcome warmth and light to their dreary situation. The river had not yet begun to fall, and wouldn't for some time.

Once it turned, Nathaniel had Jeb Jr. start staking its retreat.

~

"Do you think we ought to alert the National Park Service that they are out there, and have been for an extended time?" Skeet asked Sam.

"Probably a good idea, though I doubt whether there is much they can do at this point. I think I know roughly where they are trapped. There are three high gravel bars in a row just above the closest takeout spot, and my guess is that once the park rangers can get a johnboat with a motor into the water they will go fetch them. Let's go down to their headquarters and report in after lunch."

Nathaniel emptied his last canteen into a plastic cup to share with Jeb Jr. He was kicking himself for not using frozen water bottles in lieu of ice like he usually did. You could drink the melt. But he hadn't because of the re-provisioning support from Skeet. What little liquid left from ice remained in the bottom of the coolers, and was tainted by the leftover foodstuffs that sat in it. They were now officially out of water, a thought that made him chuckle with all the water racing by below them.

The river was finally in retreat, though it still ran fast and brown. Nathaniel didn't like this kind of water to float on.

The Park Rangers were sympathetic to Sam's entreaties for help, but not yet able to do anything on the river. All were confident that if they had made it up high, they would be fine and the river floatable in twenty-four hours. And there hadn't been any reports of bodies or gear floating down river. Should be okay, everyone reasoned.

Their report back to the ladies did not alleviate concerns or fears. Betty Sue sobbed as tiny Mai wrapped an arm around her waist.

"Well, I reckon we're about ready to give it a go, Jeb Jr. It's still higher and murkier than I like, but we're flat out of drinking water. We'll leave all our gear here and come back for it when the water recedes. What I need from you is a calm, steady draw stroke in the bow whenever I order it. In water this fast you just steer and don't fight it. We'll be okay if we can just keep pointed downstream and avoid obstacles. We must not get turned sideways under any circumstance."

They carried "Old Gray" down to water's edge, and looked back up at their home of the past three days.

"Ready, boy?"

"Sure," responded Jeb Jr. with a hint of uncertainty in his voice.

The brown current swept them away, and downstream.

Nathaniel knew they could not be far from the next takeout spot, though it might still be underwater. He just didn't want to get swept past it before he could work his way over to the concrete boat ramp. He could never paddle back upstream, even with Jeb Jr.'s help. He didn't know if there would be anyone there to help them but wouldn't be surprised, given that they had been essentially missing for three days of intense flooding.

The river narrowed ahead and broke sharply left around blind bend, compressed into churning brown mess. Nathaniel didn't like the looks of it, particularly not being able to see what lay ahead, but they had no choice. They would plow in and pull hard to the left to avoid a partially downed tree at the corner to the turn.

Jeb Jr. gave a good strong draw on the left, moving the nose slightly across current, while Nathaniel back watered on the same side, again focused on changing direction while not getting thrown sideways.

They rounded the bend and Nathaniel gasped. A nightmare scenario loomed ahead.

A large, freshly uprooted sycamore tree blocked the narrow river passage. You couldn't get around it, you couldn't get under it, you couldn't slide over it. And its bushy limbs underwater were a certain graveyard.

"Jeb Jr., you've got to leap free of the canoe as we crash into the tree. We can't avoid it. Try to jump over it, then roll with the current feet first until you can find something to hang onto downstream. I will be right behind you. On three, boy. One, two, three, jump! Jebediah Snarkle, jump!"

He was already gone by the time Nathaniel could spit out his name. And he wasn't able to clear the tree, becoming entangled in the wad of green limbs.

Nathaniel saw his predicament and changed his exit jump accordingly to land in the limbs imprisoning Jeb Jr. He was able to embrace him briefly before the limbs began to suck Jeb Jr. down into the powerful current. Nathaniel went after him, knowing that he had to free his grandson or lose him.

Both were underwater now, unable to see through the coffee brown, but joined in a partial embrace. Nathaniel dove beneath to try and free Jeb Jr.'s legs. He gave a mighty thrust up. He then began to gulp silty water and saw his last moments of consciousness slip away.

Park Service Rangers had gotten word of the downed tree and were headed upstream from the concrete ramp, their 50-horse motor whining against the current, to try and cut part of it out before it turned into a deadly trap for someone. The old metal canoe with its bow peaking up from beneath the tree told them that they were probably too late.

Skeet and Betty Sue were not quite desperate with fear yet, but they were gaining on it. As was Layne. Sam counseled calm and Mai chanted an old Navajo verse.

The park rangers had advised them that they would be setting out from the takeout close to where Sam had pegged them holed up, and that all were welcome to wait there for their return. They sat silently in Sam's pick-up, staring into the roiling water.

As the rangers jammed the bow of their Johnboat close enough to grasp a downstream limb, one pointed to a flat rock downstream. There appeared to be a body stretched out on it. They released the tree and tried to motor cross current, almost capsizing before they were able to turn down stream and begin to slowly work their way over to the rock. They circled back out of the main current and jammed the bow of the boat on an adjoining rock, gaining stability and access.

It was a body, that of a young boy. He was soaked, but stirring. The Snarkle heir was still alive. The rangers lifted him into the boat and turned to deliver him to their warm van at the concrete slab. They would return to see if there was another survivor. They knew that two, a grandfather his grandson, had been reported missing.

Sam's pickup emptied hesitantly when the ranger boat came into view. Betty Sue gasped at the sight of her son in one of the rangers arms, unmoving, and who knew what else. Dead, or alive?

The boat pulled into the slab and the ranger handed Jeb Jr. to his father, with a slight smile.

"We found him on a flat rock along the bank, just downstream from a capsized canoe. He was moving when we picked him up, though he has drifted in and out of consciousness. He is breathing normally, and appears to have nothing broken. You probably want to get him to a doctor as quickly as possible. We need to head back up and see if we can find the other."

Jeb Jr. blinked his eyes several time and coughed up water. "Where's Grandpa?" he asked quietly.

Chapter 34

You're Okay, Son

"You're okay, son," whispered Skeet to Jeb Jr.

"Where's Grandpa?" Jeb Jr. sobbed this time.

"We don't know yet. The rangers are looking for him. We've got to get you to the doctor right now. Your great-grandfather will stay and wait. We'll come back as soon as possible."

Several hours later after the doctor had examined Jeb Jr. and declared him scared, but fit, they gathered in Skeet's living room to debrief their boy. Sam had returned with the news that there was no sign of Nathaniel, and their canoe was jammed so deep in sycamore limbs the rangers would have to wait to cut it out. They had managed to cut a narrow passage alongside the mess in case someone else, including Nathaniel, would need to squeeze through.

"What happened, son?"

An hour later the question still hung in the air. Jeb Jr. described the three days of being trapped high on the gravel bar out of harm's way, running out of fresh water to drink, shoving off into the swirling brown water against his grandpa's better instincts, rounding a sharp bend with no escape path through a mighty downed tree, ramming into the tree, trying to time his jump to clear it and falling short, and his grandpa leaping in to try and save him. Jeb Jr. had to stop to try and regain his composure through his tears.

When he picked up he couldn't recall much more. He remembered his grandfather hugging him, then diving down to try and free his tangled feet. He felt a strong push from below and then…strong hands grasping his, and pulling him free and clear of the tree. He was hazy about the rest, beyond knowing that he didn't see his grandfather again.

"Talk more about the strong hands from above," Skeet urged.

"That's all I remember."

"You never saw a face or heard a voice or even sensed a presence?"
"Not that I can think of."
"Nunnehi," whispered Sam to no one in particular.
"Rainbow Warrior," asserted Mai.

Sam had heard about Nunnehi from his father Bear Jr., who credited the mystic "travelers" who look after the Cherokee, protect them, and intervene in times of great need, with saving him and wife Sadie from murder and rape respectively, generations earlier. "A spirit race," he had called them.

Mai's version came from her Navaho roots, with Rainbow Warriors doing the same type of miraculous interventions for members of her tribe.

Jeb Jr. looked confused but grateful for the Native American ancestry that coursed through his veins from both sides of the ledger. He repeatedly gave credit to grandfather Nathaniel for the shove that freed his legs from the tangle of limbs.

They didn't find Nathaniel Snarkle until the floodwaters receded further, two days later. He was entrapped in the very subterranean limbs that he had pushed his grandson from.

Chapter 35

Halfbreeds

The Snarkle and Hensbell families shared a unique similarity. Both began their Welcome, Arkansas journeys with a heavy dose of Cherokee blood, which filtered down their respective lineages. Sunshine Snarkle was an original settler, wife of Jebediah, who started the Bear line. Dulcetta Hensbell, youngest daughter of the reclusive Native American family with no name because of fear of exportation, began the whole Tyson thing. The Snarkles sprinkled in a touch of Navajo along the way with Mai. So like many families of the early ones, pure bred was nothing but a theoretical concept. Even their pig herds occasionally mixed and mingled in those early days.

That said, Molly and L.T. took inbred to a new level. Snarkles and Hensbells shared more than just bad blood. A multi-year affair between Matilda "Tillie" Snarkle and Tyson Hensbell, III—"T3"—produced no marriage but two children. Both of the star-crossed lovers were long deceased, and it was beyond ironic that the only descendants from original lines who remained in town were genuine warring family half-breeds.

Nathaniel Snarkle's wife Layne had died shortly after he drowned in the ill-fated float trip. Most said of a broken heart.

Their son Skeet and wife Betty Sue were raising their brood, including Jebediah Jr., in Little Rock. They were just grateful to the Nunnehi or Rainbow Warrior or whatever for saving him.

Skeet's brother Solomon and Tillie's daughter Sabrina had long since moved away.

That left only Molly and L.T. from the original clans who had dominated the valley for most of its settled existence. Molly carried the name Snarkle in honor of her mother, and because her father, T3, had thankfully never married her. L.T. bore the Hensbell brand because his grandfather Tyson Jr. insisted on it if he were to carry on the family business. He had loved his

Snarkle mom, but finally succumbed to the brainwashing about her cheating on his dad, and ultimately murdering him.

Molly had tried her hand at marriage, living back east with her husband. It didn't work. Years and no children later, she moved back home to the river she grew up on and loved so dearly. She actually resurrected her grandfather Sam's float business and was making a decent living running tourists up and down and around her river. It didn't hurt business that she was easy to be with and look at, though she had to occasionally fight off the advances of a drunk customer on the backside of a gravel bar. Molly Snarkle knew how to take care of herself.

L.T. was no more than an absentee farmer, who with Jimbo Whippet's help, had stumbled into the deal of the century from his perspective. Jimbo would run all things CAFO, and L.T. would spend all earnings on his playboy lifestyle.

The clash that was coming could not have been more predictable.

Chapter 36

Pig Farm (2013)

Jebediah Snarkle, Jr. couldn't believe his nose. As he knelt on one knee above his former family plot, which once sat at the center of Welcome, Arkansas, the stench was overwhelming, and the view shocking.

The year was 2013, some 175 years after Jebediah Snarkle, Sr. first set foot on what he was said to have called "the most beautiful place on earth." 155 years after Welcome was born, 120 years after Welcome, Arkansas, ceased to exist as a small community, the eighth generation had returned to find waste and ruin. "Paradise lost," he muttered to himself.

Jeb Jr. was accompanied by his aunt Molly, and one of her friends, Larry Doobie. All were clad in camouflage. Doobie was heavily armed. It hadn't been easy to penetrate the L.T.H. Farms, LLC compound.

"Doobs, you've got to help me."

"I thought we were through, Molly."

"We are, in that way, but I need you desperately in another."

"Can we trade a little tit for tat, or something like that, just for old time's sake, Molly?"

"No, Doobs, we can't. Either you want to help an old friend, or you don't."

"Okay, okay, Molly. What and when from me?"

"As soon as possible and bring all you will need to help me and my great nephew bust into a heavily-fortressed compound here in the Ozarks."

"Sounds dangerous."

"Could be."

"Larry Doobie, meet my nephew, Jebediah Snarkle, Jr. He is the eighth-generation heir of my family in this valley, and was named after the founding father."

"Jeb Jr., this is my long-time friend Larry Doobie. Larry is an Army vet, both Iraq and Afghanistan. He's a killing machine clothed in the heart of a sweet man."

Jeb Jr.'s eyes bugged out while he tried to digest where all of this was headed. Doobie just smiled, and winked at Molly.

"Okay, we were together for a while, and I love the man with the sweet heart. But it was the PTSD hangover from his killing career I couldn't handle. So we split a while back. He has kindly agreed to help us infiltrate the Hensbell ranch and find out what in the hell they are doing."

"I know what I suspect we'll find, but I want to make sure before doing anything rash. The stench spells PIGS. The green goo that is issuing out from Large Creek into the river itself, the river I make my living from, spells PIGS. The rumor of trucks traveling through town in the middle of the night, with squeals issuing out of them, spells PIGS."

"The Hensbells have always been poor stewards of the land and water, but what is happening now would seem to exceed anything they've done before. We need to find out, and that damn Jimbo Whippit and his armed guards won't let a soul on the property. Nor can the sole blood Hensbell heir, L.T., be found anywhere. Yes, he also happens to be my brother."

"Doobs, I suggest that you scout the place out tonight, to see if you can find any weaknesses in the perimeter. You're welcome to stay with me, if you will behave yourself." Molly lit a glint of a smile.

"You drive a hard bargain, Miss, but you can count me on your team."

"Take your guns, and for God's sake, be careful. We'll meet again, once you are up, Doobs, and decide where to go next. Jeb Jr., you can crash on the couch."

"Can I have some coffee, hon?"

"Yes, and don't call me hon, Doobs." Again, a slight smile. "So what did you find out?"

"Well, they have razor wire around the whole place. And a guy in a jeep who patrols the perimeter on an hourly basis, beginning about 8 p.m. I'm guessing the fence is alarmed as well. Mini surveillance cameras at the front gate. Not sure about beyond."

"So, if we could figure out how to breach the fence, we could look around for forty-five minutes or so?"

"Yep, I think so. The way I timed it, the guy takes about fifteen minutes to make his rounds, and then goes somewhere to take a nap or something.

I only saw one human, but think I'd like to scout again tonight to make sure."

"So, how can we get in?"

"Well, I'm guessing that the fence is about eight foot tall. Got two ten-foot ladders anywhere around?"

"Nope, but I'm guessing we can get them. You go back out tonight, and we'll have your ladders by tomorrow morning."

Larry Doobie and Jeb Jr. took an immediate liking to one another. Molly took them on a run up the river, pausing only briefly at the Large Creek confluence to point out substantial algae growth.

"I don't know exactly what they have up there, but it's passing a whole lot of nitrogen and phosphorus this way. We've got to find out and stop it. Before it ruins us, all of us." Molly knew what she was talking about.

Doobie marveled at the monstrous and magnificent bluffs that loomed along both sides of the river upstream. There was one little feeder stream that they climbed up to find seven different waterfalls stair-stepping down to the river. Molly also hiked them back to what she claimed was the highest free-falling waterfall between the Rockies and the Appalachians. It was breathtaking. She threw in the colorful possibility that she had been conceived by mother Tillie and father T3 behind the curtain of falling water. A great and romantic family legend, she called it. Doobie asked if she wanted to try a curtain call, causing Jeb Jr. to laugh out loud, and Molly to shake her head firmly in the negative.

Molly's deft handling of the johnboat heading upstream through roaring rapids and occasionally thin waters amazed them both.

Jeb Jr. had simply forgotten how beautiful the upper stretches of river had always been. Doobie had never seen anything like it. They picnicked directly beneath what seemed to be the biggest bluff of them all, complete with occasional hikers traipsing out along a narrow slice of trail gouged by nature in the rock face about halfway up.

They ended the magic with a dash back to Molly's cabin to allow time for the acquisition of two ten-foot ladders and Doobie a brief rest before heading out to reconnoiter again.

His story the following morning was identical to the first version. "The guy in the jeep must have an alarm on his watch."

"No other folks around?"

"None."

"OK. We go in tomorrow after midnight."

"What do we do if we get caught?" asked Jeb Jr.

"That's why we have G.I. Joe around," Molly laughed.

"You mean I'd really have to shoot a hillbilly?"

"That would be totally up to you, but I'm guessing he would fire first. Them's the rules of the game down here where the hoot owls screw the chickens."

"Talk dirty to me, hon."

"There you go again, Doobs. Just trying to stay loose in a very stressful situation."

"Seriously, what do we do, even if we don't get caught, and find out what's going on?"

"That will depend on the gravity of the threat."

Doobie climbed one ten-foot ladder, carrying the other. Only he was strong enough to pull it off. He carefully placed the second one on the other side of the fence, stepped over and onto it, and climbed down into forbidden territory. Molly followed, and then Jeb Jr., descending slowly and carefully back into their own family history.

"Move quickly," urged Doobie.

The scene that greeted them a couple of hundred feet through the woods into a clearing was shocking to the senses. Spread out below the family graveyard was a full-fledged pig confined animal feeding operation. A real live pig CAFO. Complete with containment barns, feed towers, and the primary source of local stench and stink, a lagoon full of pig waste.

Molly burst into tears. Doobie wrapped an arm around her to comfort. Jeb Jr. knelt to one knee, and started shaking. "Paradise lost," he muttered to himself. A pig CAFO, with thousands of the little porkers sleeping head to tail beside one another. An occasional grunt or snort was all that broke the silence.

Doobie whipped out his cell phone and began capturing images. He flipped to video and scanned the whole landscape before whispering

"We've got to get going. The lone ranger will be back in the saddle in fifteen minutes. You've seen the problem. We need to figure out what to do about it." His shell-shocked compatriots nodded in agreement.

They headed back the way they came in, clamored up and over the fence taking first one, and then the second ladder with them. They crouched in the cover of woods, until the man in the jeep slipped by on his hourly rounds. No wonder they didn't want anyone to know what was going on at L.T.H. Farms.

L.T. Hensbell was awakened by the knock on his apartment door. It was Jimbo Whippet.

"Think we have a problem, son. Someone was on the property last night. They were all camo-ed up but the mini camera caught a couple of clear images. There were three of them. Your sister Molly was one, and I'm guessing the younger guy was Jebediah Jr. Not sure who the older third fellow was or how they got in, but he was heavily armed and seemed to know what he was doing. We've got problems if they got photos and share then with the community."

"What do we do now, Jimbo?"

"We've got to get rid of them, and quickly."

"Is that something you can handle?"

"Yep, I've got a man I've had to use before to create tragedies. The thing you need to know is that if you sign off, you are part of the deal. And if we ever get caught, you'll fry before me."

L.T. looked back toward the bedroom where his naked roommate peaked around the door, eyes bugging out. He then nodded. "Guess we don't have much choice, huh? Go for it, Jimbo, and keep me clear as best you can. And, by the way, sorry sis."

"Will do, and pig sooie, ma'am.

Molly, Jeb Jr., and Doobie gathered tiredly around the kitchen table.

"What do we do now?" asked Jeb Jr.

"I have an idea," answered Doobie. "We start by …."

Molly placed her hand on Doobie's, and led him away to her bedroom. "Tomorrow," she muttered, gazing listlessly beyond the open door.

"I think we should blow the whole place up as soon as possible. It won't be that hard," Doobie state matter-of-factly the next morning. "I've got a friend who can come up with the explosives on short notice. We slip in right after the lone ranger's rounds, plant our charges, and detonate remotely. It won't cost you much."

"What happens to the pigs?"

"Most will die immediately, and relatively painlessly. Those that survive will be incinerated in their pens. That will hurt a little more."

"We can't do that to all of those innocent pigs. It's too cruel. And besides, the assholes will just rebuild and restock. They already have the permit and will probably just collect insurance on a big fire of unknown origins. We accomplish nothing in the long view."

"Hmmm … didn't know you were so fond of pigs."

"Seems I slept with one last night."

"Hon … "

"Don't call me hon."

"Sorry."

"I'm sorry too, Doob. Didn't mean it, and I'm so very grateful you are here to help us. I'm just so upset by what I saw and smelled."

"Yep, they all seem to be staying in the same place. As best I can tell they're gathered around a table in the kitchen, probably plotting something nasty. I can take them now if you want? Make it look like a botched robbery? Or suicide pact?"

"No, we need this to be an unfortunate accident. Maybe burn down the house tonight? Or carbon monoxide poisoning. Something that will cause grief in the village and leave no marks."

"I can do that."

And around that kitchen table …

"Okay. Here's another idea. What does a pig locked up in a barn full of brothers and sisters want more than anything in the world?"

Silence.

"How about…freedom? I say we sneak in there tonight and turn all them pigs loose. Happy pigs, happy community. And we could have a big pig roundup later. And, the grandest barbecue in the state's history."

Jeb Jr. was laughing and nodding enthusiastically.

"You guys obviously don't live here. Or, have any intention of doing so in the near future. Do you know how much damage and degradation however many thousands of pigs that are cooped up in those barns turned loose could inflict on our water and our land before they could be "rounded up," as you call it? And how many would roam free after your great barbecue? Our water and landscape would be scarred forever. It would never recover, at least not in our lifetimes."

"So, we can't kill 'em, we can't free 'em, we can't roast 'em?"

"I do know one thing I'm gonna do, right now. Did your cell phone photos come out Doobs?"

"Don't know. I was having too much fun last night to check them out."

"Let me have it," demanded Molly, reaching for Doobie's cell.

She began to scroll through, pausing with a sigh or curse along the way. She ran the video last. "God damn my brother."

After a long silence, Molly sobbed, then spoke.

"These are outstanding. You paint a picture that will shock our neighbors and friends. I want to get these, and the video, to our local press as soon as we're at a breaking point here. I also want to try and interest the national press in the fraud and crimes against our community that are being hatched and implemented behind closed doors. My ex worked for *The New York Times* for a while when we were married and can help us get through that bureaucracy for some attention."

"You really think *The New York Times* would run a story about some little two-bit town in the Ozarks?" asked Jeb Jr. in disbelief.

"A story like this? Yes."

Chapter 37

FALLOUT

Doobie became suspicious the second time he saw, through the kitchen window, an old black pickup truck pass the house. He was trained to think like that.

He rose quickly and left the room, headed toward the front door of Molly's cabin, leaving her midway through her media blitz campaign meanderings.

He waited silently by the window as the old truck passed once again, catching an out-of-state license plate, and shushing the others as they demanded to know what was going on.

"Someone is casing the place," he said quietly. "I don't like it."

"Who could it be? Why?"

"Don't know. Don't like."

"I'm going down to the paper before we lose the evidence."

"Be careful, hon, and whatever you do, don't get into an old black pickup truck with anyone, whether you know them or not. Take this with you, just in case."

Molly let the "hon" pass this time.

Molly walked into the front door of the local paper.

Prior to leaving her cabin, she had spoken by phone to her ex-husband at length about the story unfolding in her small home town. He promised to help her anyway he could and asked if she could email him the images from Doobie's phone. He would get them over to a good friend at the *Times*, who would probably want to interview Molly as soon as possible. Secret pig CAFO, snuck in the back door of the pristine Ozarks. "What a great headline," he had laughed.

She knew the editor of the local paper well, and had in fact written some articles for him in the past. She had called ahead to make sure he was in and had time to discuss an important local story.

After formalities, she handed him Doob's cell phone, with the first of several photos pulled up. He looked confused.

"What is it?"

"A pig CAFO."

"A what?"

"Why do I get that response every time I mention that term? 'A what?' A confined animal feeding operation, this one filled with pigs. Doesn't anybody know anything about these things? Maybe that's the problem. We get all of our meat from them, they are the country's worst polluters, and no one knows anything about them. Any idea where this one is hidden away?"

"No."

"How about on the old Welcome, Arkansas site, just beneath Founder's Cemetery, on the Hensbell place, or what they call L.T.H. Farms, LLC, these days. You know that smell that settled over our village this summer? It came from here. That's a whole lake full of pig shit sitting down next to Large Creek."

"You've got to be kidding me. How many pigs are there?"

"I don't know, but it would serve you well to find that out before you start sharing this story with the community, don't you think?"

"I'll send someone out to cover this as soon as my reporter comes back from the county council luncheon. Reckon any of them know anything about it?"

"Wouldn't surprise me, but you're wasting your time sending someone down there. They will never make it through the padlocked gate, the barbed wire fence, and the heavily armed guard."

"You're kidding? How can they do that?"

"I'm not kidding. How can they do it? Private land owner rights. And if I were you, I'd go straight to the state agency that issues CAFO permits. That's where this story begins. Who owns the permit? For how many pigs? When was it issued? Were community meetings required or held? Where? When? When did construction begin? Who is monitoring? For that matter, who the hell is regulating anything?"

"So how did you get these photos and videos?"

"Forgive us our trespasses, as … ."

"You broke into this place?"

"My family used to own it, didn't we?"

"Still do, don't you?"

"I'm a Snarkle. My brother is a Hensbell. Both conceived out of wedlock, each named by choice. We might come from the same sperm bank but never confuse the two of us when it comes to stewardship of the environment."

"Can you leave these images with me?"

"No, but I'll email them to you. We need several copies anyway."

"Would you be willing to submit to an interview?"

"Thought you would never ask."

~

Molly pulled out of the parking lot downtown. She noticed her car dragging to the right. She drove to the edge of town and hopped out to take a look. It was a damn flat tire. And then she noticed the slash next to the rim. She heard someone pull up behind, and then ask if she could use some help. She turned to say thanks, and was staring at the bearded driver of an old black pickup truck.

"What do you want?"

"I want to help."

"Like hell you do. Is that why you kept driving by my cabin this morning?"

The driver opened the door and started to exit. Molly pulled out the handgun Doobie had handed her when she left, and pointed it directly at him.

"I'll shoot you if you do anything I don't like. Anything."

"Okay, okay, okay. Put it down, lady. I ain't gonna hurt you. What was you doing on Hensbell land last night?"

"Who says I was?"

"Got a picture of you and your fellow criminals."

"Well, I have a bunch of pictures of you and your fellow criminals' illegal pig CAFO, and I just gave them to the paper. I also sent them to *The New York Times* this morning. Your dirty, smelly secret is out. Tell my brother he's been busted. Who are you anyway?"

"Just a friend of Jimbo Whippet, and your brother and him didn't do nothing wrong. They followed all the laws and set out to bring economic development to the community. You ought to thank him."

"If I could find him, I would do considerably more than that. Get your ass out of here and tell brother L.T. that I will see him in court."

~

"Too late boss. I sliced her tire and pulled over to help her as she was coming home from town."

"Why did you do that, idiot? I told you no violence."

"Just wanted to scare her a little. Besides, she's the one that pulled a gun on me. The bitch said she gave cell phone photos and a video to the local paper. Claims that *The New York Times* has an interest in them, too. Wish you had let me take her out up front like I wanted to."

"Guess we could sue for trespassing and try to get the images back? Get a court gag order or something like that?"

"With *The New York Times* involved? You must be kidding."

"You're right. Guess I'd better report everything back to L.T. He is not going to be pleased. Or maybe he won't even care, unless it starts to impact his income stream. And, stay away from his sister. Okay?"

The local story ran a week later, under the simple, but provocative headline, "PIG FARM."

L.T. Hensbell even submitted to an interview. Said he was only doing what was good for the community on property that his family had farmed for well over a century. He emphasized that he had followed all the rules set out by the state in getting the permit to expand his family farm.

He reasoned that economic development would help put the little mountain town with the feminine Biblical name on the map. Maybe even draw some more family farmers to town to boost the stagnant local economy.

Ironically, some in the community sided with him. It was his land, and as one neighbor was quoted in the paper as having said, "Them's just good ol' boys trying to make a living."

Molly Snarkle joined with several community leaders to file a lawsuit demanding that the permit be revoked. Three grandmothers let the way. For their grandkids. Among other things they argued that there had not been adequate notice for public input and discussion. They also suggested that with a project so large in a nationally protected watershed, a thorough environmental impact study should have been required, though existing regulations did not demand it. They could have added that existing CAFO permitting regulations did not demand much of anything, but they didn't.

A community that had hung together through war, violence, brutal murders, the Big Lightning Fire, relocation, the Great Depression, attempts to dam their river, tragedy, and occasional triumph, was suddenly and bitterly divided.

All agreed that there would be no quick or happy outcome.

As Molly's ex-husband had promised, *The New York Times* version of "Pig Farm" ran a bit later, December 27, 2013, to be precise.

Chapter 38

Elegy

"I'm incensed, Jebediah! How could an international conglomerate sneak 10,000 pigs through the back door of state regulators under the guise of family farming in the heart of the watershed of America's first national river? And, get away with it? Money. Dirty money. Tainted money. Money that passes through powerful and self-serving trade associations, corporations and lobbyists straight into the pockets of legislators who favor them over us. Dirty money, dirty doings, dirty water."

"So, how can you get rid of 10,000 pigs, Aunt Molly? If you can't free them, if you can't kill them, if you can't pignap them, if you can't incinerate them, if you can't airlift them and their confinement barns back to Iowa, if you can't put them on a barge and ship them down to Mississippi, what can you do?"

"That's just it. Nothing."

"Nothing? There's got to be something."

"Nothing. That's the other edge of the sword. First the damage they do to the land, the water, and the community. Second, the semi-eternal nature of their presence."

"Nothing?"

"Nope. Once they are there, you can't humanely get rid of them. Except through the law. Either litigation or legislation. And since we have little of the latter the former is rendered mostly moot. This pig farm is here to stay until the lobbyists get their hands out of the legislators' pockets, until legislators pass laws that can protect sensitive water resources and vulnerable small communities from exploitation by big Ag in the name of economic development, until governors veto stupid projects, and until regulators step up and fight lax enforcement. Or, until we win a lawsuit. Even then I doubt we can shut it down, but it's worth a try. Anything is."

"Nothing? Nothing we can do, Molly? Nothing?"

"Write a book?"

"Hmmmmm … ."

Chapter 39

A Piggy Primer

A Day at the National Chick Museum and Piggy Hall of Fame

Featuring the Art of Amber Hansen
Written by Jebediah Snarkle, Jr.

Jane gently stroked the soft skin behind the little piglet's ears. It was smooth and pink, and comforting to touch. She cuddled it in the crook of her elbow. She would name it Gertrude, after her grandmother. Muffle the dog sniffed, then licked its small haunch.

Gertrude's mother lay in the corner of the barn with the rest of the litter, all eight of the fat, healthy little porkers. She had not objected when Jane had lifted one from the straw nest because she knew it would be returned unharmed. Jane's Daddy and Mama owned a small family pig farm in the rural Midwest. The year was far in the future. They owned enough mama pigs to birth nine or ten litters a year, normally eighty to one hundred piglets, to raise for food, for market, and to produce a comfortable living on their forty acres of land.

Knowing the piglets personally was part of growing up on a small family farm.

"So Daddy, what did families do for entertainment back then?" asked Dick.

"My favorite was to go on family float trips," smiled Daddy with pang of remembrance.

"My folks took all of us on a float trip by at least by age two, with overnight camping on a gravel bar around a roaring campfire a year or two later," he added.

"What's a family float trip?" asked Jane.

"Good question," responded Daddy. "Not many folks around here remember. It's when you load the whole family into canoes that slip and soar down a beautiful creek, careening off of rocks and trees, stopping to swim in cool waters, fishing for small bream, sneaking up on baby turtles to grab them on a log, shivering as water snakes swim harmlessly by, soaking up sun, the natural world at its finest."

"Why don't most remember?" puzzled Dick.

"Well, unfortunately as time went on, the creek water got sticky and gooey and it wasn't as much fun. My own Dad blamed it on really big farms and their waste but not many in town were listening. They were living happily on the money they received from selling their family farms. It took years for our neighbors to wake up and reclaim our creeks and, even more years for streams to host normal fish and critters again."

"The good news is that swimming holes are back to cool and clear and fishing for bass and green-eared sunfish has finally improved to the point of sport. I do want to take you both on a family float someday now that the water is safe again."

"It's taken this long, Daddy?" asked Jane, adding that she wanted to go. "This long, Jane, this long."

"Maybe it is time we shared the whole story with Dick and Jane," Daddy said to Mama.

Mama, Daddy, Dick and Jane are going to the National Chick Museum and Piggy Hall of Fame on a beautiful spring day to learn about the animals we eat. Cows, piggies, and chickens among others.

As they eat their breakfast of pancakes and pork sausage Mama talked about what they might see and experience.

"What a day we will have today. We will celebrate our country's great heritage of steaks, pork chops, and drumsticks."

"Why?" asked seven-year-old Dick.

"To learn about the great heroes and heroines who have made possible a steady supply of our national pride and joy—meat, " replied Daddy.

"We can also see how silly some of the things we did in the early days of making the baby back ribs you love to gnaw and the prime filet mignon we eat every Friday night available to all, and how we have advanced as a meat-eating nation."

Mama and Daddy loaded Dick and Jane into their new solar-powered pick-up truck and left on their big adventure.

As they drove through the rolling green fields sparkling with drips of a summer rain shower, the children enjoyed seeing the small herds of cows, horses, and goats grazing freely. They smiled at the barns, the chicken houses, and the pigpens that dotted the fertile landscape and even the carefully-manicured municipal golf course.It was only fifty years earlier that America had begun to transition from factory farming and large confined animal feeding operations back to the family farm model. It simply became more profitable.

This return to smaller and local had been occasioned by the severe fouling of water, air, and land around residential communities. Factory farms had drained, spewed, and sprayed tons of animal waste into rural neighborhoods, rendering many of them wastelands and occasioning large-scale migration out of traditional agricultural regions.

When government at state and federal levels stopped subsidizing large scale agriculture and shifted financial incentives from corporate farms to small family farming operations it became economically feasible for families to prosper raising their own livestock and distributing product locally and regionally. With billions of dollars of factory farm subsidization left over to reclaim the water, land and air that they had fouled, humanity thrived again. The new model was actually an old one, just aided and abetted by modern technology and methodology. The result was the

green, fragrant acreage the family drove through on the way to the museum.

As it took an hour to arrive, Daddy loaded an historical digital recording of factory farming methodology for the children to review prior to their tour of the museum. The children were shocked at the huge herds of animals packed into cramped, filthy quarters, the squeals and clucks and moos of discomfort and disenchantment, and the hazy air that engulfed it all. "I can almost smell it," commented Jane, squeezing her nose and scowling. "Why did they do it?" wondered Dick.

"This is why we are touring the CAFO Hall of Fame and Museum," muttered Daddy. He slipped into the painful memories that revisiting the past evoked, including the premature loss of his farmer grandparents to cancer that was attributed to fouled air and water on their old family farm. Yet he felt the lessons for his children would be worth his discomfort.

The family was greeted at the door of the museum by a robot dressed as a pig, clad in a uniform, and introducing himself as Perky Pig. Perky would be their guide for the rest of the day and said that he looked forward to answering their questions. He answered the first one before it could be raised. Yes, it would be okay to bring their dog along on the tour. "What is his name?" asked Perky. "Muffle," answered Dick and Jane in unison. They were relieved not to leave Muffle behind.

Perky explained that their tour would go back to the beginning of farming in the Midwest and follow its development over the past several hundred years. He warned that some exhibits would be shocking and that Dick and Jane may wish to cover their eyes at times.

Perky led them from scenario to scenario.

It all started small, Perky began, tracing the flow chart from individual farm to corn to livestock to concentration and back to the here and now.

Family farms in older times were just that, a means to feed family. They had a horse to plow and planted crops to eat. Chickens laid eggs and occasionally contributed fried goodness to special meal occasions. Pigs provided meat to smoke. Cows gave milk. Goats and sheep filled in the blanks. At one time one in four or five families lived on small family farms.

Then it became profitable to raise corn and sell it to cattle and pig farmers to feed their herds. And when profits suffered, government stepped in to guarantee a “fair” price. The “family farm” must be protected as a genuine American way of life, except family farms had less and less to do with it.

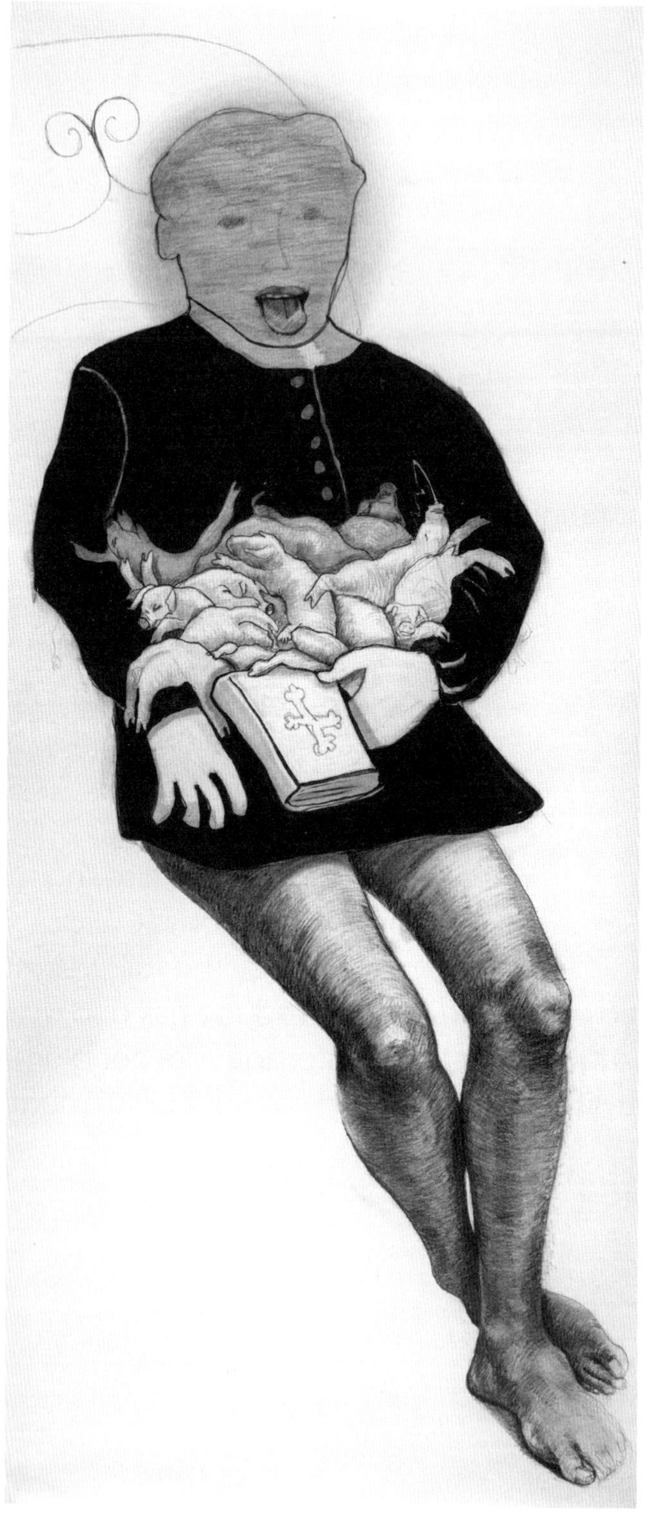

And then factory farms stepped up their game. It soon became obvious that the most efficient and cost-effective way to provide an expanding and more financially-stable population with meat was to concentrate birthing, fattening, and ultimately processing.

If corporate farmers could cram as many chickens, pigs, and cows as they could keep alive into as small of a place as possible, dose them with enough antibiotics to prevent illness, escalate the pace of weight gain, and ship them off to slaughter after shortened growing seasons, consumers would be happy and profits would soar. They could even present a pretense of family farming by allowing families to own confined animal feeding operations (CAFOs), sell them livestock, supplies and feed, and buy the full-weight finished product at a profitable price to reduce risk and assure supply for processors. Large international conglomerates could control supply, price and distribution of meat around the globe.

These CAFOs all had the same general configurations—confinements, lagoons, and spray fields.

The theory was this:

Truth One - Volume maximizes yield if you can dose the victims heavily enough to keep them breathing and growing. That is what confinement is all about.

Truth Two - Animal waste can be liquefied in pools of water, ponds, and lagoons where solids will settle and diluted liquid nutrients rise to the top.

Truth Three - Liquid waste can be sprayed or trucked to surrounding fields for general application to crop lands. Haul off the rest from time to time.

It was a neat, closed-loop system that met consumer demand, kept prices low, fed the nation and the world, and generated large corporate profits to reinvest in more of the same.

Everyone was happy except those who worried about such things as antibiotics, animal waste, and feed residue seeping into surface waters and aquifers, foul odors in the air, and hundred-year flood plains. In the end their concerns were warranted.

Generations of sycophants nursed at the bosom of Mother Ag.

"We were all guilty," added Daddy to Perky's graphic description. "We could go to any supermarket, big or small, and buy whatever meat we wanted for supper. Strip sirloins, pork tenderloins, chicken thighs and livers—the decision was weighty, and it was all ours. What would it be tonight?" muttered Daddy. "What to grill, what to sauté, what to fry? What to worry about until things turned sour at home? Like water, air, land and property values."

"One could argue all day about the ethical implications of animal confinement. But what was undeniable was the damage to land and water and host communities where CAFOs were forced into sensitive and vulnerable locations."

"And when we stood up and took our land back, and when the federal government stopped giving free rein and tax credits to corporate farmers from China to Minnesota to Illinois, to Arkansas, and when state governments regulated rather than rolled over to lobbyists and big money, and when we got to compete on a level farming field, we won! We delivered the goods in small, not gross, quantities and qualities."

"We focused locally and regionally, not internationally. We transitioned to pricing to demand not subsidized operating cost. Free market, small-scale agriculture delivered the goods. Oligopolistic pricing and market control was forced out of business. We again raised our own destiny."

Perky finished his tour with a flourish, applauding the American farmer and his ingenuity, downplaying the damage inflicted on the land and water in the process.

The CAFO Hall of Fame featured gold-embossed framed plaques with the names of the big corporate players and their logos:

- Frysomes, with a plump chicken
- Hargulls, with a cute piglet
- MySanta, with a yellow seed

After all, they had paid for it.

Mama and Daddy thanked Perky Pig for his enlightening presentation, then loaded Dick and Jane back into the solar-powered pickup and headed home to cook supper.

And the piggies, and the calves, and the chicks, and the people on their farms, and the pork chops in their frying pans lived happily ever after.

THE END

End Note

The author's grandfather to the 5th power, Abner Casey, settled and built a gristmill in the Boxley valley along the upper Buffalo River around 1840.

Abner was born in 1766. At nearly 100 years old, he died in 1865.

Abner and his wife Elizabeth were purportedly buried in the Buffalo Cemetery, Parthenon, Arkansas, near Abner's mother Mary "Polly" Wayne Casey (1752-1845).

Abner Casey did not have a pig farm, to the author's knowledge.

POLLY CASEY
DIED
in the year of
1845.

About the Author

Todd Parnell is the recently retired President of Drury University, founding CEO of THE BANK in Springfield, Mo., civic leader, environmental advocate as co-founder of the Upper White River Basin Foundation and recently retired Chairman of the Missouri Clean Water Commission, and award winning author inducted into the Missouri Writers Hall of Fame in 2012. He holds Masters degrees in Business Administration from Dartmouth University and History from Missouri State University, and an undergraduate degree from Drury University.

Parnell began writing non-fiction during his years as a banker and educator, including published works *The Buffalo, Ben, and Me, Trails of the Heart: Along the Buffalo River, Mom at War,* and *Postcards from Branson.* He tried his hand at fiction upon retiring from the Drury presidency and hasn't stopped writing since, publishing the Ozarkian Folk Tales Trilogy *{Skunk Creek, Swine Branch,* and *Donny Brook),* with a second trilogy, *Children of the Creek* in production.

His most current release, *Pig Farm,* unfolds a sweeping and rollicking historical tall tale set in the context of a real time environmental tragedy, along side America's first national river, the Buffalo. Brimming with humor and colorful characters, riddled with mystery and tragedy, and laced with money and greed, fiction merges with fact to paint a disturbing portrait of a "pig farm" over time.

Parnell was born in Branson, Mo. and is an eighth-generation Ozarker. He resides with his wife of 42 years, Betty, in Springfield, Mo. and is blessed with four children and five grandchildren.

Visit Todd's website: www.toddparnell.com

About the Illustrator

Amber Hansen is a filmmaker, muralist, visual artist and musician creating socially engaged and community-based artwork throughout the Midwest. Establishing a dialogue between her formal education and the ethics of her rural upbringing, Hansen's work promotes the value of creative engagement for all ages while raising questions about the ethics of animal welfare and humans relationship with food.

Hansen is the co-director & co-editor of the feature documentary *Called to Walls*, a film that celebrates the potential of community-based art in the Middle of the U.S. through the mural works of Dave Loewenstein.

She is currently the Assistant Professor at the University of South Dakota where she teaches painting.

Visit Amber's website: www.amberhansenart.com

Also by Todd Parnell

Mom at War (2005)

Postcards from Branson (2006)

The Buffalo, Ben, and Me (2007)

The Ozarkian Folktales Trilogy
Skunk Creek (2015)
Swine Branch (2016)
Donny Brook (2017)

Trails of the Heart - Along the Buffalo River (2017)

To Have...and Have Not - A Love Story
(release Thanksgiving, 2018)